DIVERSE ENERGIES

DIVERSE ENERGIES

EDITED BY

TOBIAS S. BUCKELL AND JOE MONTI

Tu Books
New York

Copyright © 2012 by Tobias S. Buckell and Joe Monti

Preface copyright © 2012 by Tobias S. Buckell

"Last Day" copyright © 2012 by Ellen Oh

"Freshee's Frogurt" copyright © 2011 by Daniel H. Wilson. Excerpted from the novel *Robopocalypse*, Doubleday, 2011. Reprinted by permission of Random House, Inc.

"Uncertainty Principle" copyright © 2012 by K. Tempest Bradford

"Pattern Recognition" copyright © 2012 by Ken Liu

"Gods of the Dimming Light" copyright © 2012 by Greg van Eekhout

"Next Door" copyright © 2012 by Rahul Kanakia

"Good Girl" copyright © 2012 by Malinda Lo

"A Pocket Full of Dharma" copyright © 1999 by Paolo Bacigalupi; first appeared in *The Magazine of Fantasy and Science Fiction*. Reprinted by permission of the author.

"Blue Skies" copyright © 2012 by Cindy Pon

"What Arms to Hold Us" copyright © 2012 by Rajan Khanna

"Solitude" copyright © 1994 by Ursula K. Le Guin; first appeared in *The Magazine of Fantasy and Science Fiction*. Reprinted by permission of the author.

Afterword copyright © 2012 by Joe Monti

Jacket illustration copyright © 2012 by John Picacio

TU BOOKS, an imprint of LEE & LOW BOOKS Inc.,
95 Madison Avenue, New York, NY 10016
leeandlow.com

Manufactured in the United States of America by Worzalla Publishing Company, November 2012

Book design by Ben Mautner
Book production by The Kids at Our House
The text is set in Minion Pro
The display text is set in Futura

HC 10 9 8 7 6 5 4 3 2 1
PB 10 9 8 7 6 5 4 3 2 1
First Edition

Library of Congress Cataloging-in-Publication Data
Diverse energies / edited by Tobias S. Buckell and Joe Monti.
    v. cm.
Contents: The last day / by Ellen Oh -- Freshee's Frogurt / by Daniel H. Wilson -- Uncertainty principle / by K.T. Bradford -- Pattern recognition / by Ken Liu -- Gods of dimming light / by Greg Van Eekhout -- Next door / by Rahul Kanakia -- Good girl / by Malinda Lo -- A pocket full of dharma / by Paolo Bacigalupi -- Blue skies / by Cindy Pon -- What arms to hold / by Rajan Khanna -- Solitude / by Ursula K. Le Guin.
    ISBN 978-1-60060-887-2 (hardcover : alk. paper) -- ISBN 978-1-62014-011-6 (paperback) -- ISBN 978-1-60060-888-9 (e-book)
1. Dystopias--Juvenile fiction. 2. Science fiction, American. 3. Short stories, American. [1. Science fiction. 2. Short stories.] I. Buckell, Tobias S. II. Monti, Joe.
    PZ5.D69 2012
    [Fic]--dc23
    2012016362

To the memory of Leslie Esdaile Banks, who was to be a part of this anthology, and although we only introduced her into the NYC crowd too briefly, she left a room full of boisterous joy in her wake.

And to Stacy, for creating Tu and building a bigger house.

PREFACE

by Tobias S. Buckell

I grew up in the Caribbean split between two worlds. I was son to a mother born in London, England, and a father who was born on a small island off Grenada. I looked white, but my father had an Afro. Half of my family had a Grenadan dialect, my mom British. Some of my cousins were black. And my other cousins white.

Who was I?

I didn't struggle much with that where I grew up. In the Caribbean in which I grew up, there were Palestinian and Lebanese immigrants, Indian immigrants with last names such as Singh and Patel, European expats, mixed kids like me, and a wide range of other skin tones and ethnicities.

But the books I read never looked like the world in which I lived. I read like a madman all throughout school, partly because I lived on a boat and we didn't have television. Books were my entertainment. I loved tales of fantasy, strange lands, strange worlds, strange futures, and adventure.

And over time I came to realize that most of the books I read had only one kind of hero, one kind of face on the cover.

When I moved to America, I realized why. Most politicians had that kind of face. Most actors. Most people in charge of businesses. Most Americans.

And as for my mixed identity: it confused a lot of people. But I've never been confused about it. I may fall in between the simple check boxes on a survey or in people's expectations, but as I traveled around, I found that there were a lot of people just like me.

I write adventures about the future and of future worlds, and they're populated by a diverse set of characters. Why? It's the future face of the world. It's us. All of us. And we all deserve to be seen in the future, having adventures, setting foot on those strange new worlds.

I wanted to see all the sides of my families in stories about the future, from my pale relatives to my dark-skinned ones. I wanted to see the whole human race.

When I had the chance to create an anthology of stories, I wanted to bring that wide angle I grew up with to the page. The result, the futures you hold in this book, are varied. Some are fun, many are grim. But they are all diverse, full of energy, and hopefully they will all let you sample an energetic variety of some amazing authors who today are writing the books I had once hoped to see on the bookshelves when I was young and hungry for more heroes than just the ones I was given.

The wave of the future is not the conquest of the world by a single dogmatic creed but the liberation of the diverse energies of free nations and free men. —John F. Kennedy

The Last Day

by Ellen Oh

Kenji watched his mother's care-worn hands tremble as she ladled out the morning rice gruel. His five-year-old sister, Tomoko, sat in unnatural stillness, her eyes locked on their mother's hands as if sheer force of will would keep the precious grains from being spilled.

A sudden commotion outside their apartment made them all jump. Kenji grabbed the wavering bowl from his mother's hands and placed it in front of Tomoko. His mother didn't notice the near disaster. All her attention was focused on their front door.

Several wooden sandals clacked across the hallway floor, a shrill, strident voice dominating above all others. His mother shuddered before she faced him in anguish. He recognized the voice immediately. It belonged to Mrs. Ueda, chairwoman of the Women's Brigade, and she could be here for only one reason: to claim another child's life in the name of the Emperor.

A year had passed since Mrs. Ueda's last visit to their building. A year since he'd hugged his last brother good-bye.

Within the sudden unnatural quiet of his kitchen, his family was as still as the statues of the guardian of children, Mizuko Jizo, that populated all the cemeteries—now more than ever before. Kenji didn't realize he'd been holding his breath until he heard the voice calling out for Mrs. Akita, their neighbor down the hall. He saw the tension deflate from his mother's shoulders and heard his little sister's soft, hiccuping sigh.

Their ears were assaulted by the persistent knocking on their neighbor's door and the loud calls of Mrs. Ueda and her cronies. Tomoko slapped her hands over her ears and squeezed her eyes shut. Kenji's mother set down the wooden ladle with deliberate care before rising to her feet and shuffling to the door.

Kenji watched as a tendril of steam curled up from a bowl that was not even half full. Swallowing down his hunger, he gave Tomoko a hug and pulled her hands away, motioning her to go ahead and eat. Unfolding himself from the table, he padded over to the door and placed a comforting hand on his mother's arm. She stared down at him blindly, her face a tragic reflection of the pained horror he felt himself. Moving next to her, he peered out the door and down the hallway, where three women in gray kimonos stood, their backs rigid with righteousness. After several more minutes of furious pounding, the door finally opened to reveal Mrs. Akita's frightened face.

"Good morning, Akita-san! I'm so proud and honored to announce that your youngest daughter, Michiko, has been selected to enlist in the Imperial Army of the Heavenly Father," Mrs. Ueda said.

"I'm sure there's been some kind of mistake." Mrs. Akita's voice trembled down the hallway. "My daughter is only fourteen years old! She's too young to join the army!"

"The Imperial Army never makes mistakes," Mrs. Ueda responded. "Didn't you hear the new decree that was issued earlier this week? The conscription age has been lowered to fourteen. Now we can send more of our young men and women to fight for our Heavenly Father and defeat his enemies."

Kenji heard his mother's muffled gasp. Her cold fingertips gripped his hand. Only two more years before Mrs. Ueda would come knocking on their door for him, unless the Emperor lowered the conscription age again. And then who would take care of his family? How would they survive?

"You can't take my only child! I've lost my husband and my two oldest to this war already. She's all I have left!" Mrs. Akita was weeping, trying to bar the women from entering her apartment.

Kenji couldn't see Mrs. Ueda's face, but he had no problem imagining the crazed patriotic fever that shone in her eyes. He'd seen it in too many adults. How he hated her—hated them all.

"If your daughter refuses to fight, she will be arrested and executed in the morning." Mrs. Ueda's voice was smooth, devoid of all emotion. "Your family will be branded as traitors to the Empire. All your belongings will be confiscated, and you will be homeless on the streets. It is your choice."

There was no more resistance as the three women pushed past

Mrs. Akita, leaving her to weep against the door. From inside the apartment, they could hear Michiko's frightened cries.

Kenji guided his mother away. It took all his energy not to slam the door. Not to run out into the hallway and punch Mrs. Ueda's smug face. He knew, like everyone else, that there was no choice.

His mother stood leaning against the kitchen sink, her head bowed low. He hugged her tight, his arms wrapping completely around her frail form. He breathed in the light, sweet fragrance of cherry blossoms that always seemed to cling to her. In the last few years of the never-ending war, he'd seen his beautiful, vibrant mother fade in size, age, and happiness. Each year seemed to reduce her further, her back bowing under the burden of life. It was hard to pinpoint which had been the worst blow, the loss of his father's ship at sea or the notices received on the same day of his two elder brothers' glorious deaths in separate battles. He'd been so proud that his brothers had been chosen as Tokkatai. So stupidly proud. Until his mother received their effects in small wooden boxes and their last letters filled with the regret of dreams never fulfilled. They were boys dreaming of becoming men—sixteen and eighteen years old. They died boys who would never become men.

A wave of bitterness threatened to overcome him. How foolish he'd been. They called it the highest honor—to die for your emperor in a suicide attack against the enemy. Only now did Kenji realize that there was no honor in dying.

Swallowing back his bitterness, he finished his meager breakfast and prepared to leave. His mother handed him a small bento box containing his lunch. He untied the wrapping cloth

16

and opened the container even as his mother begged him not to. Inside the small oval tin, he saw two small rice balls wrapped with a sliver of dried seaweed.

Unsurprised, he looked up to catch Tomoko's glare of hungry resentment before she dropped her gaze. Her small face was narrow, nearly gaunt as she sat staring at the rice balls, hunger pinching her face tight even as her empty breakfast bowl sat before her. Kenji bit back his angry words, knowing his mother meant well.

Taking the larger rice ball, he placed it in a bowl, ignoring the sudden increase of saliva in his mouth—the ever-present demon that ate away at his stomach.

"Kenji," his mother began.

She faltered under his gaze. Her hand fluttered up to rub the side of her face, accentuating her collarbone and emaciated form.

A desolate fury rose in him as he closed the lid to his bento box, tied it up, and threw it into his bag. Slinging the bag over his head, he ran out the door before he could change his mind.

Outside, the heat of the August sun was already bringing up the early-morning temperatures to a boil. Kenji lowered his dingy gray cap as he peered down the street.

"Almost took off without you," a husky voice said from behind. "We're gonna be late to work if we don't hurry."

Kenji turned and smiled to see his best friend, Akira Tanaka, standing in the shade of the building next door. He was a sturdy boy only a few months older than Kenji and browned by the summer sun.

"Sorry about that," Kenji said.

With a nod, Akira took off, with Kenji following close behind.

"Where are we going today?"

"Not too far," Akira said, breaking into a thudding run.

Kenji kept up but found himself tiring after the seventh block. It was the lack of food. He wished he had even a fraction of Akira's energy and stamina. But his friend was eating better than most of the others. It was why Kenji had left home earlier and was following him instead of heading to work.

The streets seemed emptier than usual. But then again, it seemed there were fewer and fewer people around. Kenji had memories of streets crowded with people—holding his father's hand as they stopped at a local street vendor selling roasted sweet potatoes. He could remember the gravelly singing voice of the old vendor as he pulled out hot, dark, purple potatoes from his wood-burning stove. The flesh was soft and sweet, and so delicious. Kenji shook his head, dislodging the memory and returning to the present. No more street vendors selling tasty treats. No more laughing families strolling down to the park.

It took ten minutes to reach Akira's destination, a small mid-rise apartment building. They entered the dingy lobby area through the unlocked front door and quietly walked up the stairs.

He followed Akira to the third floor and down a narrow hallway. They passed several doors until they reached an end unit. The sounds of apartment living could be heard through the thin, peeling walls—a baby's cry, the tinny voice of a radio announcer, muffled moans of pain or pleasure. With a quick look around, Akira pulled out a small chisel and shoved the narrow edge into the seam of the door, popping it open with one hard wrench.

Kenji took an involuntary step back, hesitating for only a

fraction of a moment before following his friend into the dark apartment. The stench of rotted food and general uncleanliness assaulted him. He pinched his nose tight and tried to keep from gagging as he followed Akira into the dirty kitchen. Several days of dishes, teacups, bowls, and pots were stacked all around the sink and countertop. A soggy rug sat in a pool of water that spread from a small icebox in the corner. Akira opened all the lower cabinets, grabbing tins and packages of food.

"Quick, get out your bag," Akira called out to him. "There's a small sack of rice that you can have."

Kenji's eyes pricked with the burning of tears at his friend's gesture. He grabbed the sack and felt it was more than half full— at least a kilo of rice left. Securing the twine on the top so not a precious grain would spill, he shoved the rice into his bag. The heavy weight was comforting.

Akira was done with the kitchen, and he moved into the bedroom. Kenji followed cautiously behind him.

"Don't come in here," Akira said. "Remember what happened the last time you saw a dead body."

Shame warred with revulsion as Kenji swallowed down his bile. He risked a quick peek into the bedroom and could see the lower half of a still body lying on a futon. The curtains were closed, leaving the room in semidarkness. His friend was poking through boxes and drawers, a thief of darkness, pocketing anything of value.

Kenji took a hesitant step forward, his eyes drawn to the stillness of the feet. *How strange*, he thought, *he is still wearing his socks*.

"How did he die?" he asked.

Akira turned and looked at the dead body, and shrugged. "Not from hunger, that's for sure. He had three additional ration coupons. That's why he had so much rice even though he was only one person."

"Then how—"

"He offed himself. Took a whole mess of pills—see." Akira kicked a few empty prescription bottles, sending them flying across the wooden floor.

"How long?" Kenji asked.

"I've been keeping an eye on him for weeks now," Akira said, rummaging in a large trunk and appraising a small music box. "I can always tell who's checking out. Their feet drag, and they walk around in a daze. Stop bathing. Lose all interest in life. This one hadn't come out of his apartment for three days. I knew he was a goner."

Akira let out a snorting laugh. "My uncle thinks it's unnatural, this knowledge I have. He said I must work for Death himself. Hey, better to work for him than to be taken by him, right?"

Staring at his friend, all Kenji could see was the flashing of Akira's teeth before he turned back into the shadows. Kenji suppressed a shudder. His friend had a talent. An unusual, terrible talent. But one that helped to keep them alive. Akira kept track of the loners, whether elderly or not—those unfortunate souls no one gave a damn about anymore. Scavenging on the dead had kept Akira and his family alive and had turned into a lucrative business.

A shiny object caught Kenji's eye. On the floor, underneath a pile of papers, there was a flash of silver. He reached down and pulled out an engraved silver lighter; an intricate pattern of designs swirled along its oblong shape. Running a finger over the cold surface, he had a vision of his father lighting a cigarette with a lighter very similar to the one in his hand. He could almost hear his mother complaining about the smell and shooing his grinning father out of the house. When they received his father's personal effects, the lighter had been missing, lost at sea along with the entire ship.

Opening the cap, he flicked the flint wheel, watching as a strong flame lit the room.

"Nice lighter," Akira said. "Silver—it would fetch a good price."

Kenji shut the lighter and curved his fingers possessively around it. It was selfish, but he didn't want to sell it. He didn't want to relinquish the small memory it gave him of his father.

Akira stepped out of the shadows and eyed him for a moment before nodding. "You should keep it. Lighters are very handy."

Kenji nodded and shoved it in his pocket—appreciating how his friend instinctively seemed to know how he felt. He owed him so much. With the deaths of Kenji's father and brothers, if it wasn't for Akira, Kenji didn't think his family would make it. It had been two weeks since Akira had called him for a hunt—two lean, hungry weeks. The comforting weight of the sack of rice was a burden he'd happily carry even with the knowledge that it came at another's death.

Several hours later, Kenji sweated under the steady blaze of the hot August sun. His shirt clung to his body as beads of sweat rolled off his hair and into his eyes. Many of his classmates had taken off their shirts, the sun beating down on their reddened backs. He worked side by side with Akira as they dug a new bomb shelter with ten other boys behind the Mitsubishi weapons factory. Foreman Masahito, an ex-soldier who'd lost a leg in battle, had already made his morning inspection rounds and was back in the cool interior of his office. The boys wouldn't see him again until lunchtime.

"Aieeee! It's so hot I feel like a boiled noodle!" Akira said. "Let's take a break and go get a drink of water."

"I hate this!" Kenji kicked at a clod of dirt.

With a loud groan, Akira stretched his arms high over his head. "Well, look at the bright side. We don't have school anymore."

"I liked school," Kenji replied.

Akira sighed. "Sometimes I don't understand how we can be best friends."

Wiping the sweat from his forehead with a small white towel from his back pocket, Kenji walked with Akira into the dark, fortified-concrete building for a respite from the heat. The old building had once been a thriving business center, with many offices and small shops. Now it was a warren of abandoned spaces. They entered the nearest room, where they found another friend, Jun, sitting on a desktop despondently playing with a red metal yo-yo.

"What's the matter with you?" Akira asked, nudging Jun with his elbow.

The smaller boy sighed. "I just don't have any energy. What's the point of it all anyway?"

Kenji nodded in sympathy.

A truck drove by. Several large speakers were affixed to its roof, and a woman's voice blared out at them.

"Hail to His Majesty the Emperor! Hail to the Living God of

Japan! We will win the war against the evil West! The Imperial Army will fight for the honor of our Emperor, our God! Long live the Tenno Heika!"

Kenji thought it was funny how they all ignored the monotonous refrain that was meant to bolster their morale. All it did was increase their resentment at the Emperor's never-ending war.

"I hate that stupid truck," Akira said. "At least when it gave out food, we had something to look forward to."

Jun groaned. "Don't remind me! A nasty tin of tuna fish, hard biscuits, and a small container of rice. It wasn't even that good!"

"You wouldn't complain about it now," Akira said with a smirk. "You'd be ripping that truck apart trying to get to the food, along with thousands of others."

"Stop talking about food!" Jun shouted. "I swear I'm glad they lowered the conscription age! Only two more years and we can start eating three meals a day."

"Hopefully the war will be over by then," Kenji said.

"The war will never be over," Akira snarled.

Kenji shook his head. "It has to end. We're dying out."

Akira stopped and stared at his friend. "What do you mean?"

Kenji was staring out the grimy windows. "It's been fifteen years that we've been fighting the West. The Emperor can't hold out against them much longer. Every year things are getting worse. They keep dropping the conscription age because we're running out of soldiers to send into battle."

After the first world war had devastated most of Europe, Asia, and South America, the remaining powers had carved up the planet, claiming countries as if they were nothing more than pawns on a chess board. Until finally there were only two powers left: the President of the West and the Emperor of the East.

"But the worst part is that whole cities are disappearing, and no one knows what's happened to them," Kenji said.

"I know, it's the strangest thing," Jun cut in. "My brother's squadron flew over Beijing last month. He wrote and said it was nothing like he'd ever seen. A whole city destroyed and empty—no people anywhere. What happened to them?"

Akira scowled. "Whole cities can't disappear. It's just crazy rumors!"

Kenji shook his head. "It's not just rumors, Akira. We had cousins living in Manila who were supposed to come home last month. They've disappeared, and there's no radio contact with Manila at all. It's like they've been wiped off the face of the earth."

"Damn it! That's just not possible!" Akira yelled. "Maybe they were bombed, and that's why they're all dead."

"But what kind of bomb wipes out an entire city? Nobody has that kind of technology!" Jun said. "And where are the survivors?" His yo-yo twirled forgotten on its string.

"What if cities are disappearing out there every day, and we don't even know about it?" Kenji asked. "What if it happens to us?"

They were all quiet. After a moment, Jun got up with a heavy sigh, winding up his yo-yo as he trudged back out into the sun. Kenji and Akira sat drinking water and fanning themselves, still too hot to move, when Akira bolted up in alarm.

"Look!" He pointed out the window. "It's a B-29 bomber! Western."

He ran to the window and looked about wildly as Kenji dashed over to his side.

"Huh, there's only one," Akira said. "What the hell is it doing out here by itself? On a suicide mission?"

He turned away with a heavy sigh. "I'm too hot and tired to care anymore."

Kenji remained at the window, staring at the plane. "Hey," he said in excitement. "It's a parachute! Maybe the pilot had engine troubles and had to abandon his plane."

Akira looked toward where Kenji was pointing, but he was too late. The parachute had already dropped beyond their view.

"I didn't see anything. Maybe it was the sun in your eyes," he said. He stomped to the back of the room and sat on the floor, where it was dark and cool.

Kenji watched his friend with amusement before turning back to the window. Suddenly, a bright flash of light filled the entire room, blinding him. He averted his face and closed his eyes. But the multicolored light was seared onto his eyeballs. In the next second, a thunderous blast threw him across the room.

Clouds of dust floated everywhere. So thick, Kenji couldn't breathe. He needed air, but he couldn't move. Opening his eyes, he felt the sting of a thousand scorpion bites prickling his skin. Looking down, he saw shards of glass protruding from his arms and legs. His body began to tremble from shock as tears of fright coursed down his face.

"Kenji! Where are you?"

He heard Akira shout for him, but the sound was muffled, as if he was underwater. Trying to stifle his fears, he called out to his friend. "Over here. I'm hurt."

From the corner of his eye, he caught a figure moving toward him, climbing over rubble. The air was thick with ash, floating particles, and something worse. He couldn't move, still stunned from the explosion. Akira cleared debris off Kenji's glass-covered body before pulling him up out of the rubble.

"We have to get out of here!" Akira said. "They might come back and bomb us again."

Kenji began to pull the glass shards from his arms and legs as Akira looked on in horrified fascination.

"Doesn't that hurt?" he asked.

Shaking his head, Kenji concentrated on removing the worst of the pieces. There seemed to be no pain, even as blood oozed from his wounds. Pulling out the final piece, he looked at his friend. Other than a film of dust covering him, Akira looked unhurt.

"What's the matter with your face?" Akira asked. "You're all red and burned on your right side."

"I don't know," Kenji said, putting up a shaky hand to touch his numb cheek. "I can't feel anything. What about you? Are you hurt?"

Akira shook his head. "My ears ache, but that's it. I guess I was lucky to be sitting in the back." He let out a shaky breath that sounded on the verge of tears. "Let's get out of here."

Stepping out of the building, the boys were stunned by the sight before them. Bodies burned beyond recognition lay every-where. Most were dead, but more frightening were the ones that moaned and wept, trembling in pain.

At his feet, Kenji nearly stepped on the charred remains of a young boy—a red yo-yo still caught up within his blackened grip.

"Jun," Kenji whispered. He blinked back tears as he tried to swallow the scream building inside him.

All around them, fire burned everything. People were rushing toward the river in a panic. Akira pulled Kenji with him into the crowd.

"Wait! My family! I have to find them," Kenji called to Akira. A group of soldiers ran by at that moment, herding people toward the hills and shouting out warnings of further attacks.

"No! We have to keep going. It's not safe. They might come back any minute now." Akira forcibly dragged Kenji away.

Kenji resisted. Pulling away, he stopped a passing soldier.

"Excuse me, sir, could you please tell me if Urakami-machi got bombed?" Kenji asked.

The soldier looked down with dead eyes. "Urakami is a burning inferno. The bomb dropped right on the cathedral. Nothing survived there. Save yourself and get the hell out of here!"

Akira pulled Kenji away, and both boys began to run as fast they could. They had not gotten far when a stabbing pain struck Kenji in his chest, slowing him down. Stopping, he pressed hot hands against swollen eyes blurred with tears.

"They can't be dead. They just can't…they just can't," Kenji said over and over as his mind repelled the thought. Akira, noticing that his friend had fallen behind, ran back and, throwing Kenji's arm around his sturdy shoulders, dragged him up a nearby hillside. Reaching a patch of green, both boys collapsed to the ground. Suddenly, Akira cried out in horror. Kenji looked up in a daze to see a large patch of skin dangling from Akira's hand. It had ripped off Kenji's shoulder in a large sheet as his friend had helped him sit down. Horror-struck by what he had done, Akira began to cry.

"Don't die, Kenji! We'll get out of here together! Please don't die," Akira wept.

"Water, I need water," Kenji said. He was disoriented and had not felt the skin rip off his shoulder.

"I'll get it. Stay here. Don't move." Akira rose to his feet and rushed toward the river.

From the hilltop, Kenji looked down on the area where the Mitsubishi factory had been.

Wake up, Kenji, you're having a nightmare, he thought. But his eyes remained open, taking in the wasteland of piles of burning rubble and dying people. Monsters climbed up the hill pleading for help. Hideous creatures whose distorted humanity made them more frightening than any tales of demons and oni. Was this what had happened to his family?

A young girl crawled up the hillside, half-naked but for the tattered remnants of her school uniform. The left side of her face was swollen and red like a balloon. The right side was blackened—the skin burned away. Her head was bald but for small patches of wavy black hair that had once been long and luxurious.

Catching sight of Kenji, she called out to him.

"Is that you, Kenji-chan? I'm so happy to find you!" Reaching out a hand to touch Kenji's foot, she collapsed at his feet. Her entire frame shuddered one last time before stilling—her eyes remained open and staring up at him. There was nothing about her he could recognize. Her face was a grotesque mask. And yet he grieved for her. It was as if she had held on until finding someone she knew, afraid to die alone.

Akira appeared, a small can of water in his hand, which he

gave to Kenji to drink.

"Who was that?" he asked when he saw the body at Kenji's feet.

"I don't know," Kenji said after drinking down the precious water. "But she knew me." He gasped. "She knew me."

"Come on, let's follow the train tracks. I hear there will be relief trains coming through if we can get to Michino-o station," Akira said.

"But that's in Nagoya. I don't know if I can make it that far." Kenji felt weak. Leaning over, he vomited up the water he had just swallowed.

"It's less than two kilometers. You can make it. I'll help you. Please! We have to try or we'll die here!" Desperation sounded in Akira's voice.

For his friend's sake, Kenji got up and began to walk down the hillside. He was light-headed and confused. Had it been hours or days since the bomb had fallen? Only Akira's sturdy arm around him felt real. Everything else was a nightmare.

They walked slowly, picking their way around downed utility lines, twisted steel girders, and pieces of broken buildings and houses. Roads were gone, and what would have been an easy route was now impassable, as dangerous live wires wreaked havoc, spreading fires through the ruins. Breathing became more and more difficult for Kenji. He felt as if a hot knife had stabbed him in his lungs.

By late afternoon, Akira was practically dragging Kenji along.

"Akira, leave me here to rest. I'm too tired. I can't make it," Kenji said, falling to the ground. Akira stood in front of him, heaving with sweat.

"No, I'm not leaving you. We're going to make it. I see the train tracks up ahead. It's clear over there, so it'll be easier to walk. We'll make it," Akira said.

"I can barely see anymore, and my face feels so hot. Please just leave me here." Kenji's face had swollen up so badly that when he touched it, he couldn't feel his own fingers. Peering up into Akira's face, he could make out his friend's scared but stubborn look.

"Akira," he whispered. "You know I'm dying. You know you can sense it."

"No! I won't let you die," Akira said. "I won't let you!" He leaned over and grabbed Kenji under his shoulder, and began walking again.

They followed the train tracks until they reached Michino-o station in Nagoya. On the platform, already crowded with shell-shocked victims, the boys lay down in a small, dirty corner at the very end of the station, uncovered by a roof.

As soon as Akira's head touched the floor, he fell into a deep sleep, exhausted by his ordeal. Kenji lay on his back, looking straight up at the darkening sky, so clear and cloudless. He couldn't see a lot, his eyes having closed to near slits. Every breath felt like a fire in his chest. All around him he could hear the sound of suffering. Closing his eyes, he pictured his mother, her beautiful face smiling at him until she morphed into a creature with melting skin.

His chest was burning inside, pain tearing, ripping with every gasping breath. Through the thudding in his ears, he heard the sound of an approaching train. He saw Akira sit up and rub his eyes, wiping away the tears that had fallen as he slept. Without a word, he lifted Kenji to his feet and began to push a path for them toward the edge of the platform. Still, they were caught in the periphery. When the train arrived, they were shoved and jostled farther away from the door until they found themselves behind the last car of the train. Kenji tripped and fell, taking Akira down with him. They were lost in a sea of bodies that was quickly leaving them behind.

"Come on," Akira said. "You have to get up!" People were climbing over them, frantic to get on the train. Akira covered Kenji's body with his, shoving the agitated mass away from them. As the crowd around them died down, Akira hauled Kenji up. He rushed forward, dragging Kenji with him, but came to an abrupt halt. His absolute stillness in the midst of the chaos was frightening.

"Something's wrong," he said, starting to back away from the train—away from the people.

"Where are we going?" Kenji asked, confused by his friend's actions. At that moment he heard the train doors open, and all movement stopped. There was an uneasy silence, broken by gasps of horror.

"What's going on?" Kenji asked.

A harsh voice began shouting, but he couldn't make out what was being said. Then the sound of bullets filled the air— thousands of bullets ripping through flesh. Bodies fell before them even as others turned to run away. Through the pandemonium Kenji could see soldiers standing in every doorway of the train, spraying the crowd with their machine guns. Blood poured, red and thick, splattering in wide arcs. He watched as it pooled on the ground—wondering how he'd ever thought red a beautiful color.

"What's wrong with them? The soldiers have gone crazy!" Akira shouted.

Kenji shook his head. Akira was wrong. It wasn't the soldiers who were crazy. It was their world.

He felt himself dragged across the pavement until he was stumbling onto his feet, held tightly around his waist by Akira. They ran behind the train, across the tracks, and over the platform. He could hear the rapid fire of the machine guns and the never-ending screams.

Kenji saw Akira point somewhere in front of them.

"There's a drainage ditch with a tunnel over there. We have to make for it now," he said.

Kenji nodded and nearly fainted in agony as his friend pulled him into a crouch and ran for the tunnel. He couldn't see where they were going. He just put one foot in front of the other.

He didn't want to live anymore. Not in this world. All his family was gone. His city was destroyed, and now he knew that his people had suffered the ultimate betrayal by their emperor. But he couldn't summon up the energy to hate him. He was too tired.

They walked in semidarkness, and the guns seemed muted. They stepped into something slick and wet. Kenji could smell old, stagnant water and the fouler stench of oil. He stumbled, falling onto his knees, one hand flung out to stop his fall. Akira pulled him up, keeping an arm around his waist. Kenji rubbed his hand on his shirt, trying to wipe off the waxy feel of the oil. They kept moving, their feet wet from the smelly water, as the tunnel got dimmer and dimmer.

He didn't know how long they had traveled. At some point

his feet stopped working, and he let his friend drag him along. He no longer cared. All he wanted was to rest. To sleep and never wake up again. To leave behind the hell his world had turned into.

"This is what happened to them," Kenji said. "A bomb like nothing else in the world. A city killer."

Next to him, he realized that Akira was crying. "It's the most horrible thing I've ever seen. Who would invent such a terrible weapon?"

"They invented it to win the war," Kenji said.

"Then why haven't they won already? Why are we still fighting?" Akira asked.

"It's the Emperor," Kenji said. "The Emperor's army comes in afterward and cleans up the city so that no one can know the danger of the bomb. That's why there are no survivors."

"But why?" Akira asked. "Why kill us?"

"So that the war can continue," Kenji said. He remembered what his father had said so long ago. War was only good for governments and always bad for the people. "If we knew about this bomb, people would revolt and stop fighting for the Emperor."

He knew this as certainly as he knew he was dying.

"Only when we are all dead will the Emperor let us free," Kenji said. His breath became more and more labored. He could feel Akira's muscles straining under his weight, his pace unsteady and slowing.

"Don't say that. We're safe now. Don't worry. Everything will be all right," Akira said.

But Kenji didn't hear him. Instead, he heard the thudding of many footsteps echoing from behind them. The soldiers had found the tunnel. Akira was breathing harshly from having to carry him. Kenji knew he wasn't aware of the danger yet. And it was getting closer.

He couldn't let his friend get caught. Akira was his best friend. The only person in the world Kenji loved as much as his own family. It would be his fault. He was the one slowing him down.

A sudden shout behind them caused Akira to jump. Using the last of his strength, Kenji pulled away and fell against the wall, nearly sliding down the curved side. With a hard shove, he pushed his friend's hands away.

"Akira, do me a favor," Kenji said, battling for breath. "Leave me. Just leave me here, and run and hide. Don't let them catch you. Don't let them kill you. You have to survive. Promise me that."

"I won't leave you!" Akira said.

"You must," he breathed. "You're strong. You can make it. Someone must remember what the Emperor is doing to us. Someone's gotta stop this war. You have to hide. Go to Uraka-mi. The soldier said that's where the bomb dropped. No one survived. They won't think to look for survivors there. You'll be safe."

He could hear the footsteps louder than ever, the harsh calls of the soldiers shouting out commands, the rapid-fire spraying of bullets. They were too close. The pain that had been so overwhelming had suddenly faded, leaving Kenji with only one thought. He pushed Akira as hard as he could.

"Run, Akira! Run now and don't look back!"

Turning from his best friend, Kenji stumbled away. He heard Akira's sobs and then the splashing of water that receded into silence. All alone in near darkness, Kenji continued to stagger toward the approaching footsteps. His vision blurred, and his breathing was painful and shallow. Propping himself up against the wall, he fumbled in his pocket until his fingers curled around the silver cigarette lighter he'd found earlier that day. He pulled it out with trembling fingers, letting his palm wrap tightly around the oblong cylinder as he flicked open the lid. The soldiers were seconds away from him, but all he could think of was his friend running for his life. Kenji knew Akira had to survive—had to somehow spread the word of the Emperor's deceit. He placed his thumb on the flint wheel and pushed away from the wall. He stood in the middle of the tunnel, listening to the approach of the soldiers.

"There he is!"

"He's just a kid!"

"Take him down, take him down!"

He didn't feel the bullets that ripped into his body. All his effort was concentrated on his thumb as it ignited the lighter. He saw the flame light up in his hand as his body fell backward—the sizzle of the oil erupted all around him. The screams of the soldiers brought a smile to his face.

Akira was safe now.

Closing his eyes, he could almost smell the fresh, light perfume of cherry blossoms in the air.

"Mother," he whispered. "Mother, I'm coming. I'm coming home."

Freshee's Frogurt

by Daniel H. Wilson

It looks me right in the eyes, man. And I can tell that it's ... *thinking*. Like it's alive. And pissed off.

Jeff Thompson

Precursor Virus + 3 months

This interview was given to Oklahoma police officer Lonnie Wayne Blanton by a young fast-food worker named Jeff Thompson during Thompson's stay at Saint Francis Hospital. It is widely believed to be the first recorded incident of a robot malfunction occurring during the spread of the Precursor Virus that led to Zero Hour only nine months later.

— Cormac Wallace MIL#GHA217

Howdy there, Jeff. I'm Officer Blanton. I'll be taking your statement about what happened at the store. To be honest, the crime scene was a mess. I'm counting on you to explain every detail so we can figure out why this happened. You think you can tell me?

Sure, officer. I can try.

The first thing I noticed was a sound. Like a hammer tapping on the glass of the front door. It was dark outside and bright inside so I couldn't see what was making the noise.

I'm in Freshee's Frogurt, elbow-deep in a twenty-quart Sani-Serv frogurt machine trying to pry out the churn bar from the very back and getting orange creme-sicle all over my right shoulder.

Just me and Felipe are there. Closing time is in, like, five minutes. I'm finally done mopping up all the sprinkles that get glued to the floor with ice cream. I've got a towel on the counter covered in the metal parts from inside the machine. Once I get them all out, I'm supposed to clean the pieces, cover them in lube, and put them back. Seriously, it's the grossest job ever.

Felipe is in the back washing the cookie sheets. He has to let the sinks drain real slow or else they flood the floor drain and I have to go back in there and mop all over again. I've told that dude a hundred times not to let the wash sinks drain all at once.

Anyway.

The tapping sound is real light. *Tap, tap, tap.* Then it stops. I watch as the door slowly cracks open and a padded gripper slips around the edge.

Is it unusual for a domestic robot to come into the store?

Nope. We're in Utica Square, man. Domestics come in and buy a 'nilla Frogurt now and then. Usually they're buyin' for a rich person in the neighborhood. None of the other customers ever wanna wait in line behind a robot, though, so it takes, like, ten times longer than if the person just got off their ass and came in. But, whatever. A Big Happy type of domestic comes in probably once a week with a paypod inside its chest and its gripper out to hold a waffle cone.

What happens next?

Well, the gripper is moving weird. Normally, the domestics, like, do the same sort of pushing motion. They do this stupid I-am-opening-a-door-now shove, no matter what door they're standing in front of. That's why people are always pissed off if they get stuck behind a domestic while it's trying to get inside. It's way worse even than being stuck behind an old lady.

But this Big Happy is different. The door cracks open and its gripper kind of sneaks around the edge and pats up and down the handle. I'm the only one who sees it because there's nobody else in the store and Felipe is in the back. It happens fast, but it looks to me like the robot is trying to feel out where the lock is at.

Then the door swings open and the chimes ring. The domestic is about five-feet tall and covered in a layer of thick, shiny blue plastic. It doesn't come all the way inside the store, though.

Instead, it stands there in the doorway real still and its head scans back and forth, checking out the whole room: the cheap tables and chairs, my counter with the towel on it, the ice cream freezers. Me.

We looked up the registration plate on this machine and it checked out. Besides the scanning, was there anything else strange about the robot? Out of the ordinary?

The thing's got scuffs all over it. Like it got hit by a car or had a fight or something. Maybe it was broken.

It walks inside, then turns right around and locks the door. I pull my arm out of the Frogurt machine and just stare at the domestic robot with its creepy smiling face as it walks toward me.

Then it reaches right over the counter with both grippers and grabs me by the shirt. It drags me over the counter, scattering pieces of the taken-apart Frogurt machine all over the floor. My shoulder slams into the cash register and I feel this sick crunching from inside.

The thing fucking dislocated my shoulder in about one second!

I scream for help. But frigging Felipe doesn't hear me. He's got the dishes soaking in soapy water and is out smoking a jay in the alley behind the store. I try my best to get away, kicking and struggling, but the grippers have closed in on my shirt like two pairs of pliers. And the bot's got more than my shirt. Once I'm over the counter it pushes me into the ground. I hear my left collarbone snap. After that it gets really hard to breathe.

I let out another little scream, thinking: You sound like an animal, Jeff dude. But my weird little yell seems to get the thing's attention. I'm on my back and the domestic is looming over me; it's sure as hell not letting go of my shirt. The Big Happy leans over, its head blocking the fluorescent light on the ceiling. I blink away tears and look up at its frozen, grinning face.

It looks me right in the eyes, man. And I can tell that it's...thinking. Like it's alive. And pissed off.

Nothing changes on its face or anything but I get a pretty bad feeling right then. I mean, an even worse feeling. And sure enough, I hear the servos in the thing's arm start to grind. Now it turns and swings me to the left, smashing the side of my head into the door of the pie fridge hard enough to crack the glass. The whole right side of my head feels cold and then warm. Then the side of my face and neck and arm all start to feel really warm, too. Blood's shooting out of me like a damn fire hydrant.

Jesus, I'm crying. And that's when...uh. That's when Felipe shows up.

Do you give the domestic robot money from the register?

What? It doesn't ask for money. It never asks for money. It doesn't say a word. What went down wasn't a tele-robbery, man. I don't even know if it was being remote-controlled, Officer...

Blanton.

Blanton.

What do you think it wants?

41

It wants to kill me. That's all. It wants to murder my ass. The thing was on its own and it was out for blood.

Go on.

Once it got hold of me, I didn't think it would let go until I was dead. But my man Felipe wasn't having any of that shit. He comes running out the back hollering like a motherfucker. Dude was pissed. And Felipe is a big man. Got that Fu Manchu 'stache and all kinds of ink running up and down his arms. Badass shit, too, like dragons and eagles and this one prehistoric fish all the way down his forearm. A "colecanth" or something. It's like this monster dinosaur fish that they thought was extinct. There are fossils of it and everything. Then one day some fisherman gets the surprise of his life when he pulls up a real live devil fish from hell below. Felipe used to say that the fish was proof you can't keep a motherfucker down forever. Someday you gotta rise up again, you know?

What happened next, Jeff?

Yeah, right. I'm on the ground bleeding and crying and Big Happy's got me by the shirt. Then Felipe comes running out the back and turns the corner of the counter roaring like a friggin' barbarian. His hairnet is off and his long hair is flying. He grabs the domestic by the shoulders, just snatches it up and throws it down. It lets go of me and falls backward through the front door, shards of glass flying everywhere. The bell chimes again. *Bing bong.* It's such a dorky sound for this kind of violent shit that it makes me smile through all the blood running down my face.

Felipe kneels down and sees the damage. "Oh fuck, Jefe," he says. "What'd it do to you?"

But I see Big Happy moving behind Felipe now. My face must tell the whole story because Felipe grabs me by the waist and drags me back around the counter without even looking at the door. He's panting and taking little crab steps. I can smell the joint in his front pocket. He drags me around behind the counter and as I watch my blood smearing behind me on the tile floor, I think, shit, man, I just mopped that.

We make it inside the doorway behind the register and into the cramped back room. There's a low row of stainless steel sinks full of soapy water, a wall of cleaning supplies, and a little cubby desk in the corner that has our punch clock sitting on it. In the very back is a narrow hallway that leads to the alley behind the store.

Then Big Happy plows into Felipe out of nowhere. Instead of following behind us, the fucker was smart enough to climb over the counter and head us off at the pass. I hear a thump and see Big Happy bash Felipe across the chest with its forearm. Not at all like getting punched by a guy; more like getting hit by a car or, like, nailed by a falling brick or something. Felipe flies backward and hits the cabinet doors where we keep all the paper towels and stuff. He stays on his feet, though. When he stumbles forward, I see a dent in the wood from the back of his head. But he's wide awake and more pissed off than ever.

I drag myself away, towards the sinks, but my shoulder is messed up and my arms are slippery with blood and I can hardly breathe from the pain in my chest.

There aren't any weapons or anything back here so Felipe snatches the mop from the filthy yellow bucket on wheels. It's an old mop with a solid wooden handle and it's been there I don't know how long. There's no room to swing the mop but it doesn't matter because the robot is hell-bent on grabbing Felipe the same way it grabbed me. He rams the mop up and gets it wedged under Big Happy's chin. Felipe isn't a tall guy but he's taller than the machine and has a longer reach. It can't get a hold of him. He shoves the machine away from us, its arms waving around like snakes.

The next part is awesome.

Big Happy falls backward onto the cubby desk in the corner, its legs sticking straight out, heels on the ground. With no hesitation, Felipe raises his right foot straight up and comes down with all his weight on its knee joint. *Snap!* The robot's knee pops and bends backward at a totally fucked-up angle. With the mop handle stuck under its chin, the machine can't catch its balance and it can't grab hold of Felipe, either. I'm wincing just looking at that knee but the machine doesn't make any noise or anything. I only hear its motors grinding and the sound of its hard plastic shell banging into the desk and wall while it struggles to get up.

"Yeah, motherfucker!" Felipe shouts before crushing the robot's other knee joint backwards. Big Happy lays on its back with both legs broken and an angry-as-fuck sweaty two-hundred-pound Mexican on top of it. I can't help but start thinking that everything is going to be okay.

Turns out I'm wrong about that.

It's his hair, you know. Felipe's hair is too long. Simple as that.

The machine stops struggling, reaches out and clamps a

44

gripper down on Felipe's dark black mane. He hollers and yanks his head back. But this isn't like getting your hair pulled in a bar fight; this is like getting caught in a shredder or a piece of heavy equipment in a factory. It's brutal. Every muscle in Felipe's neck stands out and he screams like an animal. His eyes squeeze shut as he pulls away with all his might. I can hear the roots tearing out from his scalp. But the fucking thing just pulls Felipe's face closer and closer.

It's unstoppable, like gravity or something.

After a couple seconds, Felipe is close enough that Big Happy can get hold of him with its other gripper. The mop handle clatters to the floor as the other gripper closes in on Felipe's chin and mouth, crushing the bottom part of his face. He screams and I can hear his jaw cracking. Teeth pop out of his mouth like fucking popcorn.

That's when I realize that I'm probably going to die in the back room of Freshee's fuckin' Frogurt.

I never spent much time in school. It's not that I'm stupid. I mean, I guess I'm just saying I'm not generally known for my bright ideas. But when your ass is on the line and violent death is ten feet away, I think it can really put your brain in gear.

So a bright idea comes to me. I reach behind me and bury my good left arm in the cold soaking water in the sink. In the water, I can feel cookie sheets and dippers, but I'm fishing for the drain plug. Across the room, Felipe is quieting down, making some gurgling sounds. Blood is pouring out of him, down Big Happy's arm. The whole bottom of his face is crushed in its gripper. Felipe's eyes are open and kind of bugging out, but I think he's pretty much out of it.

Man, I hope he's out of it.

The machine is doing that scanning thing again, being really still and turning its face left and right real slow.

By now my arm is going numb, the blood cut off from where I have it hooked over the lip of the sink. I keep fishing for the plug.

Big Happy stops scanning, looks right at me. It pauses for maybe a second and then I hear its gripper motors whining as it lets go of poor Felipe's face. He drops to the ground like a sack of bricks.

I'm whimpering. The alley door is a million miles away and I can barely keep my head up. I'm sitting in a pool of my own blood and I can see Felipe's teeth on the tile floor. I know what's going to happen to me and there's nothing I can do about it and I know it's gonna hurt so much.

At last, I find the drain plug and rake at it with my dead fingers. It pops out of the drain and I hear the gurgling of water draining out. I told Felipe a hundred times, if the sink drains out too fast it'll flood the floor drain and then I gotta mop in here all over again.

You know Felipe flooded that motherfucker on purpose every night for about a month before we finally made friends? He was pissed off that our boss hired a white guy for the front and a Mexican guy for the back. I didn't blame him. You know what I mean, Officer? You're Indian, right?

Native American, Jeff. Osage Nation. Try and tell me what happened next.

Well, I used to hate mopping up that water. And now I'm

46

laying on the floor counting on it to save my life.

Big Happy tries to stand, but its legs are useless. It collapses onto the floor, face down. Then it starts to crawl forward on its stomach, using its arms. It's got that awful grin on its face and its eyes are locked on mine as it drags itself across the room. There's blood all over it, like a crash test dummy that bleeds.

The drain isn't flooding fast enough.

I press my back against the sink as hard as I can. My knees are up and my legs pulled in tight. The glurg, glurg of the water draining out of the sink pulses behind my head. If the plug gets sucked halfway back in to slow it down or something, I'm dead. I'm totally dead.

The robot is pulling itself closer. It reaches out a gripper and tries to grab my Air Force One. I yank my foot back and forth, and it misses me. So it pulls itself even closer. On the next lunge, I know it's probably going to get hold of my leg and crush it.

As its arm rises, the whole robot all of a sudden gets yanked back about three feet. It turns its head and there's Felipe, laying on his back and choking on his own blood. His sweaty black hair is clinging in streaks to his ruined face. There's, like, no mouth on him anymore, just a big raw wound. But his eyes are open wide and burning with something beyond hatred. I know he's saving my life, but he looks, well, evil. Like a demon on a surprise visit from Hell.

He yanks on Big Happy's shattered leg one more time, then closes his eyes. I don't think he's breathing anymore. The machine ignores him. It aims its smiling face at me and keeps on coming.

Just then, a flood of water bubbles up out of the floor drain.

The soapy water pools up quick and silent, turning light pink.

Big Happy is crawling again when the water soaks into its broken knee joints. There's a smell of burnt plastic in the air and the machine freezes up and stops. Nothing exciting. The machine just stops working. It must of got water in its wires and, like, short-circuited.

It's about a foot away from me, still smiling.

That's really all there is to tell. You know the rest.

Thanks, Jeff. I know that wasn't easy. I got everything I need to make my report now. I'll let you get some rest.

Hey man, can I ask a question real quick before you go?

Shoot.

How many domestics are out there? Big Happys, Slow Sues, and the rest of 'em? Because I heard there were, like, two of them for every one person.

I don't know. Listen, Jeff, the machine just went willy nilly. We can't explain it.

Well, what's going to happen if they all start hurting people, dude? What's going to happen if we're outnumbered? That thing wanted to kill me, period. I told it to you straight. Nobody else might believe me, but you know what's up.

Promise me something, Officer Blanton. Please.

What's that?

Promise me that you'll watch out for the robots. Watch 'em close. And…don't let them hurt anybody else like they did Felipe. Okay?

After the collapse of the United States government Officer Lonnie Wayne Blanton joined the Osage Nation Lighthorse Tribal Police. It was there, in service of the Osage People's sovereign government, that Lonnie Wayne had the chance to make good on his promise to Jeff.

Uncertainty Principle

by K. Tempest Bradford

The world always changed around Iliana, but she never changed with it. She could always feel this when it happened: a roaring, rushing sound filled her ears, invisible tendrils gripped her chest and heart. It never lasted more than a second. So fleeting she could dismiss it except for the consequences. Because when the sound faded and the pain eased, the world around her had changed, even if she didn't know how.

This went on all her life, as far as she could tell. Even before she knew what it meant. Looking back, she recognized moments she'd dismissed or misunderstood. Like the time her mother's hair went from long to short right in front of her yet no one else noticed. Or the day her school's name changed from King to Bond Hill Elementary, and no one remembered it any differently.

But there was no mistaking what happened on the night of her seventh birthday.

Iliana's parents deemed her old enough to have a sleepover, so she got to invite five best friends. At bedtime, they all went to the basement to make pallets out of their sleeping bags and blankets. When the sound rushed up on her, she remembered thinking, *Oh no, not again*. Louder than it had ever been, the sound roared louder than a train speeding past.

She remembered how it felt—as if someone pulled her heart out of her—and cried out as it stopped for a beat. She didn't remember falling down or passing out. When she could hear again, Cara's voice yelling for her mom cut through the haze. Ripley shook her, saying, "Wake up, wake up!" while both Sarah and Nora cried.

Her mom hurried down the stairs, footsteps like thunder on the old wood. "Ili, sweetheart, are you okay? Open your eyes, *m'ija*." She didn't want to move, irrationally afraid that the pain would come back. But the fear in her mother's voice made her scared, too, so she obeyed.

"What happened?" her mom asked.

"I felt—" The girls had moved in closer, and she noticed one standing next to Ripley that she'd never seen before. "Who's that?"

"Who's who?"

Iliana pointed at the new girl, who looked both scared and a little hurt.

"That's Nivair, honey."

"But... where's Grayson?"

Grayson was her first best friend. The only girl in class with kinky curly hair like hers. She hated bananas and broccoli, loved playing basketball and braiding hair, and was two inches taller than every other girl in the second grade.

Those are the things Iliana remembers about Grayson. The only things. She held on to them. Because that night in the basement was the last time she saw her.

Both her mom and her friends said that they didn't know anyone named Grayson. But everyone knew Nivair. Iliana didn't understand. Nivair didn't look anything like Grayson or any other girl in her school. Where did she come from? How could she stand there and say she was Iliana's friend when they'd never met? Everyone, even her mom, looked at her like she was crazy.

It was the most awful feeling. Even worse than the pain in her chest. And when she wouldn't stop crying, her mother decided to take her to the hospital while her dad called the girls' parents to come get them.

In the ER she told nurses and doctors about the pain but refused to talk about Grayson. They hooked her up to machines, did tests, and found nothing.

The pain, like Grayson, must have been in her head, one doctor told her mother. Iliana knew that wasn't true, but it seemed safer to agree and stay quiet. She promised herself that's what she would do if this ever happened again.

The changing didn't stop, though it did pause for a long time. Two years went by before it happened again—just long enough for Iliana to start mistrusting her own memories. Certainty came rushing back along with that sound, now familiar and dreaded, in the middle of math class.

Less severe than the last, the pain dissipated almost as soon as she felt it. Her eyes stayed open, so she saw the classroom walls turn from white to dingy gray. The desks changed, too, now looking older and more abused than they had before. Panic bloomed in her stomach. What, or who, had she lost this time?

No one, it turned out. None of the kids she knew had disappeared. Her house was still there when she got home. Her parents came home in time for dinner, like always. But even that little change at school had to mean something, she decided. So she started keeping track.

She bought an old-fashioned pocket notebook from the paperie in the mall and wrote down all the dates and times she could remember in one column and any changes she could think of in the other. Next to her birthday she wrote just one word in bold, green letters: *Grayson*.

After the day in math class, the changes came faster. The next one happened months later, not years. Same as the one after that. Sometimes the only indication came from the sound and the pain; the differences weren't always immediately apparent. They still affected her, just the same.

The day she had to bring home a report card with a big red C next to Social Studies she wanted to tell her parents how hard it was keeping up with current events and history when the details kept changing on her. And the textbooks. But how could they possibly believe her? It's not like they or anyone else noticed how much the world changed around them.

Like the way their neighborhood went from a community where everyone knew each other to one where people barely talked and then to one where chain-link fences separated increasingly unkempt yards and the only interactions happened when someone's dog or cat violated the boundaries. Peeling paint now scarred every house on her street and the neighboring blocks. Iliana missed flowers the most and the delight of walking home from school in the spring, the air full of bees and fragrance. All over the space of four changes in middle school.

Her parents went from encouraging her to go outside and play with her friends from the block to grounding her if she didn't make it home before the 4:00 P.M. Under-13 curfew that hadn't existed just a week before.

At home, the problems always centered around money. It felt as if funding at the university where her parents worked always shrank after a change. They worried about their department downsizing or having to give up their research. Apparently things were the same at other schools, so no point in moving, according to her father.

Iliana obsessed over news feeds on the family computer or the ones at school, trying to track changes in the wider world. It sometimes took days or weeks of reading and rereading news reports, Wikipedia entries, and magazine archives to find the differences between events and people that she remembered. Though there were plenty of obvious ones.

The US went to war, then a change hit and that war didn't exist. There had been one five years before that caused a major oil shortage. Now they only had one car—an old pre-hybrid style—that they rarely drove because they couldn't afford the gas.

Cities on the coasts had to turn off all electricity during planned hours to save energy. Then a change swept through and the same had been true for Ohio and the rest of the Midwest for over a year.

By the time Iliana started high school, changes might come just weeks apart, keeping her off balance and in a constant state of anxiety. Still, she kept her log faithfully, copying it to multiple pocket notebooks after the morning she woke up to discover the furniture in her room completely rearranged. Nothing was permanent.

Tired of uncertainty, Iliana started experimenting with trying to alter the direction of the changes when they happened, just to see if it was possible. She knew they weren't all about her, of course. However, she reasoned that if she was the only person who noticed, there could be something she could do about them. Whenever the sound rushed up on her, she closed her eyes and concentrated—at first on things she wished she could revert, then later on things she wanted to happened that hadn't—only to be disappointed when she opened them again.

Then after she turned sixteen, she made it through almost a year without any change. After three, then six, then nine months without even the tiniest alteration, Iliana swayed between happiness at a predictable, if crappy, life and fear of when the nightmare would start again.

Then came election night 2048. Like everyone else, Iliana stayed up late with her parents to watch the election coverage. Poll results scrolled across the bottom of the CNN feed, and finally the numbers from Washington, Oregon, California, and the rest of the West Coast came through.

"She's ahead," her mom said.

"Don't jinx it," her dad replied, only half kidding.

Five minutes later, Aishwarya Aguda came on live to announce that all of the West Coast states were for Amirah Ellison, making her the next president of the United States.

Ili's father whooped and cheered and danced like he'd made a touchdown. Even though her mom chided him to keep it down, clearly other people were celebrating just as much. The sound of cheers and honking horns filled the neighborhood. Everyone they knew supported or campaigned for Ellison. She promised to turn the country around.

CNN had Ellison's father on—he'd been the first Muslim congressman ever elected—and Iliana's mom told them (again) about the time she'd met him years ago. Her father said something about champagne just as Iliana heard a change rushing up, yanking her hard into another reality. *No, no, no!* she thought fiercely. This wasn't allowed to be different. Not after all their hard work. *Amirah Ellison is still the president. Amirah Ellison is still the president.*

The noise out in the street ended abruptly. So did the sound from the newsfeed. Iliana opened her eyes. Instead of Ambassador Keith Ellison, Anderson Cooper's face filled the screen.

"Once again, all districts in California have reported in, and we can confidently declare that Timothy Edwards is the winner."

"No!" Iliana blurted. She didn't know this Edwards guy. He wasn't even Ellison's opponent. "What happened to Amirah?"

Her parents, who were not celebrating, turned and looked at her.

"Who?"

Under normal circumstances, Iliana would have just pretended they'd heard her wrong, or she misspoke. But the anger over losing Ellison overwhelmed her. She'd been the first person Iliana had ever really cared about being president. Now she couldn't be sure the woman even existed. None of this was fair.

"Amirah Ellison just won the election! And you don't even remember her. No one *ever* remembers. It's all changed and, and…" She wanted to scream. Everyone had worked so hard.

At first her parents just stared at her, confused. Her birthday all over again. No one would believe, she knew it.

But then her mother asked, "When did it change, Ili?"

Shocked, she answered without hedging, "Just now."

"You saw someone else elected president, then all of a sudden it changed to a different person?" her father asked, tone and voice serious.

"Yeah…"

"Has something like this ever happened before?"

Iliana thought about Grayson, and the hospital, and the doctor saying that she'd made her up. Like an imaginary friend. She didn't need to go through that again.

"No. I'm just being stupid. I'm going to bed."

Just then the electricity went out, signaling the night's black-out period, and Iliana took it as a cue to leave without saying anything more.

The next morning she avoided her parents, still not wanting to talk. The night before she hadn't slept, at first from frustration and anger, then from reading over her notebooks with a flashlight, looking for any clue that would help change things back. Nothing came to her.

All day at school she couldn't be bothered to pay attention. If everything was just going to get worse and worse and Iliana couldn't do anything about it, why care about anything?

On the walk home the funk finally lifted enough for a part of her brain to point out that her parents had tried to listen. She didn't give them a chance, just assumed they wouldn't believe her. Maybe she should have. They were scientists, after all. She needed help figuring all this out. Who better than them?

As she walked across her lawn, Iliana had resolved to tell the truth at dinner that night. Then the sound rushed up on her, so loud her head blossomed in pain almost as intensely, as the squeezing sensation in her chest. It hadn't been this bad since the night of her birthday, and that scared her more than the pain itself.

The grass beneath her, rushing up as she lost her balance and fell down, turned to concrete the moment her heart started beating again, a split second before she fell down hard on her left arm and screamed.

"Iliana!" A woman's voice cried out nearby. One of the neighbors breaking the unspoken rule only to care about what happened inside their own fences? "Are you okay, *m'ija*? What happened? You're bleeding!"

As arms helped her up, Iliana saw her arm scraped and bloody, saw the walk leading to her house on the wrong side of the yard, saw the peeling paint on the house that had changed from blue to brown.

"*Mira*! Ili, look at Mama, sweetie," the woman said. Iliana did look, but this was not her mother.

At the hospital, Iliana stayed silent except to answer the doctor's questions about her arm. The woman calling herself her mother not only looked different, but had a different name: Elena, not Adelina like her real mom. Later, a man she didn't recognize came into the curtained area: her dad. Elena called him Victor, not Malcolm. Not that he looked anything like her real father.

The only time she spoke outside of the doctor's presence was to ask for her chart. She still had the same last name—Cruz—as did Elena. Victor's was Nighthorse-Campbell, not Ahmed. None of this made any sense.

The doctor pronounced her badly bruised but free of broken or fractured bones and told Elena and Victor they could take her home. A brief impulse to tell the doctor that these weren't her parents, that something terrible had happened, to please not make her go with them rose up, then passed away quickly. Not just because no one would have believed her, but because it wasn't true. This was the change again.

Using the pain as an excuse to escape to her room, Iliana pulled out her notebooks and stared at all the pages she'd filled. Did this happen because she was about to tell her parents everything? Did she break a rule? How could there be rules if this didn't happen to anyone else? For the first time it occurred to her that maybe other people experienced this too, and whoever else noticed the changes didn't want anyone to know about it.

The thought kept her up late that night, even though the pills the doctors gave her made sleep very tempting. Still, Iliana needed to work this out. If thought didn't guide or make the change happen, it had to be something else. She needed to find out what that was so she could reverse it. She squished the idea that it couldn't be reversed.

"I will bring them back," she said to the darkness. "I have to."

"You're so quiet lately," Elena noted at breakfast the next morning. "Still zonked from those painkillers?"

"When you get better, I'll teach you to tuck and roll." Victor dropped extra bacon on her plate before sitting down next to her. "Better to get a little dizzy than break a bone."

Elena gave him a playful bump with her hip. "I've never seen you tuck and roll."

"I'm too graceful to fall down."

At least they're friendly, Iliana thought. And it was clear that they loved each other, just like her parents did. That morning she'd been a little afraid to go downstairs. What if these parents were in the middle of a divorce, or really strict, or some other horrible scenario?

While relieved that none of those fears turned out to be real, the differences between these new parents and her real ones still kept her off balance. Elena worked as a journalist for the *Cincinnati Post* and Victor as an engineer at the public radio station. Iliana could tell that Elena was mestizo, like her real mom. Victor she couldn't guess by looking, but from the award certificates on the wall in his study, she surmised that he had Native American ancestry, not Black and Arab like her real dad.

That morning, after they left, she spent a long time looking in the mirror, trying to tell if she'd changed at all. Was she still half

Black and Arab, or half Native American now? She didn't look any different—thick, curly, kinky hair; brown skin; wide nose.... A thrill ran up and down her body. Her nose still looked just like her real father's. Did that mean that whatever had changed, he still existed somewhere? Her mom, too?

"I'm going to get you back," she promised again. "No matter how long it takes."

The doctor suggested letting her take the day off from school, to which Elena and Victor agreed. So Iliana put it to good use. Even though it hurt her arm to type, she spent several hours copying the data from her notebooks into the computer in the living room, now the only one in the house besides the tablet.

She stayed offline since they still had a data restriction of just 5GB per month. She'd come home to that change two years ago, and it took a while to get used to not being able to surf as freely as before. This had apparently happened in the current reality as well, since the house account was pretty close to the limit.

Overages cost a lot of money. And she doubted Victor would be any less angry about her racking up a huge bill than Malcolm had been. Still, this was important. She needed help. And this was the best way to get it.

Once she finished typing the data, Iliana picked ten websites to post it. They had to be ones that existed across the changes— a few social networks where she still had an account, news and zine sites, blogs, and forums. To preface the odd collection of dates, times, and notes, she wrote:

The world keeps changing, but I'm not changing with it. How about you?

Text pasted in, her finger hovered over the mouse button. If telling her parents broke the rules, telling the world broke them in a big way.

"They can't make everyone disappear," she said under her breath. Before she could second-guess herself anymore, Iliana clicked SUBMIT ten times and watched as each posting went through.

A change tugged at her, so lightly she hardly felt it. A beat passed—nothing. Then Iliana heard her favorite song coming from the kitchen. Grabbing an umbrella from the closet (for defense), she carefully opened the door, not sure what to expect.

What she saw definitely didn't fit into any of her preconceived notions. A person—a girl?—stood by the stove, dressed in what looked like a wet suit except it was white and cottony. The suit covered every part of the girl except her face.

"Iliana?"

"…Yes?"

"Hi, I'm Viola. I got your message."

Viola tapped a device in her hand, and the music stopped. It looked like one of the droid handhelds Iliana used to have before her electronics downgraded, then disappeared completely.

"Sorry for the drama. I didn't think a strange voice calling your name would be a good way to start." Though she saw Viola's lips move, her voice came out of the kitchen's speakers.

Iliana's head swirled with questions, and it took a moment to sort them all out, so she blurted the first thing that came to her: "Your voice, it's…"

Viola nodded at the speakers. "I know, it's weird. I'm actually talking through your tablet because it's the only piece of technology you have that's compatible with mine. It's connected to the speakers."

"Oh." This explained nothing.

"I'm phased. You can't hear me unless I transmit." Viola continued on, seeing the *What does that even mean?* look on Iliana's face. "No one explained...? Clearly not. I'm out of sync with you by 0.1123 seconds. So I don't disturb the timeline."

None of this made any sense to Iliana, and this clearly confused Viola as much as Viola confused her.

"Didn't the walker who left the message for us tell you how this all worked?"

"What? Who?" Iliana said. "I don't know anyone named Walker."

"I mean the person who told you to post all those dates."

"No one told me to do it. I wrote those posts on my own."

Clearly Viola had a hard time believing this, though Iliana couldn't figure out why. "How did you know about those dates?"

Iliana wanted to be irritated that this girl had shown up in her kitchen and started demanding answers without providing any of her own, but she wanted more to tell her story to someone who would probably believe her. Reality changing around her wasn't any crazier than being 0.1123 seconds out of phase. She hoped. So she explained everything that had happened to her, being as detailed as possible when Viola interrupted to ask about specifics.

"So?" Iliana asked once she was done. "Do you know why this is happening to me?"

Viola didn't say anything for a long moment, her face unreadable. "I don't have a concrete answer for you. But what I think is going on... it's complicated."

64

She crossed her arms. "Try."

"All right, the short version: I'm a time walker—I travel in time. As I said, I'm phased so I don't disturb time, just observe it. Normally I'm invisible, but I made an exception here. I thought another walker was trying to reach us through you."

"Why would someone use me?"

"Your message had a lot of valuable data we've been trying to collect for a long time. Tracking down people who change time instead of just observe it."

It did not escape Iliana that Viola hadn't actually answered her question.

"Normally, when time changes, a new timeline takes its place and everyone goes on as if the new timeline had always been there. For them it has. But you...you remember all the old timelines."

"That's not normal, even for you?"

Viola considered carefully before she spoke again. "That's ultracomplicated, too. Listen—" She held up a hand to stop any more questions. "I want to help you figure this out. I need to go talk to the others. But do not worry, all right? We're going to help you."

"You can't go yet!" Iliana started to get a little panicked. "I need help. My parents disappeared. I need to get them back!"

Viola didn't get a chance to answer her. A change rushed up quickly before Iliana could voice a warning, and she disappeared.

"No time for more questions, Ili-girl."

The voice coming from the speakers had changed. Not Viola's anymore but a guy. Iliana turned and saw him standing by the kitchen table—same suit, almost the same face. A brother?

"I need to get you out of here," he said, urgency in his voice.

"What? Who are you?"

He looked up from his droid, surprised. "I'm Sebastian, Iliana."

"Where's Viola?"

A series of emotions flashed across his face. "It just happened, didn't it? A shift."

Guessing he meant a change, she nodded.

Sebastian cursed. "You've got to go before it happens again. Put on the belt."

Assuming he meant the odd-shaped bundle lying on the kitchen table next to him, Iliana picked it up but didn't put it on right away. There were a ton of reasons for her not to do what this guy said, the first being she had no idea who he was. Only one thing mattered, though.

"If I do, you'll help me get my parents back, right?"

"I will help you. But we need to hurry. One minute, forty-five seconds left," he said, looking at his droid.

Iliana wrapped the bulky belt around her, thinking it looked like something Batman would wear, and the front ends snapped together automatically. Two seconds later, every part of her body tingled. Not even in a pleasant way—more like each limb had gone to sleep, then woken up as blood rushed in.

"Fair warning: Time travel without a suit is no fun."

"Wait, I'm time traveling?"

"Only way to keep you safe."

"I can't leave! I—"

"Three . . . two . . ."

Purple light enveloped her body, intensifying the tingling

to the point of real pain. Everything around her dissolved into complete blackness. Not just dark, absolute absence of light. And air. She couldn't breathe and couldn't move, and one thought floated up: *Am I going to die?* Not a second later she felt hot air on her skin when she landed hard on the ground.

"Like I said, not the most pleasant trip."

Iliana drew in deep breaths, then immediately wished she hadn't. Not only was the air hot, it smelled foul and tasted tainted. Standing slowly on the rough, crunching leaves, her body protested every movement.

Sebastian stood a few feet away. "Sorry there wasn't time to prepare you better."

"Where...?" Shaking her head to clear the last of the darkness, Iliana tried to look around. They stood on a wooded hill filled with leafless trees. The setting sun's light had nearly gone, but the orange glow was all wrong....

"*Ay!*"

Just across a narrow river an island parted the water between two larger landmasses, covered as far as she could see with tall buildings jutting into the sky. Every one of them was one fire.

The sun wasn't setting. Rising smoke blocked it out.

"I know, not a pretty sight."

"Where are we?"

"New York City. We're in the Bronx. That"—he nodded at the flames—"is Manhattan. Or will be, from your perspective. You just traveled ten years into your future. The last year of the Oil Wars."

"Looks like we lost."

"Everyone thought so at the time." The timbre of his voice

made Iliana notice for the first time that Sebastian had changed. Before, he hadn't been much older than she. Now deep lines creased his brow and the corners of his eyes.

After another moment of looking at Manhattan, he headed into the trees. "New York City will be uninhabitable for a while. No one is likely to find us."

Iliana followed so she wouldn't have to keep looking at the burning city. As they came to the bottom of the hill, a large mansion came into view.

When they came up on the back, Sebastian tapped his droid. "Someone's at the door."

A purple pinprick of light appeared in the middle of the wall, then irised out until it was wide enough for them to step through. Beyond the light she could see Viola, also older, and a room filled with computers. Following Sebastian's lead, she stepped over the purple-rimmed threshold, the time travel tingling present for just a moment as they passed.

"Welcome to Wave Hill," he said.

The cavernous room they'd stepped into ended up being much bigger than she thought it would be. From the high ceilings, old chandeliers, and deteriorated art on the walls, she guessed it had been a sort of ballroom at one point.

"You'll be safe here," Viola said, no longer wearing a suit.

Once again there were a million questions. "Look, I appreciate you bringing me here and all, but I need to know what's going on. And I need to know what we're going to do to get my parents back."

If she'd offended them, they didn't show it.

"True. You deserve to know," Sebastian said as he peeled off his suit.

Viola hesitated. "Honestly, we're not sure if we can get your parents back."

"But you said you'd help!"

Viola flashed a momentary glance of supreme annoyance Sebastian's way, which he pretended not to see.

"We'll try," she said. "But you have to understand what happened to them."

Iliana's throat tightened—if she left home for nothing…

"In our timeline, your parents are famous," Sebastian explained. "They were the first people to travel back in time. But the tech hadn't been perfected, and they ended up stuck in 1984 for eleven months and six days. When the research team finally brought them back, your mom was pregnant. Coming back induced labor, and she had you twenty-eight minutes later.

"In the timeline we took you from, the same thing happened, except that just before the jump point opened, someone they couldn't identify shot them. They came back, but your father died a few hours later and your mom the next day. Elena is your mother's cousin. She and Victor adopted you."

Which is why she still looked the same. Her real parents still existed. Just dead. Worse than just not existing. "The people changing time, they killed them," Iliana said after processing it all. It wasn't a question, and neither of them challenged her.

"We think the reason you aren't affected by changes in the timeline is because you were born outside of time on a jump station, like the one we're in now," Viola said. "It only connects with realtime when someone goes in or out. You're the only person ever born on one."

"In our timeline, you're famous, too." Sebastian grinned a bit, somehow thinking that this news would make her happy. The smile fell off his face when he noticed the way she looked at him. "I'm going to go finish changing."

Iliana took a moment to feel overwhelmed by everything, letting grief and anger and hopelessness wash over her. Tears came, but crying wasn't going to do it. Instead, she let out a long, rough scream that didn't end until she'd poured every bit of self-pity out of her body.

"Better?"

"A little," she admitted, and wiped tears from her cheeks. "What happens now?"

"We're at an impasse, to be honest. Better off than before, though. Thanks to you, we now have a more detailed map of the changes these people made to the timelines." Viola went to one of the laptops. "Once we combined that with our existing data we pinpointed dozens of points in history where they interfered."

"Why are they doing this?"

"For control. In our timeline, time travel is administered by universities for research. The United Nations should have already drafted resolutions regulating it by the year we came and got you. Instead, it's controlled by private interests, and not many people know about it.

"With all the changes they've made, they have to be operating from a jump station, too. And because of the limitations of their technology, they can only travel seventy-three years in either direction. We're fairly sure they're based out of 1984."

"That's where my parents got stuck."

"It might even be why."

An idea occurred to Iliana. "You said that my parents are famous. You must have records on where they were back then."

"A very detailed account." Viola handed her a droid from the table. "Look at the local wiki. There's an entry."

She wasn't kidding. The entry had so much information, the table of contents had a table of contents. Iliana found the section on their time in 1984. At the end, the exact day and time they left, along with coordinates. A string of numbers that represented the moment her parents began to die.

"If you know they're somewhere in 1984, you find these people and arrest them or whatever it is you do, right?"

"Not so easy," Sebastian said, returning from a side room, now in normal clothes. "The jump station they're operating isn't one of ours, and it could exist inside any second of any minute that year."

"If we could find one of them, we might be able to pull the data from their mac," Viola said.

"What's a mac?"

"That," she said, pointing at the droid.

"Even if we pinpointed a location, transferring data between phased and unphased tech takes up to three minutes, and they'll see it happening."

"You can't drop out of phase, not even to stop them?"

"We would cease to exist." The sudden bitterness in Viola's voice surprised her a little. "Someone erased our timeline long ago. The only reason we didn't disappear is because we were on a jump station. It keeps us outside of time but means we can never leave unless we're phased."

If there was anything worse than watching the world change around you and losing the people you love, that had to be it.

"I wouldn't," Iliana said.

"Wouldn't what?"

"Stop existing. I'm not affected, right?"

Sebastian leaned in closer. "Her eyes get all fierce like yours when she's thinking hard, little sister."

Now they both shot him a look.

"No, you're not affected. But that still doesn't solve—"

"If I travel back to when we know one of these people messes with time, then I can get their droid—mac—thing and get into their jump station."

"Maybe…"

"And even if they make a change, I still exist where I am. I can still stop them!" It all fit so perfectly in her head, but Viola didn't look convinced.

"She has a point," Sebastian said. "We can teach her how to control the mac with voice commands and program it to sync with any others that come in range."

"We still don't know where to find them. Not exactly."

"Yes, we do." Iliana showed her the wiki entry. "One of them, at least."

For the second time in her life, Iliana prepared herself to travel through time. The pins and needles feeling burst through her once she put on the belt again. This time it didn't hurt as much.

Sebastian handed her the mac he'd programmed. "One more

time: When you get to the jump station, just put this on the cradle. They're using similar tech, so it will fit."

"Got it." They'd explained that the mac would force all instances of the jump station out from the fraction of a second where it existed into real time.

"We'll know exactly which moment in time to find them. If they still exist," Viola had said. Iliana tried not to think about what that last part meant.

"Let's go over the voice commands once more," Sebastian said. This would be the fifth time. But she knew she only had one chance to get this right, so she listed them all for him again.

Viola input the time and location coordinates, sending them to the belt. "Just remember, don't take that thing off for any reason. It's the only one we have, so we can't send another."

"Why only one?"

"It's tech from a time in our future. About a hundred years past our original timeline." He winked. "Not supposed to have it, but no one is playing by the rules anymore."

"Ready?" Viola asked.

No. "Yes."

The two of them stood back and glanced at each other, a million conversations in one look.

"Good luck," Sebastian said.

The mac in her hand counted down. Four...three...two... darkness.

This time the landing wasn't so rough. The lack of acrid, burning air helped, too. Instead, the first gasping breaths she took chilled her throat. December 1984. The snow on the ground threatened to seep past her jeans and socks, so she forced her aching body to stand once again.

They'd sent her back ten minutes before her parents', jump point and several yards away, so she could scope out the person with the gun. The event happened in a parking lot on Xavier University's campus that the guards only patrolled twice a night. Plenty of privacy...for anything.

Iliana walked as quietly as she could, trying not to crunch the snow too much. With the light from the lot guiding her, she kept her eyes open for her parents and anyone else around.

A crunch of gravel from the other end of the lot sent her behind a clump of trees to hide. Peering out, she saw two people, one having trouble walking, the other holding her up. A very pregnant Adelina and Malcolm. Their shabby clothes didn't look warm enough for the cold.

Just as they entered a pool of light from a streetlamp, Iliana noticed another figure in the dark. In the low light, she couldn't tell if it was a man or woman. At this point, it didn't matter. Because the person then crouched down behind the car and aimed something in her parents' direction.

Iliana did not take a moment to think.

She ran as hard and as fast as she could at the person with the gun, the slight downward slope helping her gain momentum before she plowed into their side, shoulder first. The gun flew away and something else clattered to the gravel.

Their mac.

Up close she could see the person's face: a white woman with short-cropped blonde hair. No one she recognized.

Before she could get over the shock and pain, Iliana stepped on the woman's gut and scooped up the mac, then the gun, and took off running. Having never been athletic, her newfound speed surprised her. But she knew that this wouldn't last, and she needed to get out of here fast.

"Sync!" she yelled, pressing the WAKE button on the mac in her belt.

Purple light flared to her left, and Iliana glanced over to see her confused parents. Malcolm's eyes were fixed on the car where she'd just been, Adelina's on the jump point opening for them.

"Run! Get back home, now!"

"Look out!" Adelina pointed behind her just as the blonde woman tackled Ili.

Iliana had enough forethought to pull her arms close to her chest as she fell, protecting the mac and the gun from the woman's grabbing, scratching hands.

"New jump station loaded. Add and engage?" the mac's computery voice chirped into her earpiece.

"Affirm! Engage! Go!"

The split second before the belt activated, Iliana wondered what would happen to someone touching her when it did. Would the field encompass her? Would she travel with her?

Just before the explosion of prickling sensation and darkness, the blonde woman screamed in a way that would haunt her for years. Question answered.

The room where Iliana ended up didn't have much light, only the glow from a panel of monitors along one wall. Just as Sebastian said, the room also held several computers. Dozens and dozens—too many for the low-ceilinged space. In another

75

life this could have been someone's basement. It certainly smelled like one.

After a few moments of catching her breath and assessing the room, she noticed that the arm she'd hurt before now throbbed with the promise of greater pain to come. Her shoulder also complained. Once the adrenaline had completely left her, it would get a lot worse.

"So let's get this over with," she said to the room.

Afraid that the gun might go off if she stuffed it in a pocket, but not wanting to leave it lying out just in case, Iliana settled for placing it carefully under one of the tables where it wouldn't be seen. Then she did as Sebastian had told her, transferring an app from her mac to the one she'd taken from the woman. In the center of the electronic mess, she found a cradle for it. As Viola predicted, it connected via a wire to one of the bigger computers.

She set the mac in the cradle and waited. The sync icon swirled, a notification came up: COMPLETE. Nothing.

"Is that it?"

Every monitor in the room flared red, a yellow warning triangle flashing, announcing a security breach. Half of her wanted to panic, half insisted she calm down because Viola and Sebastian knew what they were doing. The first half won out when two men in those odd white suits walked out of nothing into the room and headed right for her.

"How did she—"

"Who is—"

Then that familiar sound rushed in on her, now more turbulent and terrible than ever. Far more intense than a normal change, this one pulled at her from so many directions Iliana feared her heart would just stop. It took a while to realize that the men were gone, the room had changed, and the monitors, while still warning of security breaches, weren't so many in number.

Again out of nothing, a group of people—this time in normal clothes—appeared in the room, panic palpable in their frantic movements.

"Where did that droid come from?"

"Grab it!"

"No!" Iliana fought through the pain and the sound screaming in her head to push through them, grabbing the droid—mac—thing and holding it in the cradle. The jump station pressed in on itself even harder. Or that's how it felt.

The group disappeared. Strong hands gripped her shoulders and slipped away almost as fast. An arm wrapped around her neck, pulling, then left her gasping for breath. More shouting that died an instant later.

All the while she held on to make sure they couldn't take the device away. Soon there were just three monitors, then one, blinking the warning: IMMANENT COLLAPSE.

A strong vibration in her left hand cut through everything else somehow. She looked down, her vision hazy but still able to make out the bright white-on-black letters of the app controlling the belt.

EMERGENCY SHIFT: DATE? LOCATION?

She blurted the first date that came into her head. "November 4, 2048, sixteen hundred..." It needed longitude and latitude for the location, but she had no idea.

MAINTAIN LOCATION?

"Affirm!"

The pins and needles sensation swept through her, ending the endless pull and tug. The darkness cut her off from the sound. For a heartbeat she was at peace.

More than anything, Iliana really wanted to lie on the floor of this room and not move. The shaggy carpet underneath her felt more comfortable than the fluffiest bed at that moment. As her mind ticked over her injuries and assessed the situation, footsteps thudded above her and voices trickled down.

"...my uniform?"

"...washed it yesterday, so..."

Once again she forced herself to stand up, taking in the room around her. It looked about the size and shape of the space she'd just been in, now filled with appliances and clothes instead of computers.

"Where, on the dryer?" The voice came from the top of the stairs. *No time to gawk*, Iliana chided herself, and ducked into what she hoped was a little-used closet. Through the slats she saw a pair of long, brown legs belonging to a teenage girl trundle down the stairs. As she riffled through the clothes on the dryer, Iliana nearly gasped aloud.

Grayson.

Older, definitely. Her hair still kinky curly, pulled into short ponytails atop her head. Still tall.

Iliana wondered if they were still first best friends.

"Hurry up, Grayson!"

"Got it!" She pulled a top and shorts from the basket and ran back up the stairs.

I did it, Iliana thought. *It worked.*

She tapped at the mac, bringing up a map of the area. Her house was only ten blocks away.

Leaving Grayson's house the normal way didn't strike her as a good idea. No telling who was still upstairs. So she shared her house's coordinates with the belt control app and shifted four hours into the future, right into her own backyard.

Her house looked like it had when she was younger, before the worst of the changes. No more peeling paint, no more patchy grass, no more fences. She counted on the darkness and the chilly night to cover her arrival. No need to freak out the neighbors.

Her parents might be worried about her being out so late, but she planned to tell them everything that had happened. Now that she knew they were time travelers, too, she was sure they'd understand.

The kitchen light flicked on, and her mother came in view of the back window, carrying dinner dishes to the sink. Iliana smiled. Adelina's hair hung long and free down her back, just like the old days.

The smile slipped away a moment later when she saw herself enter the kitchen carrying another set of dishes. Adelina hugged this other Iliana and kissed the top of her head.

Viola had told her that if she collapsed the jump station, it might erase everything the time changers had done. She didn't mention that it might erase her from her own timeline.

Maybe this isn't my timeline. Maybe the one I'm from is one they messed with too.

She swallowed past the tightness in her throat and tried not to think about how utterly unfair this was.

"They're alive," she whispered. "That's what matters."

Saying it out loud didn't take the pain away.

"There she is." Broken-up audio flitted through her earpiece. "I told you we'd find her here."

"You got lucky."

Sebastian. Viola. She looked around but didn't see them.

"We probably shouldn't turn off the refractors in case someone sees us. It's bad enough someone might see you," Viola chided.

"Sorry..."

"Don't make the girl feel bad. What else was she supposed to do?"

"I know, I know."

Iliana's mac buzzed again.

"We set you to jump to the station at Xavier University," Sebastian said just as the mac buzzed again, announcing it had downloaded the new coordinates. "You can see your parents for a bit before jumping forward with us."

"What? But my parents are in there!" She pointed at the house.

"Shh! Not so loud."

Sebastian sucked his teeth, presumably at Viola. "That's a version of your parents. But the people we're taking you to see were trapped on a jump station the day after the 2048 election when their timeline disappeared. Sound familiar?"

The last version of her Malcolm and Adelina. They still existed.

Iliana hardly felt the prickling sensation this time, her mind reeling between extreme happiness and a longing to watch the Iliana in the house a little longer. When the darkness cleared and she could breathe, Viola and Sebastian stood in front of her in a giant room bordered on all sides by a persistently gray wall.

They looked young again—college age. Was this the same version of the pair that sent her off before?

"Safe and sound, just like we promised." Sebastian's grin was growing on her.

Iliana looked around the room but didn't see her parents.

"Through that door," Viola said, pointing to the far end. The wall split like a huge cargo bay, but she couldn't see anyone beyond it. "They're in the control room."

"Thank you," she said, hugging them both.

"No, thank you. You did really well." Viola squeezed her tight. "Keep the mac, and message us through it when you're ready."

"Ready to what?"

"To come back with us," Sebastian said.

Iliana pulled back. "Can't I just stay here with my mom and dad?"

Sebastian made an exaggerated shrug. "You could, but…"

"We really need your help," Viola said, holding her gaze. "This isn't over. There are others out there shifting timelines. None as crude and easy to deal with as that lot, but just as disruptive. And you're the only one who isn't affected by the shifts."

The idea didn't really appeal. Then again, what else was she going to do with her life? Iliana had her parents but no home, no school, no world she belonged in.

Because of them.

A flare of anger rose up again, and she held onto it, thinking of the other Iliana in the window. The one with the life she should have had. And of Viola and Sebastian, trapped like her parents on these jump stations forever.

"Okay. I'll do it," she said to relieved smiles.

As she walked out of the chamber to the control room where her parents waited, Iliana made one more promise to herself. That this would be the last time her life changed without her say-so.

Pattern Recognition

by Ken Liu

David knew that he wasn't always called David.

Even though he had grown up at the Volpe Ness School, he remembered a village by the sea.

The village in his memory was not like any village he read about in the novels he had stolen. It didn't have golden light or fields of hay, pecking chickens or red barns, fishing nets hung to dry, or pretty houses, each meant for just one family.

The few words he could recall of the first language he spoke, his own appearance in the mirror, and repeated consultations of the few secret reference books he had all told him that the village was in a place called "China."

He could recall only disjointed images: a tiny, noisy room perpetually in darkness, impatient hands, a dense forest of concrete towers that shot into the sky, built so close together that no sunlight reached their feet. The dim streetlights were left on around the clock.

He couldn't have been more than three or four. He and the other children were playing in the perpetual dusk of the garbage-strewn, muddy streets. All of them were equally dirty, equally hungry. They squealed and chased after a rat almost as big as he was. . . .

David startled awake. He was in his soft bed, under his warm blanket. The alarm had not gone off yet.

He looked across the room and saw that Jake, who had the bunk across from his, was still asleep. Indeed, judging by the snores, he was the only one awake of the eight boys who shared this room. He did feel hungry, but not the painful hunger of starvation, the unbearable craving of his dream.

It was a stupid dream, he thought. How could a village be full of concrete towers? It was nonsense, the product of an overactive, directionless imagination. He reprimanded himself silently. How many times had Dr. Gau explained to all of them that undirected imagination was a waste of precious youth and even more precious time.

Yet he had always been prone to temptation, to yield to his impure desires. That was why he had his hidden stash, and he thought about . . . her. His face grew hot with shame.

The loudspeaker in the corner of the room came to life. 6:00 a.m. First came the sound of tinkling bells, then drumming that gradually grew louder and more insistent, and finally, an upbeat trumpet solo that ended on a long, sustained note.

Blankets flew off the eight bunks around the room. Groaning

boys sat up, rubbing the sleep out of their eyes.

"GOOD MORNING!" a recording of Dr. Gau's voice boomed. "It's the start of another wonderful day! Come on, work awaits."

Within ten minutes the boys were dressed in their uniforms: comfortable blue tracksuits and plain white sneakers. The eight of them left the room together and joined the boys from the other rooms on the same floor in the hallway. All of them were about thirteen, fourteen. They were just one floor below the top floor, where the oldest boys lived.

Quietly, efficiently, they filed down the stairs and out of the dormitory into the exercise yard, where about a hundred boys, age five to sixteen, lined up in four neat columns over the asphalt surface, arranged by descending age.

The girls from the dormitory across the exercise yard were already in the middle of their morning run. Dressed in their yellow tracksuits, they looked like a giant caterpillar wriggling across the yard. The other two sides of the square-shaped exercise yard were taken up with academic buildings and small houses for the teachers. And then, beyond all the buildings, was the forty-foot wall that completely surrounded and protected the Volpe Ness School from the Outside.

David squinted to focus on one of the figures near the end of the yellow caterpillar. There was a certain rhythm to her movement, a pattern that made his heart beat faster.

"Let's get going," said Mr. Danziger, the morning calisthenics coach. He blew his whistle, and the boys began their jog in the cool morning air.

David stumbled, caught himself, and tried to focus on running.

"Thinking about her again?" asked Jake, who was running right next to him.

"I don't know what you're talking about," David said. They hung back a bit, near the end of the pack, so that they could talk without being overheard.

Except for the brief exchange of blessings after Temple on Sundays, boys and girls weren't allowed to talk to each other at all. Dr. Gau explained that it was so they could concentrate on their work.

"Sure you don't," Jake said, grinning. "You're getting more and more distracted these days. Did you dream about her?"

Jake's skin was darker than David's, and his hair was a bit curly. They had tried to figure out where he was from, but Jake remembered nothing of his life before the school and so they had little to work with. Almost all of the students at the school had skin like David's or Jake's or even darker (*Like...hers*, David thought) and most of the teachers did too. But a few had fair skin and hair like Mr. Danziger.

David was about to answer when the boy in front of them turned back and angrily whispered, "Shut up, you two! Haven't you gotten us into enough trouble?"

The day before, all the boys had been made to run an extra mile because Jake and David were caught talking during the run. They finished the morning exercises in silence.

Next was a quick breakfast of eggs, hot fried dough, and soy milk. At eight thirty, the boys went to the machine room, took their assigned places at the workstations, and began the morning shift, the first of three in the day.

David liked his assigned task this morning. His screen was filled with horizontal lines of tiny square blocks in various colors—red, green, blue, yellow—like beads strung on skewers. Occasionally, there were gaps between some of the squares in a line.

He could nudge the beads in each line left and right with his mouse, but he couldn't swap two beads or move them from one line to another. The goal was to shift the sequences of beads on all the skewers around until he managed to align as many of them as possible—meaning they matched in color if you drew a line from the top of the screen to the bottom.

This sounded easy but wasn't. He couldn't open up too many gaps between beads, which lowered his score and meant longer shifts and less free time in the evenings. He also had to keep the big picture in mind. If he got too greedy and focused only on matching the beads in one section, he might miss a much better, larger-scale match that required more gaps early on. Sometimes, to get the best overall match, he had to allow chaos to develop locally. It was just like Go: an easy game to learn, but hard to master.

The students were forbidden to speak while working. Around him, everything was quiet except for the clicking of mice and the clacking of keyboards. David quickly developed a rhythm and fell into the familiar flow. His eyes lost focus as he stopped seeing the individual beads but began to see only a mosaic made of four colors within which larger patterns slowly emerged.

David was very good at this game. He had been playing it since he was five.

But gradually he noticed something tugging the edge of his

consciousness. He felt the table under his hand vibrate.

taaaaaaat tat tat tat taaaaaaat

David's face flushed, and he breathed faster. He looked surreptitiously to his right. Next to him was an eight-year-old boy focusing on fitting puzzle pieces of different sizes and colors into a box on the screen. Beyond him was a twelve-year-old girl who was manipulating some three-dimensional strings on her screen, folding them into knots. And then, at the far end, was Helen, her dark skin glowing and beautiful even in the harsh fluorescent light of the machine room. She was concentrating on her screen, not looking this way at all.

tat tat tat taaaaaaat

The boy next to him frowned and looked at his mouse. The vibrations stopped. Quickly, David turned back to his screen.

tat tat

David leaned back in his chair and stretched his arms high above his head, as though trying to relieve the tension in his back. He kept his knee pressed against the bottom of the table so that he could continue to feel the vibrations. He stole a look to the right and saw that Helen's knee was pressed up against the table as well, lightly tapping.

taaaaaaaaaat tat tat

Letters appeared one by one in his mind: *D-A-V-I-D....*

Lunch was half an hour. Fifteen minutes to eat and fifteen more to use the bathroom.

David wrapped the small pile of dried lychees and apricots—his reward for getting the best score during the morning shift—in a napkin and put the package in his pocket.

David saw Jake's look and flushed. "Later, I'm saving it for…later."

Jake smiled but didn't tease him. Instead, he just finished his noodle soup and smacked his lips. "I wish it were Sunday."

On Sundays there was no school, and the children would get a treat with their breakfast: a hot dog, a sweet egg tart, or even sometimes a *bo luo bao*.

After breakfast the children would march across the exercise yard to the Temple, a large, cavernous hall filled with the smell of incense and lit by flickering candles. There were straw cushions on the hard stone floor for sitting. The boys sat on the left, the girls on the right. The ceiling of the Temple was obscured by the dark, smoky air, and the children would feel as though they were sitting below a dark, starless sky.

Then Dr. Gau would get up in front and begin the week's lesson. The children would stare, rapt, at the doctor's gaunt figure, wrapped in a dark gray suit that was so clean and stiff it looked like armor. In the dim light, his shock of white hair bobbed like a guiding light.

He spoke to them of the horrors of the Outside. The world that had been destroyed by sin, by greed. Out there, men would strangle their sons for fear that there wasn't enough to eat. And women would smother their daughters because they weren't boys. Out there was hatred, starvation, death. In some of the ruined cities, the air was scarcely breathable and water was dirty enough to melt flesh off bones.

As Dr. Gau spoke, David would recall the images from his hazy childhood and believe with every ounce of his strength that

Dr. Gau was telling the truth.

The Volpe Ness School, Dr. Gau went on, was a haven, a refuge founded by men and women of vision and faith. Here, the students were protected from the horrors of that dying world. They could spend their time pursuing their intellectual development, seeking patterns in chaos. The work that they did was intended to develop their ability to recognize important patterns, patterns that would enable them to be the future leaders of a spiritual rebirth.

It was also important, Dr. Gau warned, to resist the temptations of the Outside. They had no need for knowledge of that corrupt world. Its maps, dictionaries, books, and photographs contained nothing of use for students of Volpe Ness. Everyone was encouraged to inform the teachers if they found anyone in possession of such forbidden material, for it threatened to derail their spiritual salvation.

It was seven at night. David waited impatiently in the darkness of the cleaning supplies closet next to the boys' bathroom.

DAVID MEET SEVEN

It was a good day, David thought. Besides getting that extra serving of dried fruit, he had finished the afternoon shift with such a high score that he was granted an extra fifteen minutes for the evening break after dinner. He had time to get things ready.

The hour before the start of the evening shift at eight was really the only free time the children had all day. They could exercise in the gym, converse quietly with friends, read approved books (math books or *Dr. Gau's Thoughts*) in the library, or play board games in the recreation hall.

The door to the cleaning closet opened briefly, and the yellow light in the hallway spilled in. A dark figure slipped in and the door closed again.

"Helen?" David whispered, and swallowed hard because his throat felt so dry.

"Who else?" Her voice was like a warm breeze. He wanted to listen to her forever. He imagined the smile on her face in the darkness.

She clicked on a flashlight and set it on one of the shelves, directing the beam to bounce off the ceiling to soften the light a little.

She gasped and then laughed. David had spread out a napkin on the floor, and in the middle, the dried lychees and apricots were artfully arranged.

"Thank you," she said.

He wanted to go up and wrap his arms around her, but he didn't dare.

"You looked so intense this morning. I had to tap out the message three times before you paid attention."

"Sorry, I get like that sometimes when I'm working."

She scooted over closer to him and popped a lychee into her mouth.

Wanting this moment to last forever, but aware of how little time they had, he knelt down and pried open the loose floorboard below the bottom shelf. He took out an oilcloth package, unwrapped it, and laid its contents on the floor between them.

There was an old dictionary missing everything after *wuther*, three volumes from an encyclopedia set (Volumes B, F, and T), a folded world map that was brittle with age, a few paperback novels, and a stack of photographs of all different sizes of strangers in strange places.

These were his most treasured possessions. He and Jake had scavenged them over the years surreptitiously, from teachers who were occasionally careless about locking doors or from drawers and boxes left in forgotten corners of the school's many rooms. Forbidden objects, detritus of the world Outside, they had both thrilled the two boys and frightened them.

But only with Helen had he discovered how much joy they could bring to two people intent on building memories together.

Helen reached for the dictionary with her eyes closed and flipped it open. Her finger stabbed at a random spot on the page. She opened her eyes, and they looked at the word she was pointing to: *soccer*.

And so they began to read together. Finished with *soccer*, they looked up *football, rugby, goalie, touchdown....*

Following crumb after crumb, they picked their way through a lost world, a past that they could only imagine through words and a few black-and-white drawings. This was how they had learned Morse code, how they had read about war and peace, how they had matched the names on that old map to dry summaries and dream images.

As they read, their heads came closer together. He could smell her breath, warm, sweet, like nothing else in the world.

They had looked up *kiss* a long time ago, and tonight the reading came in handy.

It was almost time for the evening shift.

He pulled away from her reluctantly. Her face was flushed. She looked so beautiful that he wanted to kiss her again.

But she pulled back. "We have to get going."

Quickly, he wrapped up his bundle of secrets and pushed it back under the loose floorboard.

They paused at the door of the supplies closet, listening for noises outside.

"The books are nice," she said, holding his hand. "But they're old. I wish we could see…"

"What?"

She shook her head, refusing to finish.

But David was very good at seeing patterns and filling in the blanks.

David knew the snoring patterns of everyone in the room by heart. He waited until the rise and fall of snores around him were aligned just right, until he was sure all the other boys were in deep sleep.

He rose from his bunk, noiselessly jumped down to the ground, and padded his way across the room to Jake. He covered Jake's mouth so that he wouldn't make too much noise and then proceeded to poke him hard in the ribs.

A few muffled screams later, Jake finally calmed down enough to glare at David.

They made their way to the shared desk by the window, where they whispered to each other while keeping an ear out for the footsteps of teachers patrolling the halls. Being caught out of bed after bedtime was a severe offense and could subject them to a harsh public whipping. (Dr. Gau had explained that the whipping was necessary to ensure that the children were well rested for their work.)

"You have to help me, Jake. I want to do this for her."

Jake kept on shaking his head, but David wouldn't give up. They whispered long into the night.

"You'll both have to be quarantined for today," Nurse Cho said. She was a kind, middle-aged woman who could be persuaded sometimes to let a child stay in bed an extra day. "No Temple for you. I hope whatever you two ate don't make more of your classmates sick."

Right after breakfast, both Jake and David had complained of discomfort in their stomachs. Then they had thrown up one after the other, which caused all the boys at the same table to scramble out of the way.

Nurse Cho closed the door behind her. On most days she was kept busy dealing with students who suffered from dizziness and migraines from staring at computer screens all day. On Sundays she preferred to take a nap while the children were at Temple.

David waited until he was sure that Nurse Cho was asleep in her office. "Let's go."

Keeping bits of hair in their mouths and then trying to swallow until they threw up had been Jake's idea. He might have been reluctantly recruited into this operation, but once he was in, he had plenty of good ideas.

The two boys opened the window and let themselves out of the infirmary.

Since all the students and most of the teachers were at Temple, the exercise yard was empty. Quickly, the boys made their way around the infirmary so that they were behind it, in the narrow alley between the back wall of the building and the towering outer wall around the school.

None of the buildings in the school were taller than the wall, and standing in that narrow alley was like standing at the bottom of a well. The boys followed the wall toward the dining hall.

As they got closer, they heard faint voices of men talking and slowed down. Hiding in the alley between the dining hall and the recreation hall, the two peeked around the corner.

They were looking at the loading dock at the back of the kitchen. There was a break in the outer wall of the school here, and a truck was parked in the gate. While a few teachers stood around and kept watch, men, strangers, were unloading crates of food from the truck. David had figured out the delivery pattern a while ago and knew there would be one today.

The men from the Outside were dressed in dirty overalls and muddy boots. Their faces were covered by patches of grease. They looked just like Dr. Gau had described the conditions Outside: desperate, hopeless, haunted.

Whenever men like these came to deliver food and supplies or to work on some construction project, the students were kept far away and told that they could not approach the evil strangers, who would corrupt and pollute their spiritual purity.

"You ready for this?" Jake whispered.

David nodded. "Thank you." Then he grabbed Jake's arm. "Don't get into too much trouble."

Jake grinned. "If you're going to get into trouble, might as well make it big."

Then he went down the alley in which they were hiding until he was back in the exercise yard, and began to scream and laugh like a madman.

Once Jake was sure that he had the teachers' attention, he ran toward the other side of the exercise yard.

"I'm done with work!" he shouted. "Let me out of this place!"

The teachers chased after him. The Outsiders, stunned by the development, wandered down toward the exercise yard to watch the unfolding farce.

David waited until the area around the truck was clear. Then he sprinted to the truck, jumped into the cab, and began to look around for things he could take: books, pictures, anything that seemed interesting. Helen wanted to know what the Outside was really like, and he would deliver it to her.

He picked up a few loose pieces of paper with writing on them. Underneath, he saw a small slab made of smooth glass and shiny metal, like a pack of playing cards from the recreation hall. Without thinking too much, he grabbed it. He'd figure out what it was later.

By the time Jake had been caught and the Outsiders had wandered back to their truck, David was already in the infirmary, pretending to be asleep.

All the boys and girls stood and watched, stone-faced, as Jake counted out ten lashes during his public whipping. Then he was taken to solitary, where he would be given only bread and water for ten days.

David flinched with each lash and bit his tongue so hard he tasted blood.

After ten days, Jake came back to the dorm. All the other boys avoided him, except for David.

He stood next to Jake's bunk, fidgeted, and tried to speak. But no words would come.

"I think Dr. Gau rather liked that little show I put on," Jake said, his voice light. "It's been so long since anyone got out of line that he needed the practice."

David tried to laugh, but his voice choked.

"Stop acting so guilty," Jake whispered. "I agreed to help you. I know I'm not pure, and I don't care. Have you shown her what you got? Don't make me suffer for nothing."

It took two weeks before David could meet Helen at the supply closet again.

Ever since Jake's punishment, David's work had suffered. He couldn't seem to find the patterns in the colored squares, the right way to fold the knots, or the best way to pack the colored pieces into the outlined space on the screen, minimizing how long the lines between them had to be. He had to work longer shifts and sometimes had all his free time taken away.

"I'm sorry about what happened to Jake," Helen said. "I know you were close." She put a hand on his back and gently ran it down his spine.

"He got caught because he was helping me," David said, "to get this."

Helen's eyes widened as she saw the tiny metal-and-glass box in David's hands. "What is it?"

"I don't know." David's finger searched around the edge until he found a tiny protrusion and pushed it. The glass front of the box came to life, and a set of square tiles of different sizes began to drift across the screen, not unlike the puzzle pieces that the children sometimes worked with at their workstations.

"I think it's a computer," David said. "I stole it from some Outsiders."

One of the tiles looked like a small map. Helen reached out and tapped it. The screen changed to a view of a swirling blue sphere filled with tan, green, and white patches. The view zoomed in, and the white patches—clouds—disappeared. The tan patches resolved into lines between states, roads, cities. It hovered over a city labeled shenzhen and zoomed in further. Finally, the screen centered on a small patch of land with a pulsing blue dot in the middle of a square yard.

Awed, the children were unable to speak for a while.

"Is that where we are?"

"How does it know that?"

"I don't know. Maybe it's still connected to the Outside."

"I thought the Outside was dead."

Two heads bumped into each other over the tiny glass green. They giggled and, leaning against each other, their hands danced over the magical screen, exploring this portal to another world.

They saw videos of gleaming cities, of beautiful men and women dancing, of beaches full of sunlight and white sand. They saw articles, news reports—many in languages they could not read. They read posts debating the best vacation spots, celebrating the latest technological toys, urging each other to take up one cause or another.

Much of what they saw they could not understand, but they could feel a wall crumbling, the wall that had been their faith.

The Southern Weekend Journal, Letters Section

[Readers are reminded that published letters to the editor do not represent the views of the editorial staff.]

First, I'd like to thank The Southern Weekend Journal *for allowing me some space to tell my side of the story.*

By now you've no doubt seen the sensationalistic headlines screaming SLAVERY and the dramatic pictures of children walking out of a walled compound, looking dazed and confused, and yours truly led away in handcuffs. Such images do not lie, exactly, but they also do not tell the truth.

I grew up in Taipei, where I was a decent, if not exceptional, student. I went to the United States to pursue a doctorate in computer science at Stanford and to live my Silicon Valley dream.

Like most of my peers, I was trying to come up with an idea for a company that would strike gold. But nearing graduation, I still had nothing. To clear my head, I took a summer vacation through China. It was my first time there.

One day, I walked through an urban village in one of the coastal cities. My readers will know, of course, that these are unique Chinese creations, slums with Chinese characteristics.

Once rural villages, they were incorporated into city limits during urban expansion. But the city governments, having acquired cheaply all the villagers' valuable farmland for development, decided to leave the villagers where they were, stuck in their houses. So the villages became islands in the city with no way to survive other than building tall, rickety tenements to house the migrant laborers, the prostitutes, the lowly, forgotten men and women who powered China's economic miracle and whom most city dwellers feared, despised, and needed.

The authorities pretended that these places did not exist. Crime and violence were the law. A child of four came up to me and demanded that I help her. I took out a handful of coins in different currencies and asked her to pick out three and only three. She immediately went for the euros. Even at her age she could recognize the patterns in the coins that the older children favored and knew how to maximize her gain.

And there, looking around at the squalid alleys, the piles of trash, and the destitute, hungry faces of the children, an idea came to me.

As much as we've advanced the state of computing in the last few decades, some fundamental limits have not been breached. One of these has to do with the computational complexity of certain problems. Without going into too many technical details, a class of problems, called NP-complete problems, remains difficult and expensive for computers to solve.

But many of these problems are amenable to human intuition, especially the human capacity for pattern recognition. These include problems such as protein folding, logical block placement and wire routing in integrated circuit design, and multiple sequence alignment in protein and gene sequencing. While pattern recognition remains difficult for computers, humans can often come up with far superior solutions without brute-force computation.

In the vast, dark lands of China and India, there are stories of misery and suffering that the West can hardly comprehend. In these places, how a child is born is how she will die. Whether it's called caste or hukou, the children of the poor have no realistic hope of ever emerging from their lot. Indeed, the prosperity of some of their compatriots depends on their remaining poor and easy to exploit. Yet many of these children could have been brilliant researchers who could help with the search for a cure for cancer or the next energy revolution. So much human potential was wasted.

So I started the Volpe Ness Technology Group, named after my first two investors: my thesis advisor and my landlady in Palo Alto. To our investors and the public, our secret sauce was a technology that allowed us to solve complicated computational problems cheaply and quickly. In reality, we were one of the first companies to make it big in the arena of human-powered computing.

We recruit bright, promising children from the slums of India, China, Africa. We promise their parents that we would give these children a new life, a life that they could not give them. And we keep our promise: We clothe, feed, and care for the children. Our nutritional and medical staffs ensure the students have healthy meals and receive plenty of exercise. After all, they're an investment, and we have an incentive to ensure their development.

In exchange, we ask them to work. Trained from a young age to hone their pattern-recognition skills, they're experts at solving the kind of problems we specialize in. But we present the problems as computer games that they enjoy playing. Yes, the children spend all day playing games. At the same time, they're helping pharmaceutical companies, computer chip foundries, and university research laboratories with cutting-edge research at incredibly low prices. Go search through the patent database for the last ten years, and you'll see the contributions of our computational services everywhere.

Nor do we neglect the spiritual development of our children. What the media calls a "cult-like" atmosphere is misleading. These are children who have been raised without the benefit of family or *acculturation. They require the firm hand of discipline and a regi-mented lifestyle. To put it bluntly, I sometimes feel like a zookeeper.*

Some have asked what I thought would happen to the chil-dren when they were older. The truth is that I don't know. I never thought that far. Deng Xiaoping told the Chinese that they had to cross the river by feeling for stones, one step at a time, and I think that was sage advice.

There are some who seem to think that every child can be raised like a Western child. I do not know if they're foolish or ignorant: Surely they understand that progress always requires a dispropor-tionate sharing of resources and that the wealth of some demands the poverty of others? I take the world as it is. I did not make these children poor. History did.

For those of you who think I have done these children wrong, I invite you to visit the villages from which I took them. Walk through the streets, observe the scurrying criminals, and hear the cries of women in houses of prostitution. This would have been their future.

No, the children are not free, not in the way you might want. But they are free from want, from hunger, thirst, uncertainty, violence.

In a world full of suffering and exploitation, I tried to exploit a little less and ease some suffering, and for this I am crucified.

"What did you say?" David asked.

Helen shrugged. "I said no."

The men, who said they were *lawyers* (David had to look up the word), had been very kind. They had explained that all the children had been harmed, had had their lives taken away. They asked the children to help them punish Dr. Gau.

"He was all we knew," she said, "the closest thing we had to a family. The lawyers make it all sound so simple. But we now know that there's nothing simple in this world."

David let out a sigh of relief.

But Jake, who stood next to him, said nothing. He wrapped his arms around himself and felt the scars on his back.

It was Jake's turn to meet the lawyers, and he grinned at both Helen and David before leaving.

David couldn't help but feel guilty. He and Helen had continued to play with that tiny, stolen computer—he learned that it was called a "phone," though it looked nothing like the "phone" in the dictionary—and eventually found out that they could type and converse with others Outside through it. They wrote about what life was like in the school and when they were doubted, took pictures with the phone as proof. Then some reporters saw the pictures, and everything was history.

He had felt sorry for Dr. Gau as he was taken away with his hands cuffed in front of him. He had looked so frail and old, not at all like the all-powerful headmaster of the Volpe Ness School.

The lawyers had explained to David that everything Dr. Gau had ever told them was a lie. Even the Outside workers had dressed in dirty overalls only because the school had insisted. The teachers were all in on it. It was all pretend.

Yet he could not help but miss his old life, a life where he knew what was expected of him, and one in which he delighted in finding the patterns in things. He had read Dr. Gau's letter and cried. He wished he had Jake's certainty about the rightness of things.

He did not know if he could find the pattern in the world outside the walls. It seemed too big, too complicated, too overwhelming.

"We'll figure it out," Helen said. "We always do."

He took a step closer to Helen and opened his arms for a fierce hug.

Author's Note: For more on human-based computation, see *Human Computation: Synthesis Lectures on Artificial Intelligence and Machine Learning*, by Edith Law and Luis von Ahn, 2011. The multiple sequence alignment "game" played by David is modeled on the game of Phylo, available at http://phylo.cs.mcgill.ca.

Gods of the Dimming Light

by Greg van Eekhout

Now

He's going to kill me.

I'm bleeding from a gash in my right shoulder. The pain is bad, but what's worse is the blood's making my grip slippery. If I drop my sword, I'm dead. My legs feel like bags of wet cement, and no matter how much I scream at them to move, to run, to bend and leap, I can barely manage a stumble. Part of me just wants to stop, lie down, give up, and rest. This is too hard. And it's hopeless. And it's kind of silly. Of all the ways I ever thought I'd die, getting sliced up by a big Viking guy would come somewhere between having a UFO crash on my head and getting disintegrated by laser sharks. Dropping my sword and letting the universe have a good laugh at my expense makes as much sense as anything.

Then I think of my mom and dad and sister at home. It's getting late, and by now they're starting to worry. They won't know what happened to me. I'll be a missing person, forever, and along with everything else that's going on their lives, they'll have to deal with the sadness of losing their only son.

And I know them. They'll never stop looking for me. Even though they'll never find me, they'll never give up.

Egil Thorvaldsson blinks and wipes blood from his brow. I've put a pretty deep cut over his eye. But it hasn't blinded him, hasn't slowed him down. He smiles and laughs, and his laugh sounds like the roar of a bear.

"You are very brave, little boy," he says.

He's going to kill me now.

Before

There's a foot of new snow on the ground in San Diego. The bright side is that the fresh snow covers last week's sooty, muddy, sludgy snow. The cruddy side is that there's snow in San Diego.

I crunch down the sidewalk in my Baja boots, which is what we call regular shoes wrapped in newspapers and duct tape. A few people have real boots that help keep their feet warm and dry, and we have a special word for those people, too: *rich*.

There is snow almost everywhere now.

Snow in Los Angeles.

Snow in Miami.

Snow in Hawaii.

Snow in the deserts and on islands that used to glisten in turquoise waters.

It's because we burned too much oil and coal and it changed the climate.

It's because we're caught in a new part of a natural cycle.

It's because we sinned and God is punishing us.

Nobody has any clue. It's just winter all the time, and nobody knows why.

I've spent the day trudging into every open restaurant, shop, and office downtown, asking and begging and pleading for a job. I hate asking for anything. But I woke up early this morning and took inventory of the pantry. Three cans of government-relief soup. A box of crackers. Some scrapings of peanut butter. That's what's supposed to feed me and my mom and my dad and my sister.

"Got any plans today?" Dad said when I shut the last empty kitchen cupboard. He tried to hide his wince as he walked into the kitchen. His back isn't getting any better.

"Not much. Just gonna walk around a while."

He nodded and wouldn't meet my eyes. He doesn't like me to witness his guilt and shame. Dad's a proud man. Mom's a proud woman. And they can't feed their family. They sold the car when they could no longer afford gas, but all they got for it was spare-parts money. Mom sold her engagement ring. They'd sell the house if they could, even though, other than Elsa and me, it's the thing they're proudest of. But it's five rooms they can't afford to heat. More than running out of food, I fear losing electricity. The only thing worse than starving is starving in the dark.

"It'll be okay," Dad said. "Something will come through."

Yeah, something will come through. And pigs will fly. And bread and soup and electricity will come from the butts of these flying pigs.

"I know, Dad. Something will come through."

He came over and ruffled my hair, like I was seven instead of seventeen. I used to mind it when he did that. But his hand was warm, and he was trying to give me courage even though he's always afraid. There's something awful and sweet about it.

So, I'm willing to beg. Not that it does any good. We are all now a nation of beggars, and there's not much left to give.

At the bus shelter, I lower myself to the cold metal bench to rest my legs. The bus doesn't come by anymore, but I'm not alone. A wind is picking up, blowing uncollected garbage down the street, and even though this bus shelter was built to protect people from sunny days and light breezes, it's still better than nothing. After a few minutes, there's about half a dozen of us cowering in the cold.

A woman bundled in blankets, like a woolen mummy, wanders up. She's humming to herself, and then she begins saying something in a voice like a cracked glacier.

"Three winters with no summer between," she says. "The Midgard Serpent awakens, and its thrashing cracks the world. A wolf of Fenrir's kin grows to eat the Moon. Men forget the bonds of kinship and make war. Ax age, spear age, sword age, and an age of wolves till the world sinks down."

Nobody pays her much attention. People are used to all kinds of crazy these days.

"Would you like my seat?" I say.

She smiles at me from beneath the hooded shadows of her blankets. "You are a kind boy," she says. "And I smell the blood in you."

I smile back and give her my seat.

I don't feel very kind, but even if she is a crazy woman, it feels good to hear her say I'm kind. It's like a little campfire takes light in my heart. No, I don't feel kind, but I can act kind, if I can remember what it feels like to live in a world with kindness, then maybe in my own small way I can keep kindness alive for just a little bit longer.

Then I spy a white spot of hope. It comes in the form of a paper flyer taped to a lightpost. I rise on my chapped and creaking legs and step closer, and my eyes fill with dollar signs.

SEEKING PAID VOLUNTEERS FOR MEDICAL STUDY
NorseCODE Genomics
Males
Ages 18–44
Healthy with no chronic conditions
Requires screening interview and blood test, with possible
    follow-up interview
Compensation: Up to $1,000

I've heard about these kinds of jobs, where scientists pay you to be a lab rat. When school was still open, I considered going to college and getting a biology degree, and then after that I'd get a master's degree and then my doctorate, and I'd be a medical researcher, finding cures for diseases. Maybe there are still people doing that kind of thing.

The address at the bottom of the flyer is for a place about two miles from here.

I should go home, but if I do, it'll be empty-handed, and I can't blink the dollar signs out of my eyes.

I do a bad thing. I pry the flyer off the post, just in case anyone else at the bus stop reads it. I don't know how many of these volunteer positions are available, and I don't want competition.

"Men forget the bonds of kinship," says the old woman from inside her mound of blankets.

I feel small and unkind.

The wind howls like an age of wolves, and I tuck the flyer under my thin jacket and start hiking.

NorseCODE Genomics has an office on the ninth floor of a downtown skyscraper. The elevator's working, and the lights are on, a pleasant surprise. I pause before a door of frosted glass to catch my breath. The glass is etched with the NorseCODE logo, a double-helix DNA molecule growing from a tree with nine roots. Through the door I go, into a bright, warm place. For a moment I just stand there, feeling toasty. It's almost too toasty. I unzip my jacket and peel off my hat and the old sweatshirt sleeve I've been using as a scarf.

The waiting room chairs are stuffed with people filling out forms on clipboards. They are not a well-looking bunch. They are thin, stooped, tired. The room rumbles with coughs and sniffles and moans, and I wonder if I've come to the wrong place.

But I'm here for a medical study. And these people are sick. They are hungry. They are exhausted.

The flyer said they were looking for healthy people with no chronic conditions. No wonder NorseCODE's willing to pay so much. These days, healthy people are hard to find.

On closer inspection, a lot of the people are just holding their clipboards, having already filled out their forms. There's no snow in here, no rain, no shrieking wind, and the temptation to sit here until you get kicked out must be strong. But I'm eager to make some money and get home, so I ask the man in the nearest seat where to get a form. He motions me to the far wall, and there behind the desk I find the most striking woman I have ever seen.

Her skin is icicle white, with a rosy blush to her high cheeks. Blond-white hair spills over her shoulders, which look firm and strong beneath a tight sweater so soft I have to stop myself from reaching out to pet it. Must be made of some kind of fancy goat.

Standing there in my stupid Baja boots and makeshift winter gear, I feel like a troll. She knows I'm here, but she doesn't bother to look up from her computer. So I unfold my flyer and put it down on her desk. Slam it down, really.

Now she looks up. If a facial expression could kill, I'd be eviscerated. Her eyes shine at thirty below zero.

"I'm here for the study," I say.

And she stares at me.

And stares.

And stares.

"Any chronic medical conditions?" she says in an accent I can't place.

My dad has a bad back, which kept him from working even before the Long Winter began. My mom has diabetes. But I'm healthy.

"No."

And she stares at me some more. And then, just when I'm

ready to turn and run away from this pale, beautiful monster, she betrays the smallest of smiles.

"You can go in," she says, indicating a door behind her.

I'm confused and flustered. I am a flustered troll padded in too much clothing.

"You don't need me to fill out the form?"

"No, I don't. The form is just a mechanism to get people sitting down so we can inspect them. To see if they have the surface qualities we're looking for. Most of the people in this room"— she screws up her face with distaste—"they'll be sent home with ten dollars for their time."

"What surface qualities are you looking for?"

"You have them," she says.

"What are they?"

"You can go in. Through that door."

She looks down and returns to her typing, and I'm left there, trying to decide what to do.

Ten dollars is more money than I've brought home in a long time. With ten dollars, you can buy a lemon, or three slices of bread, or four vitamin-C pills. Ten dollars is nothing to sneeze at. But the flyer says the study pays up to a thousand dollars.

I step around her desk and go through the doorway.

The frosty receptionist's frosty twin takes six ampoules of my blood and instructs me to wait in another sitting room. My only company is a giant with muscles like granite and a laugh like cannon fire. He tells me his name is Gunther, and he's a merchant sailor who came to San Diego from Norway, but then the shipping company he worked for went bust, and he's been stranded here ever since. He's hoping to make enough money to buy his way on a ship back home.

"But isn't it even colder in Norway? People say the ice is locking up shipping lanes, and the blizzards are so bad the planes can't land."

He gets a faraway look. "I have family there," he says simply. "They need me."

I get it. I totally do.

We pass the time chatting. I tell him what San Diego used to be like, with blue oceans and surfers and broad beaches of sand, and how the stores used to be open and how I used to go to school and how I wanted to be a doctor of some kind. And he tells me about things he has seen—dolphins dancing off the prow of his ship, and blue whales breaching, like giant towers of life rocketing from the sea. And something he saw recently, a ridge on the horizon that didn't show up on sonar, but that through binoculars looked like some kind of impossibly large serpent.

"I don't believe in sea monsters or UFOs," he says with his powerful, cheery laugh. "It must have been an optical illusion. Also, I drink too much."

I think of what the woman at the bus shelter said: *The Midgard Serpent awakens and its thrashing cracks the world.*

I can only return his laugh with a weak smile.

A door opens, and I gasp at the sight of the woman standing there. If Miss Frost the receptionist and her twin who drew my blood were lovely and awful, this woman is some kind of terrible, beautiful goddess. She stands as tall as Gunther in a cream business suit three shades darker than her flawless skin. Red curls frame her face like flame on snow. Her blue eyes are like jewels worthy of a queen.

"Edward Darmadi?"

I make myself stand. "That's me."

She doesn't smile, but her eyes warm, and the room gets warmer with them.

"Congratulations. You've been chosen to continue with the study."

"I get the thousand dollars?"

"Within another hour, you will receive a great reward. Please come with me."

She holds open the door for me.

Gunther tries to look confident. "And me, too, right?"

The goddess barely glances at him when she speaks. "You may return to the receptionist. She will give you twenty dollars for your time. Thank you."

Gunther, this big, powerful, cheery man, seems to deflate before my eyes. He slinks off back to the main waiting room, defeated.

I have nothing to offer him but a small good-bye wave, and I go with the goddess.

She takes me down a corridor with large windows on either side. Behind the windows, technicians in lab coats labor behind workbenches arrayed with computers and biomedical equipment. I recognize some of it from my biology studies: autoclaves, centrifuges, incubators, sequencers. I suppose this place isn't too different from most medical research labs, but I wonder how many of them are staffed the way NorseCODE is. Every person

I've seen who works here—from the receptionist, to the woman who took my blood, to the goddess escorting me, to each and every one of the technicians—is a woman. They are all white. They are all tall. They are all beautiful and powerful.

"It is good to meet you, Edward. My name is Radgrid." She notices my interest in what's going on behind the windows. "Do you know anything about genomics, Edward?"

"It involves mapping genes. Figuring out the code of DNA molecules and understanding how DNA determines inherited traits. Like, why some people are blond or why they get certain diseases."

"Very good. Here at NorseCODE, we are looking specifically at Y-chromosome DNA."

"Y-chromosome…that's the DNA that we inherit from our fathers."

"Exactly. Every man's genes contain a Y-chromosome, which you received from your father. And looking at those Y-chromosomes—how they have remained the same from generation to generation, or how they have changed through mutation—has enabled us to find ancient, common ancestors of people living today. Scientists have discovered that our Y-chromosomal Adam—the most recent, common ancestor from whom all living people are descended—lived as recently as sixty thousand years ago. Research has found that sixteen million men living today are the progeny of Genghis Khan, the great warrior who ruled the vast Mongolian empire eight hundred years ago."

Radgrid's voice rises with excitement as she walks, and her pace quickens. I struggle to keep up with her long stride.

"Is that what you're doing here? Looking for descendants of Genghis Khan?

"No," she says. "We're looking for the descendants of Odin, the All-Father, chieftain god of the mighty Aesir, whose valor defends us from Ragnarok, the death of all worlds."

We step through a final door, and there, waiting for me, is a man with a sword.

He shows me a hideous, brown-toothed grin and says, "Doom."

The room is the size of a basketball court. It's all sterile white walls and a cold cement floor with a drain in the middle. The floor is wet, as if recently hosed, and the air smells of blood.

Of course, I do the only sensible thing. I turn right around and try to run. But the door we just came through locks, and when I bang on it, I only hurt my hand. It's solid steel. I'm not going anywhere.

Radgrid has been talking.

"You only remember the Aesir in lore and in your corrupted names for the days of the week. Thursday for Thor, who must die slaying the Midgard Serpent. Tuesday, for Tew, the war god who lost his arm. Wednesday for Woden, or Odin, whom I have already mentioned. They were gods of yesterday, in times of war and strife, when men and women needed help against their enemies, needed help in childbirth, needed help bringing forth crops against the starvation of the dark winters. The truth of the gods has always been bigger than stories and names."

I dig out my phone and thumb 911. But the phones haven't

worked more than a few days out of every month, and right now my mine is just a useless plastic prop. Radgrid knows this. She keeps talking.

"The gods have always known how they'll die," she says. She pulls down a plastic case from a shelf. It takes me a few seconds to remember where I've seen a case of this size and shape. It was in a sporting goods store. It's a rifle case.

I slap the walls and scream for help. Radgrid talks.

"The gods know how everything will die. It begins with three winters, and no summer between. The Fimbulwinter, it's called. You know what it is, and now you know its name. Then follow war and cruelty. Men forget the bonds of kinship. And then disaster. The Midgard Serpent stirs, raising seas and drowning the lands. Do you remember the Asian tsunami last year? Do you keep up with the news, Edward?"

I don't answer, because I'm still too busy looking for a way out, but I remember the tsunami. It killed more than a hundred thousand people.

"Then there is Fenrir, the great wolf, and one of his kin grows large enough to eat the Moon. It's an age of swords, an age of spears, an age of axes."

I turn to face her. "And an age of wolves," I say, "until the world sinks down."

"Yes," she says, nodding. "Yes, Edward. And in the end, the gods battle the giants and the other monsters, and they die, laying waste to all worlds. So it was uttered, in the beginning of days. It is fact. Nothing can change it."

The big, ugly man with the sword rolls his neck and shoulders, stretching before exercise. The way he's looking at me tells me the kind of exercise he has in mind involves butchery.

I find myself getting angry. All I wanted was some money to feed my family. "So why are you bothering me with this? I'm not from one of the places where they believe in your gods. I was born here, in San Diego. My parents are from Indonesia. I'm an atheist. And if I had a religion, it'd be my dad's, and he's Muslim."

"All gods spring from the same well," she says with a shrug, as if she's not that interested in my objection. "They change shape and color, and different peoples at different times express them differently. But now, today, in this time and place, when things are ending, they are expressed as Odin's tribe."

"You didn't answer my question. Why bother me with this?"

"You have met my sisters. They, like myself, are Valkyries. We are Odin's shield maidens. His corpse pickers. We are tasked with building his last army. Throughout history we have plucked fallen warriors from the killing fields and brought them to Odin's hall. They are called the Einherjar. There, they fight and train by day until they are cut down. Then, at sunset, they rise to spend the night in revel and feast until sunrise, when they go out to the fields to train and die once more. It is heaven."

Hope surges through me. Since I am so obviously not a great warrior, Radgrid has clearly made a mistake. This is all basically just a paperwork mix-up, and once I make her realize that, she and her sword-swinging thug will let me go.

I open my mouth, but she speaks sharply to cut me off: "The greatest of Odin's warriors share two things in common. One, they are his sons, and the sons of his sons, from the days when he walked among men and lived in their houses."

Dread dawns on me like another dark winter day. "The Y-chromosome. NorseCODE has been looking for Odin's descendants. And I'm a genome match."

Radgrid thumbs the latches on the rifle case. I flinch at the sound. "The second requirement is that the warriors of the Einherjar have died gloriously in battle. Not of sickness, not of old age. They cannot have died in bed. They must have died in blood."

I cling desperately to reason. "Why build an army when you said yourself you're going to lose the war? You said nothing can change it."

"We must act as though we have hope, Edward, even when there is none. We must pretend. To act as though we have hope is to keep hope alive."

She lifts the lid of the case, and I see what's lying there in a neatly cut foam indentation. The ugly man with the sword coughs a laugh, and I panic. I turn and throw myself against the door, and I smash my fists against steel and scream. Somehow, through all my commotion, I still hear Radgrid's chilling voice.

"Edward Darmadi," she says. "Prepare to die gloriously."

She lifts the sword out of the case and holds it out to me.

His name is Egil Thorvaldsson. He is a Viking warrior who died raiding in England in 865 A.D., and he's been one of the Einherjar ever since. He's serving as Radgrid's champion here at NorseCODE in San Diego, California, and he is offering me an opportunity to be glorious.

He is going to kill me.

There's no more time to insist that this is all a mistake, or that it's too crazy to be true. It doesn't matter that I'm not a Nordic Viking warrior. It doesn't matter that I'm the Indonesian American son of Muslims. All that matters right now are the swords.

I feel like I've been fighting him for hours, but it's probably only been minutes. Mostly, I've been running around the room, dodging the sweep of his blade. My chest heaves for breath, and my muscles ache and burn, and blood streams down my arm and makes the sword slippery in my hand.

But he's bleeding, too. I don't really remember when or how, but I cut him over his left eyebrow. The blood drips into his left eye faster than he can blink it away, blinding him. He swipes at it with a forearm the size of a hog, but the blood keeps pouring out.

It won't be enough to save me, but if I can't find hope or courage, I can at least pretend like I have them.

Egil rises to his full height, towering over me, and raises his sword high. I backpedal away, but it's like trying to escape a falling redwood when you're standing right beneath it. The blade comes down, and I rush closer to him. I move my sword in a desperate spasm, and luck or fate or doom decides that my blade will slice into his forehead above his right eye. He curses and falters as blood springs from his new wound, and I stumble away to get distance.

Now we're both sweating and breathing hard. We're both bleeding. But there's one difference between us.

I can still see.

When I was taking driver's ed, I hit a dog.

The instructor said it wasn't my fault. The dog just ran out from between two parked cars, right into my path. There was a small impact and a squeal of pain that I will never forget. I remember calmly turning off the car, putting it in park, and applying the parking brake, and I opened my door and went around to the front of the car. The dog lay there, still, its eyes open, but it was so clearly vacant of life, and I was too horrified to cry. I knew that a life had been subtracted from the world, and the sense of its absence never left me.

I feel the same thing when I dart around Egil Thorvaldsson and run my sword through his back.

Standing over his lifeless body, I turn to Radgrid.

"You made me kill a man."

She waves this off. "He's Einherjar. He's died before. He will rise and die again. There are ways," she says. "Ways to bring the living to the afterworld. You still draw breath, and though you have not achieved a glorious death, you have fought gloriously. With your leave, I will take you to Valhalla. There you will train with the greatest warriors the world has ever seen for a fight whose day draws ever closer. There you will drink the ale of gods and be counted among the greatest of men, ever. You will eventually die, as all things do. Every animal, every human, every god, must one day end. But such grand meaning will your death have."

I think about the waiting room outside, filled with coughs and moans. I think about the cold world outside, getting darker and darker every day until the sun refuses to rise. Things will end not with a bang but with a sniffle.

I release my sword and let it clang against the cement floor.

"I want my thousand bucks."

Radgrid said the long, dark winter won't lift. I hear the blowing wind outside, and a hard rain patters the window. I sit with my mother and father and sister in our little living room, eating roast chicken by the light of a low-energy bulb. Maybe this is cowardice. Monsters are coming. I can't see them yet, or hear them, but I know they're out there, lurking beyond a stranger horizon than I ever dreamed possible. Maybe it's cowardice to stay here at home.

But maybe, sometimes, heroism is doing whatever you have to do to stand guard over your family. Sometimes heroism is just paying the electricity bill to keep the lights burning one more night.

Next Door

by Rahul Kanakia

At 3 A.M., the itching got so bad that Aakash rolled off his mattress and crawled across the garage floor to the bug-free patch of concrete where Chandresh and Rishi were sleeping. But after a shivering hour next to his restless brothers, he got up and trudged to the bed. He was just crawling in when he spotted a black speck on his pillow. Shuddering, he flung the bedding away and huddled atop the bare plastic with which he'd shrink-wrapped the mattress.

At first he kept the light on, but then Chandresh started rustling around on the floor, so he switched it off. In the dark, he felt the featherlight touches all over his skin, running up his legs and across his chest, pausing on the tip of his nose and then jumping into his hair. He knew that most of the sensations were probably just imaginary bugs, conjured up by his anxiety. He needed to relax. They'd only had the bugs for a few weeks. His boyfriend, Victor, had lived in a bug-ridden squat for two years, but he'd gotten used to them after a few months. "They're no worse than mosquito bites," Victor had said.

But Aakash couldn't stop *feeling* them. Finally, he gave in and raked his nails over his neck, arms, legs, chest, stomach, armpits, and groin. But the scratching brought no relief. The points of itchiness multiplied until he didn't have enough fingers to deal with them. He screamed silently and beat on the mattress, but then his mother, Deepa, sleepily murmured, "What? Who?" so Aakash clenched his hands together. There was no sense in waking her up too.

Fighting tears of frustration, he got off the mattress and went to the far corner of the garage. He crossed his legs and sat down next to the spigot that provided their water. He was surrounded by junk: skis, a lawnmower, three bicycles, boxes of Christmas ornaments, books, and old clothes. It all belonged to the family of strangers who owned this garage. Whenever Aakash tried to move any of it, little bots would sizzle out of the junk and sound a warning beep until Aakash moved away.

Chemicals couldn't get rid of the bedbugs—modern bugs were immune to most all pesticides—but those tiny little bots could run through the garage and zap them all in an instant. Aakash looked upward and mouthed a silent prayer to the owners of the garage. He was right on the verge of cranking open that garage door and walking up to the big house and knocking on the door and begging the owners to make that tiny adjustment to the bots and set Aakash's family free from this menace. But Aakash stepped back from the edge. He was a squatter. He didn't have any rights.

In most squats, the strangers were so zonked out that their squatters could make them do anything, but Aakash's strangers were a little more awake than most. They seemed to understand and accept that there were people living in their garage, but they'd also set firm boundaries; whenever Aakash tried to move into their house, he found that everything was firmly locked and secured. Aakash couldn't risk what would happen if they decided to withdraw their unspoken invitation. No, the answer was the same as always. He had to move out. He had to find a new squat: a bug-free squat.

So he called Victor.

Victor always kept late hours. He answered the call immediately, "Hey there."

"I can't take another day with these bugs," Aakash whispered.

"Stay strong. We'll have our own squat soon enough."

"How? When? We've been looking for a year."

"It'll happen."

"The new place will probably get the bug, too. Every place has them nowadays."

"Not our place. I'll make sure of it. I got a surprise for you."

Aakash smiled. "What?"

"I'll show you tomorrow. Go to sleep. Make sure you rest up."

"I can't sleep for shit. Come on, what is it?"

"What, you really want me to ruin the surprise?"

As they whispered back and forth, Aakash grew drowsy and finally fell asleep.

He awoke when the garage door rolled up and let in a stream of morning light. A stranger—the man who owned the house—

stood in the doorway, saying to himself, "Hold on. Hold on. I think I put it in the bin marked RADICAL SELF-EXPRESSION IN GROSSLY MATERIALIST CONTEXTS."

Aakash glanced at his phone. It was 8 A.M. Victor's last text said, *Hope you're finally asleep. I love you.*

Aakash's mother ran forward and pulled sleepy Chandresh and Rishi out of the way as the stranger stepped into the garage. The stranger was walking blindly, using his fingers to manipulate keyboards and windows and graphical elements that no one else could see. Their visual implants allowed the strangers to see much more than was actually there, but it also meant they mostly ignored the real world.

Bots—tiny tangles of wire—wriggled out of the stranger's hair and radiated across the concrete floor, emitting low-powered zaps. One of the bots zapped a speck of dust. Aakash pulled out his phone, and it identified the speck as a bedbug.

The stranger clattered through the junk in the back corner. Finally, he said, "Found it!" and pulled out a large machine.

The bots wouldn't go farther than three feet from the man, but when he passed Aakash's bed, hundreds of them crawled into it. Aakash's heart leaped.

Aakash sucked in his stomach and tiptoed behind the man, trying to get within the bots' range. The bug-killing bots leaped directly from the stranger's hair onto Aakash. They crawled all over his body. Each time he felt a tiny static shock, Aakash sighed with relief.

As the man left, Aakash tiptoed behind him. He was close enough to kiss the man. His mom and brothers were looking at him with shocked expressions. A half-dozen would-be squatters were gathered around the garage door with bedrolls and bags. They were clearly hoping the garage would empty out so they could snake the squat for themselves. A few of them laughed at Aakash's absurd dog-step.

"What the hell are you doing?"

The interjection came from another stranger: a teenager with the wispy hint of a beard.

"Be patient, Joel!" the man said. "I *just* found the laser-saw."

"I wasn't talking to you, Dad," Joel said. "Can't you see this guy riding your ass?"

The man glanced back. His face was just a foot from Aakash's. Aakash smiled but didn't pull back. The bots were still working.

"Oh, it's just a street person." The dad handed over the laser-saw. "All right... are you ready to reclaim your cultural heritage?"

The son pulled Aakash back by the arm. "Jesus, give my dad some room," Joel said. Aakash could hear the powered-up hum of the personal-defense system embedded in the son's shirt. He was probably getting ready to unleash an arc of electricity that would shock Aakash into unconsciousness.

"Don't worry about him," the father said. "The street people are harmless."

The father snapped his fingers, and the garage door started closing. Aakash shouted to his mother, "I'm coming in. I'll stay today."

"No, no," his mother yelled. "Victor will be waiting for you! You need to keep searching!"

Aakash ran in and grabbed his bag from the high shelf, then rolled out and under the door. When he got up, the father and son were walking away.

One of the would-be squatters standing by the garage door said, "I hate that kid. I can't wait until he finally goes to sleep."

"At least he doesn't ignore us," another said.

"Man . . . if they didn't ignore us, how could we live with them?"

Aakash looked at the pair. He'd seen them around, but he didn't know their names. Aakash said, "C'mon, guys, what're you waiting around for? Didn't you hear? Our squat has the bug."

One of them said, "So what? My bedroll has the bug, too. At least you've got a roof."

Aakash shook his head. Someone had to stay behind to stop these guys from stealing the squat, but why did he always let his mom do it? His mom never got a break from being eaten alive in there. He knew he ought to slap on the door of that garage and make her hoist it up from the inside using the manual override. He needed to pull his weight and do his time. But then he felt the phantom touch of a bug crawling across his neck. He texted Victor, *I'll be there in an hour.*

As he trudged toward the bus stop, Aakash fell in with the tens of thousands of other homeless people who were wandering the streets of L.A. County. Every street corner was a marketplace. Street stalls sold crude handicrafts to the few passersby who looked as if they had any money. People delved into collapsed buildings, pulling out copper wire, aluminum coils, rags, and paper and piled their goods into shopping carts for resale at some distant recycling center. At red lights, children ran into the crowds of sleek, self-driven cars, begging the occupants for dollars until the lights turned green and they were stranded in the middle of the lane by the zooming rivers of cars.

And every few blocks, crowds of hundreds of people surrounded a dispensary. With the bots, manufacturing was cheap and easy. Many strangers—acting singly or as part of organizations—had set up points of distribution to give away clothes, canned goods, shoes, prepaid cell phones, or whatever else they could program their bots to churn out. Aakash spent most days waiting in long, slow lines so he could accumulate something to take back to his family.

Not today, though. Today they had enough food stockpiled back in the squat. Today Aakash was going to engage in the other major pastime of the streets. He was going to head up into the hills to look for a new squat.

With their visual implants, the strangers spent more and more time in their own realities, so they didn't much care what happened to their houses. Most of them weren't as awake as the one who owned Aakash's squat. Usually, a house's owner was just a wired-up body lying in a bed, dreaming for twenty-three hours a day. So it wasn't hard for a squatter just to move right into the spare rooms. Sometimes the owner even got carried down to a cellar or something if the squatters needed more space.

But the owners were starting to die. And an ownerless house soon shut off; the electricity, the water—even the doors—stopped working. Eventually ownerless squats fell apart, and their occupants had to look for another place.

And there weren't many places left. In this part of the Hollywood Hills, there were more rubble-filled lots than upright houses.

Aakash knew that his odds of finding his own place were pretty bad. Hell, some people would say that he was a fool for wanting to leave the garage. But he couldn't stop searching for something better. Something clean and spacious and graceful: a place fit for a human being.

Victor and Aakash never went to each other's squats. Instead, they began their daily search by meeting in an abandoned steam pipe nexus underneath Griffith Observatory. To get there, Aakash passed through a long corridor whose wall was covered in frescoes of the exploding universe and whose floor was cluttered with food wrappers, broken bottles, and used condoms.

The dark corridor was a popular meeting place. In one corner, two voices were whispering.

One said, "We're evaluating your kid today, aren't we? You excited?"

The other voice said, "I just hope he does his duty. Sometimes he seems a little...careless."

"I'm sure he'll be fine." A moment of silence, then "Should we clear out the street people before your kid arrives?"

"No...he needs to learn how to deal with them."

Aakash kept walking. Lingering over someone else's secret rendezvous was against the corridor's etiquette.

The temperature in the steam pipe room was more than a hundred degrees. Victor, stripped to his shorts, sat cross-legged on their mattress and gulped water from a plastic bottle. He rose and leaned forward to kiss Aakash, only to be pushed back.

"No," Aakash said. "I'm probably *covered* in bugs."

Victor's smile threw strange shadows in the shaky light they'd dangled from an exposed wire. "So what? Now we both have them," Victor said.

Aakash said, "What if, in a few hours, we crack open a door

and come up in an abandoned mansion! A place with running water and electricity and three thousand square feet of space. And what if, with our first footsteps, we infect it?"

Aakash hung his clothes from a blisteringly hot steam pipe. Then he gingerly reached for the steam valve. The jet of steam had burned him once, but that'd been six months ago. He was more careful now. They had to heat the room to more than 120 degrees and then stand here for an hour to make sure the bugs died.

"Wait!" Victor grabbed him by the waist and pulled him back. "You haven't asked about your surprise yet!"

Victor pressed an aluminum canister into his hand. Aakash held it up to the light. The aerosol can was covered in Chinese characters.

"Pesticide? We've already tried *everything*. We have the chemical-resistant bugs."

"They're not resistant to *this*," Victor said. "It's never been used in the US. It's illegal here."

"Shit, then it'll kill us."

"No, it's just illegal because it kills birds or something. One treatment shouldn't hurt us. In China, they spray this on kids to kill lice."

"Where did you get this?"

Victor kissed Aakash. "I started looking for it on the day when you first told me your place had gotten the bug. You never blamed me, but...I felt so guilty."

"But you could use this on your own place...to help your own family...."

"No. This is for our new life. We'll find a place, spray it up, close the door, and lock our troubles on the other side."

Aakash hugged Victor, but he couldn't stop thinking about the closed door that his mom was locked behind.

A light momentarily blinded them. A stranger had entered, holding a powerful lantern. He glanced at the nearly naked pair and rolled his eyes. The stranger dragged in a chair from the hall. Aakash and Victor stepped to the side of the room. The stranger flipped their mattress up into a corner, then he hopped onto the chair and examined the ceiling.

"Hey," Aakash said. "I think that's the son of the stranger who owns my squat."

"What?"

"Yeah, I see him all the time. His name is Joel."

The teen looked down and said, "Can't you guys swish it up somewhere else?" He pulled a machine from his bag and held it up to the ceiling.

"Is that a laser-saw?" Victor whispered.

"Keep it down!" Joel said. "This is hella dangerous."

"Umm...what are you doing?" Aakash ventured. He'd lived under the boy for years, but he'd never said a word to him before.

"None of your damn business," Joel said.

Aakash whispered, "I think he's trying to break into the observatory."

"Really?" Victor said. "By lasering through the floor? Seems like someone would notice. This guy's going to go to jail."

"It's Sunday. The place is closed and empty," Joel said.

"But there are guards," Aakash said.

"There's one guard," Joel said. "I've had cameras in there, watching him, for the past two weeks. We're under the atrium right now. There's an hour-long window when he doesn't ever look into it."

Victor said, "Couldn't this kid just—" but Aakash shushed him.

"I bet I can get in there before you do," Aakash said.

"Sure...right. When the guard arrests you guys, that'll be a great distraction. Now, can you leave me alone?"

"If I get there first, you need to program your bots to zap your entire garage for bedbugs."

"What? You're bug infested? That's disgusting."

"Is it a bet?"

"No. Of course not. What would be in it for me?"

"I'm not some random punk. I know who you are. I know where you live."

"Sure," Joel said. "My shirt is a Shield S400. It'll shoot an arc that can lay you out before you—"

"I think the cops might be pretty interested in what you're doing."

"You wouldn't. You'd lose your nice little squat."

"I don't care. Those bugs are...I don't care."

Joel's face reddened and contorted. "Fine. Whatever. It's a bet."

They hastily donned their steam-pressed clothes. In the corridor, Aakash bounced up and down and whispered, "Mom will be so happy! We'll be bug free forever!"

"Wow, that kid was a straight-up fool," Victor said. "I guess strangers aren't too used to having to think."

The hallway's exit emerged from a fenced-off hill. They hopped the fence and landed in a silent park. Unblinking strangers peddled lazily on bikes that steered themselves. Some tapped on invisible keyboards as they rode. No one looked at Victor and Aakash.

Strangers didn't usually spend much time outside, but Griffith Observatory was a popular enough L.A. landmark that it managed to attract a few dozen visitors every day. Several strangers were sunning themselves on the grass. Some were walking virtual dogs that only they could see. Others were jogging or throwing balls. But all of them were seeing far more than Aakash and Victor could see. Their data displays were so dense and information rich that the world of grass and concrete and flesh was only a minor part of their visual field.

When Aakash took a running start and leaped up onto the lip of the observatory's first story, no one looked up. He gave a hand to Victor. They shinnied around to the front of the observatory and—in full view of almost fifty people—clambered up to the open slit of the dome. Then Aakash stepped onto the thin mezzanine that was just inside the dome. Below them, the guard was walking his rounds, but he never looked up.

"This is nice," Victor said. "I could def live here. Why did we strike this place off the list?"

"It's only two feet wide."

"Oh. Right."

When the guard moved away, they dropped down.

A floor tile rose, and a head poked up. Joel stood, then pulled out three gadgets. Aakash and Victor crouched down next to him. "Is that to, like, identify laser trip wires?" Victor said.

Joel opened his mouth, closed it, and then nodded.

Aakash laughed. "This place doesn't have any laser trip wires."

"Well, it's got them installed," Victor said. "But I think the guard deactivated them. Too many false positives."

Joel pulled himself out, then handed his camera to Aakash. "Fine, you win. Just take some pictures of me, all right? I gotta prove I was here."

By the time they'd dropped back into the steam-pipe room, Joel was laughing. "Wow, you guys really schooled me," he said.

"No!" Aakash stepped forward. "Actually...you...umm, definitely have skills. We just...well, it could've gone either way."

"My dad mostly taught me computer stuff," Joel said. "I guess he kind of overlooked the basic skills. Or maybe I was supposed to know them already...."

"Your dad?" Victor said.

"Yeah, this is kind of a family business for us," Joel said. "After I pass my evaluation, he and I are gonna set up shop down here and pop up at night to secretly restore the telescope. It's a great early-twentieth-century piece, but when the lens broke, the curators just hung up a do not touch sign and let it fall to pieces."

"Why?" Victor said.

"Money. They don't care whether it—"

"No...why do *you* care?"

"That's what we do. We keep things preserved after the sleepers abandon them. We're doing it for you...so you'll have some kind of history left."

"Look," Aakash said. "About those bugs. It's just a little thing. It won't be a problem to reprogram the bots, right?"

Joel's phone buzzed. He looked at it, then grimaced.

"What? Is it the next task?" Victor said.

The kid looked up at them with moisture-filled eyes; it was as if he'd never seen them before in his life. "My dad saw me with you in the atrium," Joel said. "He says that my carelessness could've compromised the mission."

Aakash cranked his mind. How could he convince this kid to pay up on the damn bet?

Joel's eyes widened. He tapped at his phone for a long while.

Then Aakash got a call. His mom was shouting, "The lights turned off! And I tried to pull open the doorway, but the rope snapped! You need to come home. I don't know what's happened. Oh God, I knew it was wrong to stay in this country; I knew we didn't belong here; I knew…"

As Aakash talked his mom through her panic, Joel's face became grimmer. When Aakash hung up, the stranger said, "It will be a while before my dad notices that power is out in the garage. Your family might be trapped for days."

"What did you do?" Aakash said.

"I'm sorry that I had to do that," Joel said. "My dad says that I'm not adaptable enough for front line work…but I'm gonna show him. And if you want your mom to get out safely, then you're gonna help me."

Joel wanted to hack the observatory's computers and insert himself into their HR database. With his finger-, voice-, and retinalprints on file, he'd be able to go in and out whenever he wanted. Then his dad would *have* to come around. Joel promised that once the operation was successful, he'd restore power to the garage.

As they walked around the building, Joel outlined a long plan that involved knocking out the lights and executing a lightning-fast, perfectly timed run. They'd memorize the floor plan, descend on wires from the ceiling, run inside in total darkness, switch the lights back on, hack the computers, and then hide until morning and leave—just like any other tourist—after the observatory opened to the public.

Aakash's stomach was churning. His mom was trapped...in the dark...with the bugs. "Fucking Christ!" he interjected. "Why bother with all that spy shit? The reason there's only one guard is because no one gives a damn whether we break in or not."

Aakash pulled three sticks of gum out of his bag and started chewing. Then he spit out the wad, took a deep breath, and ran up to the front gate of the museum. He pressed buttons and pummeled the door with his fist. Five long minutes passed before the guard opened the door.

Aakash held up his bag. "Hey, I'm sorry to bother you, but I was wondering if you could let me pick through your bins."

The guard said, "We got a guy who takes out the cans. He's a big, bald fella."

"Yeah, I know," Aakash lied. "But he only does cans. He spotted some copper coils in there, though, and tipped me off about them."

"Jeez, I don't think..."

"Please...I need this. My tooth's been killing me for months." Aakash opened his mouth and touched the blackened incisor he hadn't thought about since the bugs had come. "I need a big score to pay for pulling it."

The guard rubbed his own jaw. "Well, all right, but I gotta watch you." As he entered, Aakash stuck the wad of gum against the door's locking mechanism.

Aakash followed the guard down a set of stairs. His phone buzzed. A text from an unknown number: *We're in.*

As they walked down a corridor, Aakash's practiced eyes could see the patch where the door that led to the exploding galaxy hallway had been sealed off entirely. Steel chains secured by a big combination lock barred a set of doors that said JAMES LICK MEMORIAL IMAX THEATER.

"You ever catch a movie?" Aakash said.

"No," the guard said. "That was already locked up when I started working here. Makes sense. What we've got is way better than IMAX." The guard laughed and tapped at the visual implant pasted to his temple, but then he looked at Aakash's bare brow and said, "Well, the implants also have downsides. After you've got them for a while, the ordinary world starts to seem a little...dull."

It was hard to stay impassive while rooting around in the Dumpster at the loading dock. The theater was all that Aakash could think about. The theater probably still had electricity. And they wouldn't have to stay inside it twenty-four-seven to keep it from getting snaked by someone else. The guard would keep everyone else out!

The guard's phone rang. Red lights flashed. A raucous alarm echoed from wall-mounted speakers. Aakash tensed up.

But the guard just waved his hand. "Oh man, this happens all the time," the guard said. "Some bird probably hit a window, and now I gotta go disable the alarm." The guard looked over Aakash's shoulder. "Damn...you haven't found the coils yet, have you?"

Aakash winced and rubbed the side of his face. "No...I...I

guess I'll go," he said. "Thanks for everything you've done. He said it was pretty far down at the bottom...but if you've gotta..."

The guard said, "Look. You don't mind if I lock you down here, do you? I'll be back in just a second."

When the guard left, the electronic lock clicked behind him. And why shouldn't the guard feel safe? There was no way that some street kid could break a top-of-the-line cryptographic lock.

But Aakash wasn't going in through that door. Instead, he took a slab of plywood from the Dumpster and manually levered up the vehicle gate a few inches so he could reach inside with a stretched-out wire hanger and hit the button to open the gate.

The lock barring the theater was idiotically simple. It must've been put in before they replaced everything with electronic locks. He pulled down on the lock to put pressure on the internal mechanism and slowly rotated the numbers until the tumblers clicked into place.

The theater was a paradise. A tall ceiling. A long silver screen. Hundreds of padded chairs. The lone glow of an emergency light meant readily available power. The dust was thick and undisturbed. Aakash was the first person to step inside here in years. And no people meant no bugs.

Footsteps echoed outside. Aakash gasped. The alarms had just gone silent. Was he going to be trapped in here? He forced himself to calm down. He listened. There were two sets of footsteps. He opened the door. Joel and Victor were running down the corridor.

"In here, you idiots."

"Alarms, cops, caught," Joel gasped.

Victor pulled Joel inside. Aakash stepped out, closed the

doors, slapped the padlock back on, and forced himself to walk, briskly but quietly, back to the loading dock.

When the guard returned, he said, "Yeah...some kind of bird or something. Oh...you haven't gotten the coils yet? Look, I'm sorry, but...I think I gotta take you back."

As they passed the theater door, Aakash smiled. He and Victor had finally found their new home.

Over the next day, Joel sent him a stream of increasingly frantic texts:

What the FUCK are you waiting for?

Get me out of here or your mom's fucking going to jail!

Don't THINK about ratting me out. My dad knows people. He can get me off, no prob.

Aakash's mother called a few times, too, and he had to soothe her as well. He was being torn in a dozen directions. Even after he saved Joel, how could he leave his family under the teen's thumb? How was he going to placate that kid?

But he wasn't going to screw this up by acting rashly. He texted with Victor, and they both agreed to wait. Night fell, and still Aakash waited. He felt guilty when he lined up at a dispensary for his meal. Victor and Joel had to be getting pretty hungry right now. He knew he could probably run inside and rescue them, but he'd looked for that place for years...for his whole life. He couldn't risk setting off the alarm again and making the guard suspicious.

When morning came, he was cold, damp, and hungry. But he was the first person in the ticket line. The guard had changed, so no one recognized him. He sauntered down that corridor and picked the padlock unhurriedly.

Victor embraced him, and Joel clawed for the door. Aakash restrained Joel. "Wait a second. I saved your ass here. You gotta admit that you owe—"

The doors reopened. Two strangers—Joel's father and some woman—walked in.

"Congratulations," the father said. "This will be a fine base of operations."

"We'll be moving in our equipment throughout the day," said the woman.

Joel was shaking. "Then...I passed?"

The father said, "Your method of handling these street people was unorthodox, but it got results. I've never been prouder." He embraced his son.

"I...I also put you and me into the staff database," Joel said. "We can come and go whenever we want."

"What the fuck?" Victor said. "You guys can have the telescope, but this theater is *ours*."

"You can stay in the garage," Joel said. "I'll reprogram the bots. It's no problem."

Aakash groaned. He'd known this was gonna fall apart somehow.

"No!" Victor said. "We *need* this place. We want to live here, do you understand? We're not just pulling some kind of guerrilla art stunt...we're talking about staying alive."

His father glanced at Joel. Aakash wondered if that hug could be taken back.

"No, wait!" Joel said. "These two, they're good. They want to join us."

"Fuck you guys," Victor said. "You're *really* going to snake this from us? We have nothing at all, and you're really gonna…"

"Calm down," Aakash said. "Let's just get out of here."

Joel said, "Come on. What's wrong with letting them live here and help us? Aren't they the ones who'll inherit all our work?"

His father said, "You don't need to placate them. They're probably illegal. I'll arrange to have them deported."

Joel's mouth opened. "C'mon, Dad… that's not funny."

"You know that I'm in favor of helping the street people whenever we can, but these two have already proven themselves to be dangerous and untrustworthy," his father said. "From the beginning, they threatened to compromise you. Finally, you had to extort them into helping you. If we let them go, they'll sell us out for a quick payday."

"No, I'm *not* backing down," Victor said. He held up the can of Chinese pesticide. "You can all eat bug spray." He pulled the tab, and gas billowed from the top of the can. The strangers' eyes got big and their shirts flashed and bots swarmed out of their hair. What were their informational overlays telling them about this gas? The smoke enveloped Victor.

"Crazy bastards, that stuff is—" Joel's father said.

"We need to go!" the woman said.

Joel took one last backward look before he followed them. The doors slammed behind them, and the padlock clicked. Joel's father probably thought he was locking them in to face a fatal poison. Aakash fell to his knees, took off his shirt, wetted it with a water bottle, and shoved it against the door to stop the smoke from seeping out and setting off god-knows-what alarms.

From within the smoke cloud, Victor laughed. "What a bunch of posers," he said.

The smoke reached Aakash. He tried not to breathe it in, but it was everywhere. He reached for Victor. "Is this really happening?" Aakash said. "Have we really done it?"

"They won't bother us again. I'll send out a few messages and tie them up in knots, thinking we got killed by this stuff. They won't want to come within five miles of this place."

"But…what about…"

"That kid isn't going to mess with your family…not after what he's already done to you."

"But he won't help them either. The bugs…"

"We could be alone: here, together, forever. No one would ever bother us. If we bring our families, we'll be in danger every day. Who knows who might try to take it from us? Or whether someone would attract the guards? Are your brothers really gonna be quiet for weeks, months, years? We'll have to think about their food and their water. We'll have to make dispensary trips every day; each trip means another chance of getting caught. And we'll have to—"

Victor's speech was broken up by a long fit of coughing. Aakash's throat and lungs were also feeling ill-used by the pesticide, but hopefully the pain would fade soon enough.

Victor continued, "We'll have to build toilets and find some way to get running water. And what if they bring more bugs? Do you really think we can live like that? Do you really think that'll work?"

"Not really," Aakash said. "But…we have to try. I can't be

happy here knowing Rishi and Chandresh are growing up in that place."

Victor was silent for a long moment. Aakash could feel his boyfriend giving up that old dream and trying to orient himself to the new one. Could he do it? Or would he leave?

"Fine," Victor said. "We'll open this place up to everyone and your mother."

After they kissed, Aakash turned and spit out the toxic dust he'd picked up from Victor's lips.

"You're amazing," Aakash said. "I'll text my mom and—"

"Wait," Victor said. "Do it tomorrow. Can't we have it to ourselves for at least one day?"

The ceiling was so high and dark that it looked like the night sky. The pesticidal dust on the carpet was so white that it looked like frost. And the two lovers lay down next to each other so tenderly that, for a moment, they looked carefree.

Good Girl

by Malinda Lo

"You look like a good girl. Aren't you a little far from home?"

Those were the first words she said to me. That was the day I finally got up the nerve to squeeze through the crack in the wall near Lucky Grocery that everybody knew about but nobody admitted to. Inside, the gray afternoon light shone faintly over a flight of half-broken stairs. I waited until my eyes adjusted to head down into the dark, because, like an idiot, I hadn't thought to bring a flashlight.

Her words came at me through the murky half-light like a gunshot, and I actually ducked. "Who's there?" I heard my voice quivering.

A dim, yellowish bulb hung from the ceiling about ten feet away from the bottom of the stairs, revealing dirty, chipped tiles on the walls and a grimy concrete floor. I heard footsteps, and a few seconds later a figure stepped out from the shadows and into the cone of light. I knew she was a girl from her voice, but she didn't look like any of the girls I knew. Her head was shaved clean, and her scalp was tattooed with strange symbols. Her left eyebrow was pierced twice, rings ran up both of her ears, and I saw the traces of tattoos on her throat, too. She held a knife in one hand, and the other was balled up in her jacket pocket. She was dressed in army-green cargo pants tucked into beat-up combat boots, and she didn't look friendly.

"What do you want?" she asked.

"I—" The words stuck in my throat as she glared at me. Heat crept up my neck.

"Can't hear you," she said in a low, singsong voice, and took a step closer.

I reached into my pocket, and quicker than I could take another breath she had her knife at my throat, twisting me around so that her other arm was wrapped tightly across my body. My heartbeat pounded in my ears, and I gasped against the sharp blade. I smelled the metallic tang of sweat on her skin.

"What're you reaching for?" she muttered.

"I brought money," I squeaked. "That's all, I swear."

When she let me go, I scrabbled my hand in my pocket again and pulled out the folded twenty-credit note. I held it out to her with shaking fingers.

"You're new at this, aren't you?" she growled. "First you tell me what you want and *then* I name the price."

Embarrassed, I tried to put the money away, but she snatched it from my hand. "How do I know you won't just report me?" I asked.

She came closer. She was a few inches taller than me, so I had to raise my eyes to hers. She had the features of someone who was mixed: Something about the shape of her cheekbones marked her as not entirely Asian; something about the color of her skin marked her as not entirely African. And to my shame, I found her face—even with its tattoos and piercings—entirely beautiful.

I blushed.

"Do I look like I'm Patrol material?" she asked sharply.

"No," I whispered. Everyone in Patrol was pure-blooded. Nobody down here in the Tunnels was. Not my brother, and not me. I was lucky that my Asian genes were predominant, and if I kept quiet, people didn't notice.

"Then tell me what you're looking for, good girl."

Her words stung. Good girls didn't come down to the Tunnels. "My name is Kyle," I said.

She smirked. "All right. Kyle. What are you looking for?"

I felt like my face was on fire. I lowered my gaze. "I'm looking for my brother. Kit Lin. He disappeared almost a year ago."

"And you think he's down here?"

"I don't know. Maybe."

"I haven't heard the name."

She was watching me warily when I looked up in desperation. "Can't you ask around? I have money—I can pay you—"

She took a step back, her face falling into shadow, and raised one hand as if to stop me. "I'll take the name to my boss. But that's all I can do."

Relief poured through me. But I remembered to ask, "How much will it cost?"

"Fifty credits to take the name."

"*Fifty?* I only brought twenty—it's just a *name*."

"That's the rate, *Kyle*. If you don't have fifty, I'm not taking the name."

"But—"

She stepped into the light again so that I could see the expression on her face, hard and cold. "That's the rate. We gotta eat down here. You don't have fifty, you come back when you do."

I stared at her, my mind racing as I tried to figure out how I could get another thirty credits. I only made two credits a week in my part-time job at the restaurant, and my mother made me put half of that into the emergency account. I had saved up for five months to get that twenty. It would take almost eight months to save thirty, and I couldn't wait that long. The more time passed, the harder it would be to find Kit. "Please," I said. "I can trade you something instead. I'll give you the twenty, and you can have thirty credits' worth of—of—"

She sighed. "What do you got worth thirty credits?"

I remembered what she had just said, and an idea clicked in me. "*Food*. You said you've got to eat. My mother owns a restaurant. The Emerald Garden in Chinatown. Come by, and I'll give you thirty credits' worth of food." That much would feed her for at least one month. I just hoped I'd be able to smuggle it out without my mother noticing.

I could tell that she was surprised by my offer. She didn't say anything for a minute, but her slate-colored eyes searched my face to see if I was lying. What she saw must have satisfied her, because she said, "I'll think about your offer. Come back tomorrow, and I'll tell you my decision."

"How do I know you won't just take the money and do nothing?" I asked before I lost my nerve.

She cocked her head at me. "You don't."

I swallowed. A droplet of sweat trickled down my cheek.

"You better get home to your mama before I change my mind."

My stomach knotted. I didn't really have a choice. I was stupid to have come down here expecting anything other than to get robbed.

I knew she was watching me as I climbed back up the half-broken stairs, grabbing onto the rebar and pipes jutting from the walls to haul myself over the missing steps. Up above I saw the crack in the wall that led out into the world—or what's left of it—and after my time down in the Tunnels, the gray daylight was so bright I had to squint.

All I could think about the next day at school was whether or not I should go back down to the Tunnels that afternoon. I knew that the rational thing to do was to stay away from that place at all costs. That girl wasn't going to help me. She was a criminal.

But I owed my brother.

He had always watched out for me. He kept people from teasing me when I was little; he warned me about the Tunnel gangs; he taught me how to blend into the crowd so the Patrol wouldn't notice me. He taught me how to be perfectly average. And then, almost one year ago, he disappeared.

The thing is, plenty of people have disappeared. And from what I've heard, plenty of the disappeareds ended up in the Tunnels. Nobody knew for sure if they got there on their own or if the Patrol forcibly relocated them as punishment for any number of crimes against the state.

The day that Kit disappeared had been the day of his government assignment. He went out that morning on an errand before the ceremony and never came back. At first I told myself he was just delayed. Sometimes there were long lines at the stores, especially on assignment day, when families wanted to make a special meal for their children. As I waited, I remembered that he had come to my room earlier, before the lights came on, and said, "It's going to be a long day. Make sure you eat something."

Had that been his good-bye? He always took care of me. It wasn't unusual for him to say something like that, but there might have been something in the tone of his voice or the way he touched my arm before he left—gently, his hand lingering—that I should have recognized as a sign. When I finally realized he wasn't coming back, I ran downstairs to our mother in a panic. But she didn't seem surprised. She seemed tired.

She filed a missing-person report with the Patrol, but that was it. A couple of months later she stopped mentioning him at all; it was like he had never been born. But I knew he had, and that's why I had to go back. Because what if Kit was in the Tunnels? I needed to know.

Besides, I was less than two months from high school graduation. Less than two months from getting my own government assignment. Some of my classmates looked forward to it eagerly: the start of their adult lives. But it just left a sick, sinking feeling in my stomach. I couldn't help but attach that day to Kit. What had happened to him?

After school I took off my uniform of gray trousers and white blouse and pulled on dark work pants and a beat-up denim jacket that Kit had found in an alley when we were kids. On the way to Lucky Grocery, I passed a fresh banner affixed to the giant bulletin board in Confucius Square, the letters a garish red against the steel-gray dome of the sky. TREASURE OUR DIVERSITY! GENETIC DIFFERENCE IS THE KEY TO HUMANITY'S SURVIVAL. A rash of mixed-race births had happened a few months ago, and the government was running a new campaign to raise awareness about the dangers of not following the birth plans determined by the Health Ministry.

On the news they said the babies had contracted Multigenetic Immunodeficiency Disorder and died, and their bodies were cremated to prevent further infection. But not every mixed baby gets sick and dies. I hadn't, and neither had my brother or that girl in the Tunnels. But nobody talked about that, because nobody wanted to be sent to the reeducation center in the Bronx sector, where the dome was always malfunctioning.

I pulled the collar of my jacket up around me and hurried past the square, trying to avoid making eye contact with the Patrol officers on duty. The air was cold today, which meant the generators must be off for recharging. Out of the corner of my eye I saw the officers gathered together over a portable heater to ward off the chill, flaunting their luxuries as the rest of us shivered. I didn't let my disgust show on my face until I found the crack in the wall and knew they wouldn't be able to see me.

The Tunnels supposedly snaked beneath the entire city; some said that trains used to run through them, carrying people from the southernmost tip of the island all the way up north past Central Farms. I saw some of the old tracks once, on a school trip to the reeducation center. Most of the entrances have been blockaded and put under surveillance. But the crack in the wall in Chinatown has been there for a while. I wasn't sure if the Patrol didn't know it was there or if they didn't care. Chinatown wasn't a wealthy sector. The higher-ups probably thought we were barely a step above the Tunnel mutts ourselves.

At the bottom of the broken stairway, the Tunnels stank of old piss. The yellow light flickered slightly in its socket, and at first I thought she wasn't there. All I could hear was my own breath, rattling around scared in my chest like a rat in a cage.

From nowhere a hand reached out and clamped down over my arm, dragging me into the dark lurking near the wall, and another hand slammed over my mouth just before I was about to scream. She pushed me down to my knees and shoved me through a hole in the wall. My hip scraped against jagged concrete, and I yelped.

"Shh," she whispered, her breath hot against my ear as she immobilized me again. I reached up and locked my hands over her forearm, trying to tug her hand away from my mouth—I could barely breathe—but she wouldn't budge.

"Stop it," she said, her voice so low I could only hear it because she was speaking directly into my ear. "Patrol's coming."

I froze. As my ears adjusted to the sound around me, I heard footsteps approaching. Had they followed me through the crack? Light beams—flashlights—scattered over the far wall. We were crouching beneath a low ceiling in what looked like some kind of filthy nest. There was a mattress on the floor, and a blanket, and a cardboard box full of rags that might have once been clothing. Behind me her chest rose and fell against my back. There were rings on her hand, still clamped over my mouth. The smell of old pennies on her skin.

I didn't notice when the Patrol passed. When she let me go, moving away swiftly, I felt cold where she was no longer touching me. She flicked on a dim battery-powered lantern that shed a ghostly light over the space we were in. I realized we were hiding under a counter, like in the ticket booth at the cinema where they showed ancient movies every weekend. She crawled out and sat down on the edge of the mattress, knees propped up and facing me.

"I'll do it," she said. "Thirty credits' worth of food, and I'll take your brother's name to my boss."

My mouth went dry. The absence of her hand was like a ghost touching my face. "You'll do it?" I whispered.

"That's what I said. When do I get the food?"

I had thought about it, of course, because she couldn't come over in the middle of the day. Not the way she looked. People would notice, and they would call the Patrol. "Come to the back of the restaurant—the Emerald Garden, on Mott Street—at one in the morning. We close at ten, and my mother's asleep by midnight. I'll meet you by the trash bins in the alley."

"Okay. I'll see you tonight then."

I was dismissed. I scrambled out from beneath the counter. Above it was a cracked glass window, painted black except for some places where the paint had been scratched away to create a few peepholes. I turned around, but I couldn't figure out how to get out. "How do I—"

"Through there," she said, pointing to a dark slit in the wall half-hidden by the edge of the counter.

I squatted down, preparing to leave, but before I slid through I glanced at her and asked, "What's your name?"

She just looked at me, and I thought for a while that she wouldn't tell me. But finally she said, "Nix."

"See you tonight, Nix," I said, and before she could see my face turning red, I hightailed it out of there.

Thirty credits of food was a lot. I couldn't give it to her all at once. My mother would notice, and then she would ask questions. So when Nix came the first night, I only gave her leftovers from that night's dinner: a box of rice and two boxes of mixed vegetables and tofu.

She showed up wearing a skullcap over her tattooed head, but she still didn't look like someone who belonged in Chinatown. "This isn't thirty credits' worth," she said as I gave her the take out bag.

"I know. It's all I can do right now. Or else my mother will find out."

She shook her head. "You're saying I have to come back here?" She glanced around, and even though the alley behind the restaurant was empty, I could tell she was out of her element.

"Sorry. But it's better this way anyway—thirty credits' worth would spoil, and then the food would be worthless."

She opened the box of mixed vegetables. It was cool by now, but it still smelled good, and I heard her stomach rumble. I handed her a pair of chopsticks. She took a tentative bite and then began to shovel the food into her mouth as if she hadn't eaten in a week. Maybe she hadn't.

She was halfway through the box before she realized I was still standing there in the alley with her, watching her. I could swear that she blushed, but the light was bad. She folded the box shut and said, "Fine. I'll be back tomorrow night."

I kept track of how much food I was giving her and how much it was worth. Some nights there were more leftovers than others, but at the rate I was going, she'd be paid off within four weeks, and then I would ask her again about Kit. For now I let it go, because she was so obviously starving every time she came.

I began to heat up the leftovers just before she arrived. She began to sit on the back stoop with me to eat some of it before it cooled off. It was kind of like feeding a stray cat. Eventually they stopped freaking out when you approached them. Eventually I got the feeling that she kind of liked having me sit with her while she ate.

I tried not to stare, but I would watch her out of the corner of my eye as her ringed fingers raised the chopsticks to her mouth. I had always assumed that anyone who lived in the Tunnels must be covered in filth, but her hands were always clean. I wondered what her life was like underground. Did she live in that dirty ticket booth at the bottom of the stairs? I wondered where she had been born, and how she had ended up in the Tunnels, and whether it hurt to get those tattoos inked onto her scalp. But I never asked.

She would eat in silence, and when she was ready to go, she'd box up her food and say, "See you tomorrow night, Kyle."

And that was that. She didn't know that I sat there on the back step long after she had gone, feeling the prickles that rose on my skin when she was nearby slowly fading. Sometimes I would rub my hands over my arms, as if that would bring the tingling sensation back. Sometimes I closed my eyes and remembered the way she felt when she had shoved me into that dirty little nest behind the wall, the muscles of her arms taut as she held me silent.

I knew it was a stupid thing to do: to nurse a crush on a criminal who was only there because I was paying her.

The night I reached thirty credits' worth of food, I thought about not giving her the full amount so that she'd have to come back. But she would know I was cheating her, and I didn't want to piss her off.

As we sat on the back step in the light from the kitchen window, I said, "So you'll ask your boss about my brother now?"

"I've already asked."

Surprise rushed through me. "You have?"

She nodded as she took another bite of kung pao chicken. "Nobody's heard of him."

For a minute I just gaped at her. "You—nobody?"

"Nobody."

"Who did you ask?"

"I asked around. Kit Lin's not in the Tunnels."

"But…" A buzzing sound filled my ears. That couldn't be the end. I dug my nails into the palms of my hands. "Where is he, then?"

She shrugged and began to fold the box shut. "I don't know." She stood up and I followed, reaching out and grabbing her arm before I knew what I was doing. She froze, hard as stone beneath my hand, and cold shot through me when she turned to look at me. "Let go," she said.

My heart raced. I snatched my hand back. "I'm sorry."

Something in her face shifted, as if a shadow slid away. The rings in her left eyebrow glinted in the light from the window. I licked my lips, feeling the hairs on my arms rising. Nobody had ever studied me so intensely, as if she were peeling back my skin, and I relished the feel of it: her eyes scraping against my flesh. I wanted her to see the real me, to see that I wasn't a good girl.

"Nix," I whispered.

I knew it was a bad idea, and that's why I did it. I had to do something. She was leaving, all paid up, and I had no information about Kit at all. In another month I'd get my assignment, and it would probably be a monotonous job at the restaurant, and then the rest of my life would unspool ahead of me according to a government-mandated plan that I had nothing to do with. I was only a warm body, doing my part to move humanity forward one more generation until we could finally leave this city of refugees.

But Nix wasn't part of the plan.

She jerked her head away when I touched her cheek. "What are you doing?"

I leaned forward on my toes and brushed my lips over hers. She didn't move. I felt as if I might shatter into a thousand dusky moths, wings sounding a staccato beat in the still air, and the only thing that would hold me together was a kiss from this girl.

I curved my hand around her neck to tug her down toward me, and her muscles were tight as steel bars beneath her skin. I thought she would resist, but all of a sudden her mouth pressed hard against mine. She tasted slightly of soy sauce, but there was a stud in her tongue and it sent a ripple through my entire body as the metal clicked against my teeth. I could dissolve right there.

I could melt into the wet dark concrete of the alley and no one would ever find me again. I reached up. Her scalp was surprisingly soft under my hands; the stubble of her hair pushed against my palms like fur.

When she shoved me away I couldn't breathe, and her face was wild with panic. "Not a good idea," she muttered.

"Wait," I gasped, but she was already gone. She had even left the takeout containers behind. I sank down onto the back stoop, my body reeling with adrenaline and woozy from her kiss.

A fuse had lit inside me. I had to see it through to the end.

I brought a pound of rice with me when I snuck down to the Tunnels the next day. I stood there with the plastic bag swinging in my hand, and I whispered, "Nix?"

She was there, a shadow in the dark a few feet away.

I moved toward her, holding out the bag. "I brought you some rice."

"You shouldn't have come," she said, but she took the rice.

This time I heard the Patrol the same instant she did, and I followed her through the crack in the wall, where we crouched on the grimy concrete beneath the counter, trying to disappear into the dark as flashlight beams pierced the broken window above. I wondered if the Patrol ever actually caught anyone down here. I hadn't heard of any Tunnel mutts being caught in a long time. Maybe it was all for show now—a show for those of us who had to live aboveground and endure the endless campaigns for genetic purity and political order and whatever other crap initiative the premier and his ministers came up with.

But Nix seemed plenty worried about it. She didn't relax until the Patrol was long past, and then, like last time, she swung around and sat on the edge of the mattress and turned on the electric light. "What do you want?" she asked bluntly.

I crawled over to her and did what I had been thinking about since the night before: I kissed her. And she didn't resist.

The mattress was lumpy, but it was better than the floor. She wouldn't let me peel off her jacket, and the metal buttons hurt a little when they dug into me, but I liked it. I liked how rough her hands were, and I let her touch me, and I shoved my mouth against her neck so that I didn't make a sound.

The next night she came to the alley at one in the morning. I had been hoping she would come, but she didn't tell me she would. All day I had been in a daze. Even my friends at school had noticed, but I didn't tell them a thing. I enjoyed having my secret. Everybody said I was so good, such a perfect student and daughter and citizen. I liked being a liar.

When she arrived, I opened the kitchen door. "Don't you want a cup of tea?" I asked.

She smiled—the first smile I'd seen from her, though it was gone in a flash. "Sure," she said.

I made the tea: one teaspoon of precious jasmine leaves in the cracked blue porcelain teapot. I opened the spout on the kettle so that it wouldn't whistle and wake up my mother. Then I heated up leftovers for Nix, who sat down at the kitchen table—the table where I had done my homework every day after school, obediently, for years—and wolfed down rice and pork and pickled turnips. When the tea was ready, I poured it, steaming and fragrant, into one of our chipped teacups and placed it in front of Nix. I felt like a little wife preparing dinner for my criminal of a lover.

We made out on the kitchen table afterward, carefully moving all the dishes aside first so that we wouldn't smash them and make a noise. But I must have forgotten where I was, because the next thing I knew, Nix was pulling away from me, her eyes looking behind me, where I heard my mother's voice: "—are you? What are you doing to my daughter?"

Nix's face was dazed, but an instant later that expression vanished behind a blank, hard mask, and she turned and left. The kitchen door had already banged shut by the time I managed to sit up, pulling my shirt closed. My mother was yelling at me, but I barely heard her words over the pounding of my heart. I saw her mouth opening and closing as she berated me, the flash of her teeth, the rising tide of red in her cheeks.

I buttoned my shirt. My fingers barely shook at all.

My mother lunged forward and slapped me.

I reeled, one hand rising to cup my stinging face, and I slid off the table and backed away from her.

"Don't ignore me," my mother said, spitting out the words. "What have you done? Do you know what could happen to our family if someone found out? You're a good girl, Kyle—how could you do this? With a *Tunnel mutt*. You're only one month away from assignment! If you get pregnant, I can't afford to buy you an abortion, much less pay off the government. I'll lose the restaurant. We'll lose everything. Is that what you want?"

I flinched involuntarily. "I'm not going to get pregnant."

"Where are you getting money for birth control? Are you stealing? Whatever you buy under the table won't work. And if you keep seeing this boy, you *will* get pregnant." Her hands clenched into fists.

Everything I had never said to her—all the times I bit my tongue when she warned me to stay away from non-Asian boys; all my frustration over her emotionless reaction to Kit's disappearance—it all exploded out of me, and I said the worst thing I could think of. "Are you afraid I'm going to be just like you?"

My mother's eyes bulged.

"I know my father wasn't Asian," I continued relentlessly. "Do you really think I don't know that you did everything you tell me not to?"

I braced for a blow, but instead my mother's shoulders slumped, and tears slid down her cheeks as if a dam had broken. She sat down in a chair, cradling her head in her hands, and I saw the white streaks radiating out from the crown of her head. She suddenly seemed so old and tired, and guilt began to seep through me. I said in a quieter voice, "I know that's what happened to you, but it's not going to happen to me because Nix is a girl."

She raised her head. "What?"

"She's a girl. The person who was just here. As far as I know," I said, sarcasm lacing my words, "she can't get me pregnant."

My mother stared at me. I heard the hum of the refrigerator in the background. The creak of her chair as she shifted in her seat. I pulled out the other chair—we only had two, since there were only two of us—and sat as well. The clock hanging over the door ticked. It was just after three in the morning.

"Well," she said finally, "that's almost a relief."

Tears welled up hot and urgent at the corners of my eyes, and suddenly I found it difficult to breathe.

"Are you doing this because of your brother?" she asked.

I recoiled. "What are you talking about?"

She raised her eyebrows. "Sneaking around after midnight with a Tunnel mutt. Girl or not, that's still not safe. You could ruin everything, Kyle. Not only for you, but for me too."

I hunched over. "I'm not going to ruin everything."

"I hope not." She didn't sound like she believed me.

I glared at her, wiping away my hot tears. "Why don't you ever talk about Kit? You act like he never existed."

She let out a broken sigh. "Of course he existed. He was my baby boy." She sounded wistful, and a smile flitted over her face. "He was a good boy, too. Never cried or fussed the way you did." She got up to put the kettle on the stove. "I thought he would be assigned somewhere outside Chinatown, he was so good at school. But I guess my status is still a problem."

"What do you mean?" My mother had never said so much about this before.

"The government only let me keep you two because my parents paid them off," she said, preparing a fresh pot of tea. She didn't use the jasmine, just the regular black tea.

"Really?"

"Oh, yes. It was a disgrace when Kit was born—I was lucky he looked Asian, because his father certainly wasn't pure-blood. But I loved him, Kyle. Every minute I had with your father was worth it."

My mother sounded unexpectedly fierce, and I was taken aback. I had never thought of my father as a real man; he had always been a distant idea to me, flimsy as the paper of my birth

162

certificate, on which he wasn't even named. The knowledge that my mother had loved him opened a new ache inside myself. But how could I suddenly long for someone I had never known?

"What happened?" I whispered. "Why didn't they sterilize you after Kit?" That was the standard procedure for girls who gave birth outside the Health Ministry's plans. I never should have been born.

My mother poured boiling water into the teapot and sat down again. "Your grandfather was a decorated military officer, so the government was willing to overlook the indiscretion. That might have been the end of it. I might have been able to continue at my assignment at the Defense Ministry. But I was too young, and too much in love. When you came along, my parents had to bribe the officials. It was expensive, and I had to submit to sterilization then. I was reassigned here, and I never saw your father again."

"Why didn't you ever tell me this before?"

She shrugged. "It's ancient history. Nothing to be done about it. Besides, when Lao Yan died and asked that I be given the restaurant, it seemed like I was getting a pretty good deal. We have food, Kyle. We're lucky. And we have a roof over our heads, and because I own this place now I can sweep it for bugs. We can talk freely inside here. I have more freedom now than I've ever had before. If you get assigned to Chinatown, you should remember that."

"Kit didn't want to be assigned here."

"No. Kit didn't. He had dreams—" My mother gave an impatient sigh. "He didn't understand his place."

"Did he tell you that he was leaving? Did he tell you why?"

She poured two cups of tea and slid one across the table to me. "No."

"Don't you miss him?" I demanded. "Don't you want to know where he went? What if he was taken in by the Patrol and imprisoned for being mixed? Shouldn't we look for him?"

Red splotches darkened my mother's cheeks, but her voice was measured when she answered me. "I did look for him. I've done more to look for him than you know. Is that why you found this Tunnel mutt? Because you thought Kit joined a Tunnel gang?"

"Don't call her a mutt. Kit and I are mutts, too."

Her face hardened. "No, you're not. Don't ever say that—not even to me at home. You're my children; you're not a mutt living in the filth below everybody else."

"They only live there because the government won't let them live aboveground."

"Who's giving you these ideas? They're criminals!"

"Wasn't my father a criminal?" I shouted, and then I winced. I hadn't expected my words to come flying out so loudly.

My mother's face went white, and she stood up, shoving her chair back so forcefully it fell over, clattering, onto the floor. "You don't know what you're talking about," she said, her voice so thick with fury that I felt as if she had slapped me in the face again. "Go to your room. And never bring this up again."

I stood, my legs shaking. "You can't treat me like a child forever. I deserve to know the truth."

Instead of going to my room, I ran out the back door, letting it slam shut just as Nix had.

164

* * *

I had never been out after closing time, and the streets of Chinatown were deserted and eerie, lit by dim street lamps that left pools of thick darkness in between. As I rounded the edge of Confucius Square, I heard the wail of Patrol sirens, and I instinctively ducked into a doorway, hoping their bright floodlights wouldn't find me. If they caught me now, with no work papers giving me a reason to be out after curfew, that would be the end of my life as I knew it. They'd test me for MID and even if I came up negative, I bet they'd disappear me, or at least send me to Bronx sector. There was no excuse for being out this late, and I didn't think it would be brushed off as a minor offense—especially given my mother's record.

I squeezed my eyes shut, cold sweat prickling over my skin. But just as panic was about to paralyze me completely, I realized the sirens were fading. I opened my eyes to see the last of the floodlights sweeping out of sight. I sucked in the cool air in a ragged gasp, relief searing through me. With it came a kind of reckless confidence: I was lucky tonight. As soon as I was sure the Patrol was gone, I sprinted toward the crack in the wall.

When I arrived, I was surprised to see a dim glow coming from below, and then I remembered that after dark the Tunnel gangs ruled the underground. I was about to walk into their territory, and I hadn't even brought a bribe with me.

But I couldn't go home. I wouldn't. And I also couldn't stay up here, because the Patrol would be back.

At the bottom of the broken stairs, a group of men were

standing together, joking and drinking by the light of electric lanterns set on the ground. I didn't see Nix. But the men saw me, and one of them called out, "You lost, little girl?"

Another clicked on the bright beam of a flashlight and shone it directly at me. I threw my hand up to block the glare.

"I'm looking for Nix," I said.

They laughed. "Who? You *sure* that's what you're looking for?"

The guy holding the flashlight came toward me and put his big hand on my chin and jerked my face up. He had light-brown skin and curly hair, and his breath stank of liquor. "You're a pretty little girl. You shouldn't be out this late alone."

I tried to pull away, but his fingers just dug deeper into my face. "I need to talk to Nix," I said again. I knew he could hurt me—they all could—but I didn't care. "Let go of me," I snapped.

His eyes narrowed, his forehead wrinkling. "Smart-ass lazy bitch. Shut up."

"Hey, take it easy," someone said from behind him.

The man glanced over his shoulder. "You wanna deal with this rich girl? Go ahead." He dropped his hand from my face, but not without shoving me back so that I sat down, hard, on the edge of the stairs. I bit back a cry of pain.

"You want to talk to Nix?"

This man was younger—maybe only a few years older than me—and his head was also shaved and tattooed like Nix's. The expression on his face was wary but not unkind. "Yeah," I said, rubbing my jaw. It felt like that man's fingerprints were permanently indented in my chin. I pushed myself to my feet. "Where is she?"

He looked at me for a while, and I glared back. He laughed. "I'll take you to her."

166

I had only ever heard rumors about what the Tunnels were like: dank, disease-ridden sewers crammed full of stinking mutts and their gang leaders. Unending darkness, full of the scrabbling noise of rats. None of the rumors prepared me for what I saw: an entire city underground, layer upon layer of board-covered walkways, black iron pillars and rainbow-colored tiled walls lit with scavenged lanterns. A honeycomb of wonders, all safely tucked away beneath the streets. I would never be able to find my way out without a guide. I knew I should be afraid, but I wasn't. I was overwhelmed by the evidence before my eyes: There was an entire world down here, and it was full of people. Healthy people.

I'd learned in school that mixing genes of different races would almost certainly lead to MID and early death, but these people seemed stronger than some of my classmates. And there were so many of them. They were working: laying boards across abandoned train tracks; slapping laundry in giant steel vats of water; frying noodles in a shallow pan, a line of mixed-blood children waiting with bowls in hand. As we walked past, the kids swiveled their heads to look at me. Here, I was the oddity, not them.

We walked for about twenty minutes before we arrived at our destination: a giant underground room as grand as a government hall, with marble walls and dark chandeliers hanging from the ceiling. A few lights still shone from above, giving the whole space a dim yellow glow. All along the perimeter, the walls were covered with bits of paper, and as we approached I realized they were mostly photos. Some were decorated with ribbons or notes, some with plastic flowers, others with wilting grasses or weeds that must have been brought down from above. People were scattered all around the hall, looking at photos or decorating them.

"There she is," he said, pointing to the left, where I saw Nix standing with her hands in her pockets, staring at something on the wall I couldn't make out.

"Thanks," I said, and then I went to join her.

She was looking at a tiny photo of a man and a woman—one African, one Asian—taken by what appeared to be an automated photo booth camera. There was one on the corner of Mulberry and Canal in Chinatown; I'd scrunched inside with my school friends once, making faces at the camera as it clicked and flashed. In this photo, the man and the woman were smiling at each other, not at the camera. They seemed happy.

"Nix," I said.

She didn't look at me. "Did your mother kick you out?"

"No."

"Then what are you doing here?"

"What is this place?" I asked instead of answering her question.

"It's the Wall," she said as if I should know.

"Why are there so many photos here?"

"They're photos of people who have disappeared." She finally glanced at me. "What are you doing here?"

"I—I had a fight with my mom." My face burned.

She cocked her head. "So you ran down to me? I can't do anything for you, Kyle."

"I don't want anything from you," I insisted.

Her eyebrows rose. "You don't?"

My blush deepened.

"There's nothing for you down here. You're better off up above."

"My mother won't tell me the truth," I blurted out. "I need to know the truth."

"About what?"

"About...everything." I gestured to the photos on the walls. "Who are all these people?"

"I don't know who they all are. But these are my parents." She pointed to the couple in the photo.

"Who put the photo there?"

"I did. When someone disappears, one of us who remains puts up a memorial to them."

I looked around at the photos; there were thousands of them. Some of the people in the photos were mixed, but others were pure. One photo, of an Asian girl with shoulder-length hair in a school uniform, reminded me of myself. I shivered.

"Why does the Patrol allow these photos to stay up?" I asked.

"The Patrol never makes it this deep into the Tunnels." She glanced one last time at the photo and touched my elbow. I jumped in surprise. "Come on. Let's get out of here."

Nix took me through the maze of tunnels, passing other people bearing the same tattoos she did. They nodded to each other, their gazes sweeping over me briefly, dismissing me. I wasn't one of them.

She led me to a little square room with plywood walls built in a row of rooms along an abandoned train track. Inside, she pulled a string to turn on a hanging overhead bulb. The place was small but clean, with a mattress elevated on concrete blocks and stacked crates that contained neatly folded clothes and a few other items: a leather-bound book, a carved wooden box. This must be her home, not that dark nest beside the stairs. There was one ancient spindle-legged chair in the corner next to an overturned crate that served as a table. On the crate was a can of jasmine tea.

I would have recognized that can anywhere. It had come from my mother's kitchen. I looked at Nix, my pulse speeding up. "Did you steal that from us?"

She didn't seem perturbed. "It'll bring in a good price."

My mouth fell open. She was a thief. I had paid her fifty credits to take my brother's name to her boss, and I had gotten nothing out of it. And then she had robbed me. When had she had the opportunity? When we were clearing off the table? Before she—before we—

My insides went hot, remembering how distracted I had been. I never would have noticed.

"Hey, you don't need that tea," she said easily.

"But it's not yours!" My voice screeched like a schoolgirl's.

She shrugged. "It's not yours, either. It's your mother's."

I sat down on the chair beside the can of tea in shock. "What's my mother's is mine." A lump rose in my throat as I said the words. Guilt welled up again, bitter and coarse.

"I thought you two had a fight." Nix sat on her bed, and the wooden board supporting it creaked.

My mother had scrimped and saved for months to buy that can of tea. We only drank it on special occasions, like my birthday or when the government issued us special rations for Chinese New Year. And I had taken it out tonight just to impress this girl, who had promptly stolen it.

"I'll tell you something," she said, grinning briefly. "You've got some balls for a good girl."

My stomach fell. I had trusted her. *I had trusted her*, and I had invited her into my home.

"Most girls come wandering down here in the middle of the night, and they'd never be seen again. I'm impressed you made it out to the Wall. It's a good thing you ran into Rio."

"Rio?"

"The guy who brought you."

"Oh." Why hadn't I asked his name? I was too focused on Nix. On getting here, to this place that was obviously her home, where she was sitting on her bed and watching me with glinting dark eyes, a foot away from the tea she had just stolen from my house.

"So, Kyle, you want the truth?"

Hearing her speak my name made my whole body tremble. I nodded.

"The truth is, I don't believe a thing the government says. All those campaigns for maintaining racial diversity, all those warnings about MID. What a bunch of shit. Nobody's died of genuine MID for generations. Maybe once it was real—I don't know. I never had the benefit of a scientific education. But what I do know is that I'm alive. I'm alive, and so are thousands of people who live in these tunnels, and none of us fits, the definition of *pure.*"

I had never heard anyone say these things out loud, and it shocked me. "You think the government is lying to us?" I asked. "Why would they do that?"

"People like power," she said simply. "And once they have it, they don't want to give it up. They'll do just about anything to keep it. There are plenty of us down here in the Tunnels, but compared to the population of the whole city, we're a drop in the bucket. And we serve a purpose. We take in your outcasts. We give the Patrol work to do. We eat your garbage and we do your dirty work. You have no idea how much money there is to be made making the government happy."

I was horrified. Part of me wanted to believe her, and part of me didn't. "But the government is trying to keep us—humanity—alive for the future. They're trying to keep us safe."

She snorted. "You know how the government says we can't ever leave this place? All those posters everywhere saying you'll die of radiation poisoning if you even try to get out of here."

"Yes." Of course I knew; they drilled it into us every day at school. After decades of war and human misuse had destroyed most of the world, a few safe havens had been built. We were the last enclave on the eastern coast of North America.

The government had built a safe zone around our city—an atmospheric shield that would protect us while the planet healed. There were other enclaves across the continent, but since we couldn't risk traveling outside the dome, we might as well be alone. It would take twenty generations before we could walk on the earth again instead of on the concrete of this city. I was generation eleven. I would never see the real sky.

And then Nix said: "There's a tunnel that leads out of here. All you need is a thousand credits. You pay the toll, you get out."

I stared at her in disbelief. "But what's on the other side? It could be a wasteland. It probably is."

"I don't know what's on the other side, but my parents went through the tunnel, and so did most of the people on that wall. And I'm getting out of here, too." She paused, glanced at the jasmine tea. "All I need is another fifty credits. That tea will buy it for me."

My stomach churned. I was going to be sick. I was such an idiot. "You just said you'd help me because you wanted the money. For the toll."

She shrugged. "Don't take it personally."

I ground the palms of my hands against my eyes to push back tears. "I thought you liked me," I said, my voice breaking, and then the hot nausea of shame flooded through me.

I felt her hands tugging at mine, pulling them away from my eyes. When I blinked through the tears, I saw her kneeling on the floor in front of me. If she had looked at me with pity, I think I would have fled. But I didn't see pity in her face. I saw sadness, and the slightest trace of regret.

"I do like you, Kyle," she said, her voice barely louder than a whisper.

So I kissed her. I kissed her so hard that I bit her lip, making her cry out in surprise, and she backed away, raising a hand to her mouth.

"Fuck," she said.

We stared at each other. I wanted her so badly. It scared me how much. There, deep underground, beneath the streets of the only world I had known, I wanted this girl who had just robbed me.

"I'm sorry," I said, not sure if I was apologizing to her or to myself.

Her face softened, and she said, "Come here," and pulled me over to the bed.

This time she took off her coat.

When I woke up, she was gone.

I sat up in the dark and felt for the string attached to the bare bulb and pulled, and the room sprang into harsh yellow light. The can of tea was gone. The crates were empty. But there was something lying on the chair.

I got up. It was a photo of Nix scowling at the camera, the flash reflected in her eyes and making her skin look washed-out and pale.

I sat down on the chair, my legs shaking.

Outside Nix's room, Rio was waiting on the edge of the abandoned train tracks, sitting on an overturned crate. When he saw me, he said, "She asked me to take you back out."

"Did she really leave?" I was hollow inside.

"Yeah, she left." He gave me a sympathetic look as he got up. "Let's go."

By the time I crawled out of the stairwell, it was late afternoon. I walked back home to find my mother and the Emerald Garden chef preparing for the dinner rush. She gave me one short look and barked, "Get changed for work."

I went upstairs and buried the photo of Nix in my top dresser drawer, between folded uniform blouses, and then I put on my work clothes.

My mother told me to focus on my studies, that my assignment was coming soon. "You've always been a good girl," she said. "Just forget about what happened."

But I couldn't. I thought about what Nix had told me every time I saw one of the Patrol. I wondered if that tunnel to the outside was real. I wondered if Kit had paid the toll, too.

One weekend morning when my mother was out at the market, I went into her room and pulled down the box she kept hidden on the top shelf in her closet. It contained my birth certificate, her deed to the restaurant, and various other government-issued papers, but I knew it also contained a slim photo album. I had caught her looking at it a few times surreptitiously, but she had never let me see it. I hoped it had photos of my father in it.

I recognized him because he looked like Kit, except older. He had short, curly hair and medium-brown skin. He didn't have any gang tattoos—at least none that were visible—but he was obviously mixed. He never would have blended into the crowd. Kit and I were lucky that we hadn't inherited his hair. I pulled out a picture of him standing beside a brick wall, a faint look of surprise on his face.

On the next page was a collection of small photos of Kit and me as babies. Seeing us together made my heart sink, and I had to turn the page. There was Kit in the ceremonial photo taken a week before his assignment day, wearing his school uniform and a fixed, fake smile. I missed him so much.

I didn't think I would ever see him again.

I took a few deep breaths. I peeled Kit's photo off the page and pocketed it along with the picture of our father. Then I went back down to the Tunnels.

* * *

Rio had taken over Nix's post, and he recognized me. "What are you doing back down here?" he asked.

"I need to go to the Wall."

His face didn't change expression, and I remembered how Nix had been at first: so cold and blank and hard. "You'll have to wait. I don't get off duty till lights out upstairs."

"I'll wait." I ducked into the dark room behind the tunnel wall and sat on the edge of the mattress, and I remembered the last time I had been there.

I could tell that Rio thought I was insane, but he didn't ask any questions. When his shift ended, he took me through the maze of tunnels again until we ended up in the vast ruin of a train station, the bits of paper layered onto the walls like feathers on a bird.

"You gonna need someone to take you back?" he asked.

I could stay down here. I could find a way to live in the Tunnels, just like Nix.

But I couldn't abandon my mother.

I was a good girl.

"Please," I said. "Will you wait for a little while?"

He shrugged. "It'll cost you twenty credits."

"Okay." I didn't have twenty credits, but he didn't know that— did he? He gave me a look that suggested he knew I was lying.

He snorted. "Five minutes."

I walked around the perimeter of the hall until I found the photo that Nix had been looking at. There wasn't much room around it, but there was enough. I pulled three tacks from my pocket and stuck the photos onto the wall. My father, whose name I didn't even know. My brother, with that fake smile on his face. I wondered if he had known, when that photo was taken, that he would be leaving soon afterward.

And Nix. Her photo was the smallest. I pushed the pin through the left side margin so that it didn't cut off any of her face. "I hope you made it out," I said. She seemed to glare at me through the photo, all hard edges and metal, just like the smell of her skin.

A Pocket Full of Dharma

by Paolo Bacigalupi

Wang Jun stood on the rain-slicked streets of old Chengdu and stared up into the drizzle at Huojianzhu. It rose into the evening darkness, a massive city core, dwarfing even Chengdu's sky-scrapers. Construction workers dangled from its rising skeleton, swinging from one section of growth to the next on long rap-pelling belts. Others clambered unsecured, digging their fingers into the honeycomb structure, climbing the struts with care-less dangerous ease. Soon the growing core would overwhelm the wet-tiled roofs of the old city. Then Huojianzhu, the Living Architecture, would become Chengdu entirely.

It grew on lattices of minerals, laying its own skeleton and following with cellulose skin. Infrastructure strong and broad, growing and branching, it settled roots deep into the green fer-tile soil of the Sichuan basin. It drew nutrients and minerals from the soil and sun, and the water of the rancid Bing Jiang; sucking at pollutants as willingly as it ate the sunlight which filtered through twining sooty mist.

Within, its veins and arteries grew pipelines to service the waste and food and data needs of its coming occupants. It was an animal vertical city built first in the fertile minds of the Biotects and now growing into reality. Energy pulsed from the growing creature. It would stand a kilometer high and five wide when fully mature. A vast biologic city, which other than its life support would then lie dormant as humanity walked its hollowed arteries, clambered through its veins and nailed memories to its skin in the rituals of habitation.

Wang Jun watched Huojianzhu and dreamed in his small beggar-boy mind of ways and means that might lead him out of the wet streets and hunger and into its comforts. Already sections of it glowed with habitation. People, living high and far above him, roamed the organism's corridors. Only the powerful and wealthy would live so high above.

Those with *guanxi*. Connections. Influence.

His eyes sought the top of the core, through the darkness and rain and mist, but it disappeared long before his eyes could find it. He wondered if the people up high saw the stars while he saw only drizzle. He had heard that if one cut Huojianzhu, its walls would bleed. Some said it cried. He shivered at the rising creature and turned his eyes back to earth to continue pushing with his stick-thin limbs and bent posture through the Chengdu crowds.

Commuters carried black umbrellas or wore blue and yellow

180

plastic ponchos to protect them from the spitting rain. His own hair lay soaked, slicked to the contours of his skull. He shivered and cast about himself, seeking hard for likely marks, so that he nearly tripped over the Tibetan.

The man squatted on the wet pavement with clear plastic covering his wares. Soot and sweat grimed his face, so that his features sheened black and sticky under the harsh halogen glare of the street lamps. The warped and jagged stumps of his teeth showed as he smiled. He pulled a desiccated tiger claw from under the plastic and waved it in Wang Jun's face.

"You want tiger bones?" He leered. "Good for virility."

Wang Jun stopped short before the waving amputated limb. Its owner was long dead so that only the sinews and ragged fur and the bone remained, dried and stringy. He stared at the relic and reached out to touch the jerky tendons and wickedly curving yellowed claws.

The Tibetan jerked it away and laughed again. There was a tarnished silver ring on his finger, studded with chunks of turquoise, a snake twining around his finger and swallowing its tail endlessly.

"You can't afford to touch." He ground phlegm and spit on the pavement beside him, leaving a pool of yellow mucus shot through with the black texturing of Chengdu's air.

"I can," said Wang Jun.

"What have you got in your pockets?"

Wang Jun shrugged, and the Tibetan laughed. "You have nothing, you stunted little boy. Come back when you've got something in your pockets."

He waved his goods of virility at the interested, more moneyed buyers who had gathered. Wang Jun slipped back into the crowd.

It was true what the Tibetan said. He had nothing in his pockets. He had a ratted wool blanket hidden in a Stone-Ailixin cardboard box, a broken VTOL Micro-Machine, and a moldering yellow woolen school hat.

He had come from the green-terraced hills of the countryside with less than that. Already twisted and scarred with the passage of plague, he had come to Chengdu with empty hands and empty pockets and the recollections of a silent dirt village where nothing lived. His body carried recollections of pain so deep that it remained permanently crouched in a muscular memory of that agony.

He had had nothing in his pockets then and he had nothing in his pockets now. It might have bothered him if he had ever known anything but want. Anything but hunger. He could resent the Tibetan's dismissal no more than he might resent the neon logos which hung from the tops of towers and illuminated the pissing rain with flashing reds, yellows, blues, and greens. Electric colors filled the darkness with hypnotic rhythms and glowing dreams. Red Pagoda Cigarettes, Five Star Beer, Shizi Jituan Software, and Heaven City Banking Corporation. Confucius Jiajiu promised warm rice wine comfort while JinLong Pharmaceuticals guaranteed long life, and it all lay beyond him.

He hunkered in a rain-slicked doorway with his twisted bent back and empty pockets and emptier stomach and wide-open eyes looking for the mark who would feed him tonight. The glowing promises hung high above him, more connected to those people who lived in the skyscrapers: people with cash and officials in their pockets. There was nothing up there he knew or understood. He coughed, and cleared the black mucus from his throat. The streets, he knew. Organic rot and desperation, he understood. Hunger, he felt rumbling in his belly.

He watched covetously as people walked past and he called out to them in a polyglot of Mandarin, Chengdu dialect, and the only English words he knew, "Give me money. Give me money." He tugged at their umbrellas and yellow ponchos. He stroked their designer sleeves and powdered skin until they relented and gave money. Those who broke away, he spat upon. The angry ones who seized him, he bit with sharp yellow teeth.

Foreigners were few now in the wet. Late October hurried them homeward, back to their provinces, homes, and countries. Leaner times lay ahead, lean enough that he worried about his future and counted the crumpled paper the people threw to him. He held tight the light aluminum jiao coins people tossed. The foreigners always had paper money and often gave, but they grew too few.

He scanned the street, then picked at a damp chip of concrete on the ground. In Huojianzhu, it was said, they used no concrete to build. He wondered what the floors would feel like, the walls. He dimly remembered his home from before he came to Chengdu, a house made of mud, with a dirt floor. He doubted the city core was made of the same. His belly grew emptier. Above him, a video loop of Lu Xieyan, a Guangdong singer, exhorted the people on the street to strike down the Three Wrongs of Religion: Dogmatism, Terrorism, and Splittism. He ignored her screeching indictments and scanned the crowds again.

A pale face bobbed in the flow of Chinese. A foreigner, but he was a strange one. He neither pushed ahead with a purpose, nor gawked about himself at Chengdu's splendors. He seemed at home on the alien street. He wore a black coat which stretched to the ground. It was shiny, so it reflected the reds and blues of neon, and the flash of the street lamps. The patterns were hypnotic.

Wang Jun slid closer. The man was tall, two meters high, and he wore dark glasses so that his eyes were hidden. Wang Jun recognized the glasses and was sure the man saw clearly from behind the inky ovals. Microfibers in the lenses stole the light and amplified and smoothed it so that the man saw day, even as he hid his eyes from others in the night.

Wang Jun knew the glasses were expensive and knew Three-Fingers Gao would buy them if he could steal them. He watched the man and waited as he continued up the street with his assured, arrogant stride. Wang Jun trailed him, stealthy and furtive. When the man turned into an alley and disappeared, Wang Jun rushed to follow.

He peeked into the alley's mouth. Buildings crowded the passageway's darkness. He smelled excrement and dead things moldering. He thought of the Tibetan's tiger claw, dried and dead, with pieces nicked away from the bone and tendons where customers had selected their weight of virility. The foreigner's footsteps echoed and splashed in the darkness, the even footsteps of a man who saw in the dark. Wang Jun slid in after him, crouching and feeling his way blindly. He touched the roughness of the walls. Instant concrete. Stroking the darkness, he followed the receding footsteps.

Whispers broke the dripping stillness. Wang Jun smiled in the darkness, recognizing the sound of a trade. Did the foreigner buy girls? Heroin? So many things for a foreigner to buy. He settled still, to listen.

The whispers grew heated and terminated in a brief yelp of surprise. Someone gagged and then there was a rasping and a splash. Wang Jun trembled and waited, as still as the concrete to which he pressed his body.

The words of his own country echoed, *"Kai deng ba."* Wang Jun's ears pricked at a familiar accent. A light flared and his eyes burned under the sharp glare. When his sight adjusted he stared into the dark eyes of the Tibetan street hawker. The Tibetan smiled slowly showing the encrustations of his teeth and Wang Jun stumbled back, seeking escape.

The Tibetan captured Wang Jun with hard efficiency. Wang Jun bit at the Tibetan's hands and fought, but the Tibetan was quick and he pressed Wang Jun against the wet concrete ground so that all Wang Jun could see were two pairs of boots; the Tibetan's and a companion's. He struggled, then let his body lie limp, understanding the futility of defiance.

"So, you're a fighter," the Tibetan said, and held him down a moment longer to make his lesson clear. Then he hauled Wang Jun upright. His hand clamped painfully at Wang Jun's nape. *"Ni shi shei?"* he asked.

Wang Jun trembled and whined, "No one. A beggar. No one."

The Tibetan looked more closely at him and smiled. "The ugly boy with the empty pockets. Do you want the tiger's claw after all?"

"I don't want anything."

"You will receive nothing," said the Tibetan's companion. The Tibetan smirked. Wang Jun marked the new speaker as Hunanese by his accent.

The Hunanese asked, "What is your name?"

"Wang Jun."

"Which '*Jun*'?"

Wang Jun shrugged. "I don't know."

The Hunanese shook his head and smiled. "A farmer's boy," he said. "What do you plant? Cabbage? Rice?" He laughed. "The Sichuanese are ignorant. You should know how to write your name. I will assume that your 'Jun' is for 'soldier.' Are you a soldier?"

Wang Jun shook his head. "I'm a beggar."

"Soldier Wang, the beggar? No. That won't do. You are simply Soldier Wang." He smiled. "Now tell me, Soldier Wang, why are you here in this dangerous dark alley in the rain?"

Wang Jun swallowed. "I wanted the foreigner's dark glasses."

"Did you?"

Wang Jun nodded.

The Hunanese stared into Wang Jun's eyes, then nodded. "All right, Little Wang. Soldier Wang," he said. "You may have them. Go over there. Take them if you are not afraid." The Tibetan's grip relaxed and Wang Jun was free.

He looked and saw where the foreigner lay, facedown in a puddle of water. At the Hunanese's nod, he edged closer to the still body, until he stood above it. He reached down and pulled at the big man's hair until his face rose dripping from the water, and his expensive glasses were accessible. Wang Jun pulled the glasses from the corpse's face and laid its head gently back into the stagnant pool. He shook water from the glasses and the

Hunanese and Tibetan smiled.

The Hunanese crooked a finger, beckoning.

"Now, Soldier Wang, I have a mission for you. The glasses are your payment. Put them in your pocket. Take this"—a blue datacube appeared in his hand—"and take it to the Renmin Lu Bridge across the Bing Jiang. Give it to the person who wears white gloves. That one will give you something extra for your pocket." He leaned conspiratorially closer, encircling Wang Jun's neck and holding him so that their noses pressed together and Wang Jun could smell his stale breath. "If you do not deliver this, my friend will hunt you down and see you die."

The Tibetan smiled.

Wang Jun swallowed and nodded, closing the cube in his small hand. "Go then, Soldier Wang. Dispense your duty." The Hunanese released his neck, and Wang Jun plunged for the lighted streets, with the datacube clutched tight in his hand.

The pair watched him run.

The Hunanese said, "Do you think he will survive?"

The Tibetan shrugged. "We must trust that Palden Lhamo will protect and guide him now."

"And if she does not?"

"Fate delivered him to us. Who can say what fate will deliver him? Perhaps no one will search a beggar child. Perhaps we both will be alive tomorrow to know."

"Or perhaps in another turning of the Wheel."

The Tibetan nodded.

"And if he accesses the data?"

The Tibetan sighed and turned away. "Then that too will be fate. Come, they will be tracking us."

The Bing Jiang ran like an oil slick under the bridge, black and sluggish. Wang Jun perched on the bridge's railing, soot-stained stone engraved with dragons and phoenixes cavorting through clouds. He looked down into the river and watched styrofoam shreddings of packing containers float lazily on the thick surface of the water. Trying to hit a carton, he hawked phlegm and spat. He missed, and his mucus joined the rest of the river's effluent. He looked at the cube again. Turning it in his hands as he had done several times before as he waited for the man with the white gloves. It was blue, with the smoothness of all highly engineered plastics. Its texture reminded him of a tiny plastic chair he had once owned. It had been a brilliant red but smooth like this. He had begged from it until a stronger boy took it.

Now he turned the blue cube in his hands, stroking its surface and probing its black data jack with a speculative finger. He wondered if it might be more valuable than the glasses he now wore. Too large for his small head, they kept slipping down off his nose. He wore them anyway, delighted by the novelty of daysight in darkness. He pushed the glasses back up on his nose and turned the cube again.

He checked for the man with white gloves and saw none. He turned the cube in his hands. Wondering what might be on it that would kill a foreigner.

The man with white gloves did not come.

Wang Jun coughed and spit again. If the man did not come before he counted ten large pieces of styrofoam, he would keep the cube and sell it.

Twenty styrofoam pieces later, the man with white gloves had not come, and the sky was beginning to lighten. Wang Jun stared at the cube. He considered throwing it in the water. He waited as *nongmin* began filtering across the bridge with their pull-carts laden with produce. Peasants coming in from the countryside, they leaked into the city from the wet fertile fields beyond, with mud between their toes and vegetables on their backs. Dawn was coming. Huojianzhu glistened, shining huge and alive against a lightening sky. He coughed and spit again and hopped off the bridge. He dropped the datacube in a ragged pocket. The Tibetan wouldn't be able to find him anyway.

Sunlight filtered through the haze of the city. Chengdu absorbed the heat. Humidity oozed out of the air, a freak change in temperature, a last wave of heat before winter came on. Wang Jun sweated. He found Three-Fingers Gao in a game room. Gao didn't really have three fingers. He had ten, and he used them all as he controlled a three-dimensional soldier through the high mountains of Tibet against the rebellion. He was known in Chengdu's triad circles as the man who had made TexTel's Chief Rep pay ten thousand yuan a month in protection money until he rotated back to Singapore. Because of the use of three fingers.

Wang Jun tugged Three-Fingers's leather jacket. Distracted, Three-Fingers died under an onslaught of staff-wielding monks.

He scowled at Wang Jun. "What?"

"I got something to sell."

"I don't want any of those boards you tried to sell me before. I told you, they're no good without the hearts."

Wang Jun said, "I got something else."

"What?"

He held out the glasses and Three-Fingers's eyes dilated. He feigned indifference. "Where did you get those?"

"Found them."

"Let me see."

Wang Jun released them to Three-Fingers reluctantly. Three-Fingers put them on, then took them off and tossed them back at Wang Jun.

"I'll give you twenty for them." He turned back to start another game.

"I want one hundred."

"Mei me'er." He used Beijing slang. No way. He started the game. His soldier squatted on the plains, with snowy peaks rising before him. He started forward, pushing across short grasses to a hut made of the skin of earlier Chinese soldiers. Wang Jun watched and said, "Don't go in the hut."

"I know."

"I'll take fifty."

Three-Fingers snorted. His soldier spied horsemen approaching and moved so that the hut hid him from their view.

"I'll give you twenty."

Wang Jun said, "Maybe BeanBean will give me more."

"I'll give you thirty, go see if BeanBean will give you that." His soldier waited until the horsemen clustered. He launched a rocket into their center. The game machine rumbled as the rocket exploded.

"You have thirty now?"

Three-Fingers turned away from his game and his soldier perished quickly as bioengineered yakmen boiled out of the hut. He ignored the screams of his soldier as he counted out the cash to Wang Jun. Wang Jun left Three-Fingers to his games and

190

celebrated the sale by finding an unused piece of bridge near the Bing Jiang. He settled down to nap under it through the sweltering afternoon heat.

He woke in the evening and he was hungry. He felt the heaviness of coins in his pocket and thought on the possibilities of his wealth. Among the coins, his fingers touched the unfamiliar shape of the datacube. He took it out and turned it in his hands. He had nearly forgotten the origin of his money. Holding the datacube, he was reminded of the Tibetan and the Hunanese and his mission. He considered seeking out the Tibetan and returning it to him, but deep inside he held a suspicion that he would not find the man selling tiger bones tonight. His stomach rumbled. He dropped the datacube back into his pocket and jingled the coins it resided with. Tonight he had money in his pockets. He would eat well.

"How much for *mapo dofu?*"

The cook looked at him from where he stood, swirling a soup in his broad wok, and listening to it sizzle.

"Too expensive for you, Little Wang. Go and find somewhere else to beg. I don't want you bothering my customers."

"*Shushu*, I have money." Wang Jun showed him the coins. "And I want to eat."

The cook laughed. "Xiao Wang is rich! Well then, Little Wang, tell me what you care for."

"*Mapo dofu, yu xiang* pork, two *liang* of rice and, Wu Xing beer." His order tumbled out in a rush.

"Little Wang has a big stomach! Where will you fit all that food, I wonder?" When Wang Jun glared at him he said, "Go, sit, you'll have your feast."

Wang Jun went and sat at a low table and watched as the fire roared and the cook threw chilies into the wok to fry. He wiped at his mouth to keep from drooling as the smell of the food came to his nose. The cook's wife opened a bottle of Five Star for him, and he watched as she poured the beer into a wet glass. The day's heat was dissipating. Rain began to spatter the street restaurant's burlap roof. Wang Jun drank from his beer and watched the other diners, taking in the food they ate and the company they kept. These were people he might have previously harassed for their money. But not tonight. Tonight he was a king. Rich, with money in his pocket.

His thoughts were broken by the arrival of a foreigner. A broad man with long white hair pulled back in a horse's tail. His skin was pale and he wore white gloves. He stepped under the sheltering burlap and cast alien blue eyes across the diners. The Chinese at their tables stared back. When his eyes settled on Wang Jun's bent form, he smiled. He went to squat on a stool across from Wang Jun and said, in accented Mandarin, "You are Little Wang. You have something for me."

Wang Jun stared at the man and then, feeling cocky with the attention of the other Chinese said, *"Ke neng."* Maybe.

The foreigner frowned, then leaned across the table. The cook's wife came, interrupting, and set down Wang Jun's *mapo dofu*, followed quickly by the pork. She went and scooped out a steaming bowl of rice broader than Wang Jun's hand, and set it before him. Wang Jun picked up chopsticks and began shoveling the food into his mouth, all the while watching the foreigner. His eyes watered at the spiciness of the *dofu* and his mouth tingled with the familiar numbing of ground peppercorns.

The wife asked if the foreigner would eat with him, and Wang Jun eyed the foreigner. He felt the money in his pocket, while his mouth flamed on. He looked at the size of the foreigner and assented reluctantly, feeling his wealth now inadequate. They spoke in *Chengdu hua*, the dialect of the city, so that the foreigner did not understand what they said. The man watched as the wife scooped another bowl of rice and set it in front of him with a pair of chopsticks. He looked down at the white mountain of rice in his bowl and then looked up at Wang Jun. He shook his head, and said, "You have something for me. Give it to me now."

Wang Jun was stung by the foreigner's disregard of the offered food. Because he was unhappy he said, "Why should I give it to you?"

The pale white man frowned and his blue eyes were cold and angry. "Did not the Tibetan tell you to give me something?" He held out a white-gloved hand.

Wang Jun shrugged. "You didn't come to the bridge. Why should I give it to you now?"

"Do you have it?"

Wang Jun became guarded.

"No."

"Where is it?"

"I threw it away."

The man reached across the small table and grasped Wang Jun's ragged collar. He pulled him close. "Give it to me now. You are very small, I can take it or you can give it to me. Little Wang, you cannot win tonight. Do not test me."

Wang Jun stared at the foreigner and saw silver flash in the man's breast pocket. On impulse he reached for the glint of sliver and drew a thing up until it was between their two faces. Other people at nearby tables gasped at what Wang Jun held. Wang Jun's hand began to shake, quivering uncontrollably, until the Tibetan's severed finger, with its tarnished silver and turquoise ring still on it, slipped from his horrified grasp and landed in the *yu xiang* pork.

The foreigner smiled, an indifferent, resigned smile. He said, "Give me the datacube before I collect a trophy from you as well." Wang Jun nodded and slowly reached into his pocket. The foreigner's eyes followed his reaching hand.

Wang Jun's free hand reached desperately out to the table and grabbed a handful of scalding *dofu* from its plate. Before the man could react, he drove the contents, full of hot chilies and peppercorns, into those cold blue eyes. As the foreigner howled, Wang Jun sank his sharp yellow teeth into the pale flesh of imprisoning hands. The foreigner dropped Wang Jun to rub frantically at his burning eye sockets, and blood flowed from his damaged hands.

Wang Jun took his freedom and ran for the darkness and alleys he knew best, leaving the foreigner still roaring behind him.

The rain was heavier, and the chill was coming back on Chengdu, harder and colder than before. The concrete and buildings radiated cold, and Wang Jun's breath misted in the air. He hunched in his box, with its logo for Stone-Ailixin Computers on the side. He thought it had been used for satellite phones, from the pictures below the logo. He huddled inside it with the remains of his childhood.

He could still remember the countryside he had come from and, vaguely, a mud-brick home. More clearly, he remembered

194

terrace-sculpted hills and running along those terraces. Playing in warm summer mud with a Micro-Machine VTOL in his hands while his parents labored in brown water around their ankles and green rice shoots sprouted up out of the muck. Later, he had passed those same terraces, lush and unharvested, as he made his way out of his silent village.

Under the cold instant-concrete shadows of the skyscrapers, he stroked his toy VTOL. The wings which folded up and down had broken off and were lost. He turned it over, looking at its die-cast steel frame. He pulled out the datacube and stared at it. Weighed the toy and the cube in his hands. He thought of the Tibetan's finger, severed with its silver snake ring still on it, and shuddered. The white man with the blue eyes would be looking for him. He looked around at his box. He put the Micro-Machine in his pocket but left his ratted blanket. He took his yellow *anchuan maozi*, the traffic safety hat children wore to and from school, stolen from a child even smaller than he. He pulled the yellow wool cap down over his ears, repocketed the datacube, and left without looking back.

Three-Fingers was crooning karaoke in a bar when Wang Jun found him. A pair of women with smooth skin and hard, empty eyes attended him. They wore red silk *chipao*, styled from Shanghai. The collars were high and formal, but the slits in the dresses went nearly to the women's waists. Three-Fingers glared through the dim red smoky light when Wang Jun approached.

"What?"

"Do you have a computer that reads these?" He held up the datacube.

Three-Fingers stared at the cube and reached out for it. "Where did you get that?"

Wang Jun held it out but did not release it. "Off someone."

"Same place you got those glasses?"

"Maybe."

Three-Fingers peered at the datacube. "It's not a standard datacube. See the pins on the inside?"

Wang Jun looked at the datasocket.

"There's only three pins. You need an adapter to read whatever's on there. And you might not even be able to read it then. Depends what kind of OS it's designed for."

"What do I do?"

"Give it to me."

"No." Wang Jun backed off a step.

One of the women giggled at the interaction between the mini mob boss and street urchin. She stroked Three-Fingers's chest. "Don't worry about the *taofanzhe*. Pay attention to us." She giggled again.

Wang Jun glared. Three-Fingers pushed the hostess off him. "Go away."

She made an exaggerated pout, but left with her companion.

Three-Fingers held out his hand. "Let me see it. I can't help you if you don't let me see the *tamade* thing."

Wang Jun frowned but passed the datacube over. Three-Fingers turned it over in his hands. He peered into the socket, then nodded. "It's for HuangLong OS." He tossed it back and said, "It's a medical specialty OS. They use it for things like brain surgery, and DNA mapping. That's pretty specialized. Where'd you get it?"

Wang Jun shrugged. "Someone gave it to me."

"*Fang pi.*" Bullshit.

Wang Jun was silent and they regarded each other, then Three-Fingers said, "Xing, I'll buy it off you. Just because I'm curious. I'll give you five yuan. You want to sell it?"

Wang Jun shook his head.

"Fine. Ten yuan, but that's all."

Wang Jun shook his head again.

Three-Fingers Gao frowned. "Did you get rich, suddenly?"

"I don't want to sell it. I want to know what's on it."

"Well, that makes two of us now."

They regarded each other for a time longer. Three-Fingers said, "All right. I'll help you. But if there's any value to what's on that, I'm taking three-quarters on the profit."

"*Yi ban.*"

Three-Fingers rolled his eyes. "Fine. Half, then."

"Where are we going?"

Three-Fingers walked fast through chill mist. He led Wang Jun into smaller and smaller alleys. The buildings changed in character from shining modern glass and steel to mud-brick with thatched and tiled roofs. The streets became cobbled and jagged and old women stared out at them from dark wooden doorways. Wang Jun watched the old ladies with suspicion. Their eyes followed him impassively, recording his and Three-Fingers's passage.

Three-Fingers stopped to pull out a box of Red Pagodas. He put one in his mouth. "You smoke?"

Wang Jun took the offered stick and leaned close as Three-

Fingers struck a match. It flared high and yellow and then sank low under the pressure of the wet air. Wang Jun drew hard on the cigarette and blew smoke. Three-Fingers lit his own.

"Where are we going?"

Three-Fingers shrugged. "Here."

He jerked his head at the building behind them. He smoked for a minute longer, then dropped his cigarette on the damp cobbles and ground it out with a black boot. "Put out your smoke. It's bad for the machines."

Wang Jun flicked the butt against a wall. It threw off red sparks where it bounced and then lay smoking on the ground. Three-Fingers pushed open a wooden door. Its paint was peeling and its frame warped so that he shoved hard and the door scraped loudly as they entered.

In the dim light of the room, Wang Jun could see dozens of monitors. They glowed with screen savers and data. He saw columns of characters and numbers, scrolling, connected to distant networks of information. People sat at the monitors in a silence broken only by the sound of the keys being pressed at an incessant rate.

Three-Fingers pulled Wang Jun up to one of the silent technicians and said, "He Dan, can you read this?"

He nudged Wang Jun and Wang Jun held up the datacube. He Dan plucked it out of Wang Jun's hand with spidery graceful fingers and brought it close to his eyes in the dimness. With a shrug he began to sort through a pile of adapters. He chose one and connected it to a stray cord, then inserted the adapter into the datacube. He typed on the computer and the borders and workspaces flickered and changed color. A box appeared and he hit a single key in response.

"Where am I?" The voice was so loud that the speakers distorted and crackled. The technicians all jumped as their silence was shattered. He Dan adjusted a speaker control. The voice came again, softer. "Hello?" It held an edge of fear. "Is there anyone there?" it asked.

"Yes," said Wang Jun, impulsively.

"Where am I?" the voice quavered.

"In a computer," said Wang Jun.

Three-Fingers slapped him on the back of the head.

"Be quiet."

"What?" said the voice.

They listened silently.

"Hello, did someone say I was in a computer?" it said.

Wang Jun said, "Yes, you're in a computer. What are you?"

"I'm in a computer?" The voice was puzzled. "I was having surgery. How am I in a computer?"

"Who are you?" Wang Jun ignored Three-Fingers's glowering eyes.

"I am Naed Delhi, the nineteenth Dalai Lama. Who are you?"

The typing stopped. No one spoke. Wang Jun heard the faint whine of cooling fans and the high resonances of the monitors humming. Technicians turned to stare at the trio and the computer which spoke. Outside Wang Jun heard someone clear their throat of phlegm and spit. The computer spoke on, heedless of the effect of its words. "Hello?" it said. "Who am I speaking to?"

"I'm Wang Jun."

"Hello. Why can't I see?"

"You're in a computer. You don't have any eyes."

"I can hear. Why can I hear and yet not see?"

He Dan broke in, "Video input is not compatible with the software emulator which runs your program."

"I don't understand."

"You are an artificial intelligence construct. Your consciousness is software. Your input comes from hardware. They are incompatible on the system we have installed you."

The voice quavered, "I am not software. I am the Dalai Lama of the Yellow Hat sect. The nineteenth to be reincarnated as such. It is not my fate to be reincarnated as software. You are probably mistaken."

"Are you really the Dalai Lama?" Wang Jun asked.

"Yes," the computer said.

"How—" Wang Jun began, but Three-Fingers pulled him away from the system before he could phrase his question. He knelt in front of Wang Jun. His hands were shaking as he held Wang Jun by the collar of his shirt. Their faces nearly touched as he hissed out, "Where did you find this cube?"

Wang Jun shrugged. "Someone gave it to me."

Three-Finger's hand blurred and struck Wang Jun's face. Wang Jun jerked at its impact. His face burned. The technicians watched as Three-Fingers hissed, "Don't lie to me. Where did you find this thing?"

Wang Jun touched his face. "From a Tibetan, I got it from a Tibetan who sold tiger bones, and a man from Hunan. And there was a body. A big foreigner. They were his glasses I sold you."

Three-Fingers tilted his head back to stare at the ceiling. "Don't lie to me. Do you know what it means if we've got the

Dalai Lama on a datacube that you've been carrying around in your pocket?" He shook Wang Jun. "Do you know what it means?"

Wang Jun whined, "I was supposed to give it to a man with white gloves, but he never came. And there was another man. A foreigner and he killed the Tibetan and took his finger, and he wanted mine too, and I ran and—" His voice rose in a babbling whine.

Three-Fingers's hands settled around Wang Jun's neck and squeezed until Wang Jun's ears rang and blackness scudded across his eyes. Distantly, he heard Three-Fingers say, "Don't cry to me. I'm not your mother. I'll take your tongue out if you make my life any more difficult than it already is. Do you understand?"

Wang Jun nodded in his haze.

Three-Fingers released him, saying, "Good. Go talk to the computer."

Wang Jun breathed deeply and stumbled back to the Dalai Lama. "How did you get inside the computer?" he asked.

"How do you know I am in a computer?"

"Because we plugged your datacube in and then you started talking."

The computer was silent.

"What's it like in there?" Wang Jun tried.

"Terrible and still," said the computer. Then it said, "I was going to have surgery, and now I am here."

"Did you dream?"

"I don't remember any dreams."

"Are you leading a rebellion against my homeland?"

"You speak Chinese. Are you from China?"

"Yes. Why are you making people fight in Tibet?"

"Where is this computer?"

"Chengdu."

"Oh, my. A long way from Bombay," the computer whispered.

"You came from Bombay?"

"I was having surgery in Bombay."

"Is it lonely in there?"

"I don't remember anything until now. But it is very still here. Deathly still. I can hear you, but cannot feel anything. There is nothing here. I fear that I am not here. It is maddening. All of my senses are lost. I want out of this computer. Help me. Take me back to my body." The computer's voice, vibrating from the speakers, was begging.

"We can sell him," Three-Fingers said abruptly.

Wang Jun stared at Three-Fingers. "You can't sell him."

"Someone wants him if they're chasing you. We can sell him."

The computer said, "You can't sell me. I have to get back to Bombay. I'm sure my surgery can't be completed if I'm not there. I must go back. You must take me back."

Wang Jun nodded in agreement. Three-Fingers smirked. He Dan said, "We need to unplug him. Without some form of stimuli he may go crazy before you can decide what to do with him."

"Wait," said the Dalai Lama. "Please don't unplug me yet. I'm afraid. I'm afraid of being gone again."

"Unplug him," said Three-Fingers.

"Wait," said the computer. "You must listen to me. If my body is dead, you must destroy this computer you keep me in. I fear that I will not reincarnate. Even Palden Lhamo may not be able to find my soul. She is powerful, but though she rides across an ocean of blood astride the skin of her traitorous son, she may not find me. My soul will be trapped here, unnaturally preserved, even as my body decomposes. Promise me, please. You must not leave me—"

He Dan shut off the computer.

Three-Fingers raised his eyebrows at He Dan.

He Dan shrugged. "It could be that it is the Dalai Lama. If there are people chasing the beggar-child, it lends credence to its claims. It would not be hard to upload his identity matrix while he was undergoing surgery."

"Who would do that?"

He Dan shrugged. "He is at the center of so many different political conflicts, it would be impossible to say. In a datacube, he makes a convenient hostage. Tibetan extremists, Americans, us, perhaps the EU; they would all be interested in having such a hostage."

Three-Fingers said, "If I'm going to sell him, I'll need to know who put him in there."

He Dan nodded, and then the door exploded inward. Splinters of wood flew about and shafts of light illuminated the dim room. Outside there was a whine of VTOLs and then there were bright lights lancing through the door, followed by the rapid thud of heavy boots. Wang Jun ducked instinctively as something seemed to suck the air out of the room and the monitors exploded, showering glass on the technicians and Wang Jun. People were shouting everywhere around him and Wang Jun smelled smoke. He stood up and pulled the datacube out of its adapter and rolled underneath a table as a barrage of pellets ratcheted across the wall above him.

He saw Three-Fingers fumble with something at his belt and then stiffen as red blossoms appeared on his chest. Other technicians were falling, all of them sprouting bloody stains on their bodies. Wang Jun huddled deeper under the table as forms in black armor came through the door. He put the datacube in his mouth, thinking he might swallow it before they could find him. More explosions came and suddenly the wall beside him was gone in a cacophony of bricks and rubble. He scrambled over the collapsed wall as shouts filled the air. Hunched low and running, he became nothing except a small child shadow. An irrelevant shadow in the rain and the play of lights from the troops left behind.

He crouched in a doorway's shadow, turning the datacube in his hands, stroking its blue plastic surface with reverential fascination. Rain fell in a cold mist and his nose dripped with the accumulated moisture. He shivered. The datacube was cold. He wondered if the Dalai Lama felt anything inside. People walked along the side-street, ignoring his small shadow in the doorway. They rose as forms out of the mist, became distinct and individual under the street lamps and then disappeared back into shadows.

He had seen the VTOLs rise from a distance, their running lights illuminating their forms in the darkness. He had watched their wings lower and lock above the wet tile roofs. Then they were gone in a hissing acceleration. Against his better judgment he had returned, joining other residents in a slow scavenging across the rubble of the destroyed building. They moved in a methodical stooped walk. Picking at brick. Turning shattered monitor screens. Fumbling at the pockets of the bodies left behind. He had found no trace of Three-Fingers and doubted he was alive. He Dan he found, but only in pieces.

He turned the datacube again in his hands.

"Where did you get that?"

He jerked skittishly and moved to run, but a hand was holding him and he was immobile. It was a Chinese woman and she wore white gloves. He stared at the hand which held him.

"Do you have something for me?" she asked. Her Mandarin was clear and educated, perfect, as though she came from Beijing itself.

"I don't know."

"Is that yours?"

"No."

"Were you supposed to give it to me?"

"I don't know."

"I missed you at the bridge."

"Why didn't you come?"

"There were delays," she said, and her eyes became hooded and dark.

Wang Jun reached out to hand her the datacube. "You have to be careful with it. It has the Dalai Lama."

"I know. I was coming to you. I was afraid I had lost you. Come." She motioned him. "You are cold. There is a bed and food waiting for you." She motioned again and he followed her out of the doorway and into the rain.

She led him through the wet streets. In his mind, the images of VTOLs and exploding monitors and Three-Fingers's blossoming red mortality made him wary as they crossed intersections and bore along the old streets of Chengdu.

The woman held his hand firm in hers, and she bore him with direction and purpose so that no matter how many twists and turns they took, they were always closer to the organic skeleton of the city core. It rose above them, glowing. Dwarfing them and the constructors who swung from it on gossamer lines. They swarmed it as ants might, slowly growing their nest.

Then they were under its bones, walking through the wet organic passageways of the growing creature. Wang Jun smelled compost and death. The air grew warm and humid as they headed deeper into the architectural animal. Glowing chips embedded in the woman's wrists passed them through construction checkpoints until they came to a lift, a cage that rose up through Huojianzhu's internals, sliding on smooth organic rails. Through the bars of the cage Wang Jun saw levels completed, shining and habitable, the walls with the appearance of polished steel, and fluorescent lamps, glowing, in their brackets. He saw levels where only the segmented superstructure of the beast existed. A monster with its bones exposed; wet slick things sheened with a biological ooze. Hardening silicon mucus coated the bones, flowed, and built up successive layers to form walls. Huojianzhu grew and where it grew the Biotects and constructors oversaw, guiding and ensuring that its growth followed their carefully imagined intentions. The beautiful woman, and Wang Jun with her, rose higher.

They came to a level nearly complete. Her feet echoed in a hallway, and she came to a door. Her hand leaned gently on the surface of the door and its skin moved slightly under her pressure so that Wang Jun was unsure if the door molded to her hand or reached out to caress it. The door swung open and Wang Jun saw the luxury of the heights of which he had always dreamed.

In a room with a bed so soft his back ached and with pillows so fluffy he believed he smothered, he woke. There were voices. "—a beggar. No one," she said.

"Then blank him and turn him out."

"He helped us."

"Leave his pocket with money, then."

Their voices became distant, and though he wished he could stay awake, he slept again.

Wang Jun sank into the enveloping cushions of a chair so deep that his feet could not touch the polished elegance of the real wooden floors. He was well rested now, having climbed finally out of the womb of bedding and pillows which had tangled him. Around him, *shanshui* paintings hung from smooth white walls, and recessed shelves held intricately fired vases from China's dynasties, long dead and gone. The kitchen he had already made acquaintance with, watching the lady who looked Chinese but wasn't as she prepared a mountain of food for him on burners that flared like suns, and made tea with water that scalded as it came from the faucet. In other rooms, lights glowed on and off as he entered and departed, and there was carpet, soft expanses of pale fiber that were always warm under his feet. Now he sat in the enveloping chair and watched with dark eyes as the lady and her foreign companion paced before him. Behind them, the Dalai Lama's cube sat on a shelf, blue and small.

"Sile?"

Wang Jun started at the sound of her voice, and he felt his heart beating. Outside the windows of the apartment thick Chengdu mist hung, stagnant and damp. No more rain. He struggled out of the chair and went to look out the windows. He could not see the lights of Chengdu's old city below. The mist was too thick. The woman watched him as her counterpart spoke. "Yeah, either the Chinese or the Europeans blew his head full of holes. They're just annoyed because they lost him."

"What should we do?"

"I'm waiting for an indication from the embassy. The Tibetans want us to destroy him. Keep whining about how his soul won't be reborn, if we don't destroy it."

She laughed. "Why not write him onto a new body?"

"Don't be sacrilegious."

"That's how they see it? Fanatics can be so—"

"—intractable," he finished for her.

"So this whole mission is a waste?"

"He's not much good to us without his body. The Tibetans won't recognize him if we write him onto a new body and he's no good as leverage against the Chinese if he doesn't have a following."

She sighed. "I wish we didn't have to work with them."

"Without the Tibetans, we wouldn't even have known to look for the kid."

"Well, now they're threatening that if we don't give him back, the Pali Lama is going to flay our skins, or something."

"Palden Lhamo," said the man.

"What?"

He repeated, "Palden Lhamo. She's a Tibetan goddess. Supposed to be the protector of Tibet and our digital friend." He jerked his head at the datacube sitting on its shelf. "The paintings of her show her riding a mule across seas of blood and using the flayed skin of her son as a saddle blanket."

"What a lovely culture they've got."

"You should see the paintings: red hair, necklaces of skulls—"

"Enough."

Wang Jun said, "Can I open the window?"

The woman looked over at the man; he shrugged.

"*Suibian*," she said.

Wang Jun undid the securing clasps and rolled the wide window open. Chill air washed into the room. He peered down into the orange glow of the mist, leaning far out into the air. He stroked the spongy organic exoskeleton of the building, a resilient honeycomb of holes. Below, he could just make out the shifting silhouettes of constructors clambering across the surface of the structure. Behind him the conversation continued.

"So what do we do?"

He waved at the datacube. "We could always plug his eminence into a computer and ask him for advice."

Wang Jun's ears perked up. He wanted to hear the man inside the computer again.

"Would the Chinese be interested in a deal, even if his body is gone?"

"Maybe. They'd probably keep his cube in a desk drawer. Let it gather dust. If he never reincarnated, it would be fine with them. One less headache for them to deal with."

"Maybe we'll be able to trade him for something still, then."

"Not much, though. So what if he does reincarnate? It'll be twenty years before he has an effect on them." He sighed. "Trade talks start tomorrow. This operation's starting to look like a scrub at the home office. They're already rumbling about extracting us before the talks begin. At least the EU didn't get him."

"Well, I'll be glad to get back to California."

"Yeah."

Wang Jun turned from his view and asked, "Will you kill him?"

The pair exchanged looks. The man turned away, muttering under his breath. Wang Jun held in his response to the man's rudeness. Instead he said, "I'm hungry."

"He's hungry, *again*," muttered the man.

"We only have instants, now," said the woman.

"Xing," said Wang Jun.

The woman went into the kitchen and Wang Jun's eyes fastened on the dark blue sheen of the datacube, sitting on its shelf.

"I'm cold," said the man. "Close the window."

Wang Jun sniffed at the aroma of frying food coming from the woman and the kitchen. His belly rumbled, but he went to the window. "Okay."

The mist clung to him as he clung to the superstructure of the biologic city. His fingers dug into its spongy honeycomb skin and he heard the rush of Chengdu far below, but could not see it through the mist. He heard curses and looked up. Light silhouetted the beautiful woman who looked Chinese but wasn't and the man as they peered out of their luxury apartment window from high above.

He dug a fist deeper into the honeycomb wall and waved at them with his free hand, and then climbed lower with the self-confident ease of a beggar monkey. He looked up again to see the man make to climb out the window, and then the woman pulled him back in.

He descended. Slipping deeper into the mist, clambering for the slick safety of the pavement far below. He passed constructors and Biotects, working late-night shifts. They all hung precariously from the side of the mountainous building, but only he was so daring as to climb the skin of the creature without the protection of a harness. They watched him climb by with grave eyes, but they made no move to stop him. Who were they to care if his fingers slipped and he fell to the infinitely distant pavement? He passed them and continued his descent.

When he looked up again, seeking the isolated window from which he had issued, it was gone. Lost in the thickness of the chill mist. He guessed the man and woman would not follow. That they would have more pressing concerns than to find a lone beggar boy with a useless datacube somewhere in the drizzling streets of Chengdu. He smiled to himself. They would pack and go home to their foreign country and leave him to remain in Chengdu. Beggars always remained.

His arms began to shake with strain as his descent continued. The climb was already taking him longer than he had guessed possible. The sheer size of the core was greater than he had ever imagined. His fingers dug into the spongy biomass of Huojian-zhu's skin, seeking another hold. The joints of his fingers ached and his arms trembled. It was cold this high even though the night air was still. The wet mist and the damp spongy walls he clung to chilled his fingers, numbing them and making him unsure of his handholds. He watched where he placed each hand in an agony of care, seeking stability and safety with every grip.

For the first time he wondered how long it would be until he fell. The descent was too long, and the clinging chill was sinking deeper into his bones. The mists parted and he could see the lights of Chengdu proper, spread out below him. His hopes sank as he saw finally how high he hung above the city.

He dug for another handhold and when he set his weight against it, the spongy mass gave way and he was suddenly dangling by a single weak hand while the Chengdu lights spun crazily below him. He scrabbled desperately for another handhold. He dug his feet deep into the spongy surface and found one. He saw where his slipping hand had torn away the wall. There was a deep rent, and from it, the milky blood of the bio-structure dripped slowly. His heart beat faster staring at Huojianzhu's mucus wound and he imagined himself slipping and falling; spattering across the pavement while his blood ran slick and easy into the street gutters. He fought to control his rising panic as his arms trembled and threatened to give way. Then he forced himself to move his limbs and descend, to seek some respite from the climb, a hope of survival on the harsh skin of the core.

He spoke to himself. Told himself that he would survive. That he would not fall and die on the pavement of the street. Not he. Not *Xiao* Wang. No. Not *Xiao* Wang at all. Not Little Wang anymore. Wang Jun; Soldier Wang. Twisted and bent though he was, Soldier Wang would survive. He smiled to himself. Wang Jun would survive. He continued his descent with shaking arms and numbed fingers, picking each hold carefully, and eventually when he began to believe that he could climb no more, he found a hole in Huojianzhu's skin and swung himself into the safety of the ducts of the animal structure.

Standing on a firm surface he turned and looked out at Chengdu's spread lights. In a few more years all of Chengdu would be overwhelmed by the spreading core. He wondered where a beggar boy would run then. What streets would be left open for those such as he? He reached into his pocket and felt the hard edges of the datacube. He drew it from his pocket, and gazed on its smooth blue perfect surface. Its perfect geometric edges. So much consternation over the man who lived inside. He hefted the cube. It was light. Too light to hold the whole of a person. He remembered his brief interaction with the Dalai Lama, in a dark room under the glow of monitors. He squeezed the cube tight in his hand and then went to the edge of the duct. Chengdu lay below him.

He cocked his arm to throw. Winding it back to launch the Dalai Lama in his silicon cell out into the empty air. To arc and fall, faster and faster, until he shattered against the distant ground and was released, to begin again his cycle of rebirth. He held his arm cocked, then whipped it forward in a trajectory of launch. When his arm had completed its swing, the datacube and the Dalai Lama still sat safe in his palm. Smooth and blue and undamaged.

He considered it. Stroking it, feeling its contours in his hand. Then he slid it back into his pocket and swung himself out, once again onto the skin of Huojianzhu. He smiled as he climbed, digging his fingers into the living flesh of the building. He wondered how long this infinity of climbing would last, and if he would reach the streets whole or as a bloody pulp. Chengdu seemed a long way below.

The datacube rested in his pocket. If he fell, it would shatter and the Dalai Lama would be released. If he survived? For now he would keep it. Later, perhaps, he would destroy it. The Dalai Lama was asleep in the cube, and would not overly mind the longer wait. And, Wang Jun thought, who in all the world of important people could say, as he could say, that he had the Dalai Lama in his pocket?

Blue Skies

by Cindy Pon

---

yao: to want; pronounced "yow." • *you:* to have; pronounced "yo."

I watched the two *you* girls from the corner of my eye as the crowds surged around me. Eleven o'clock on a balmy summer evening, and the Shi Lin night market in Taipei was spilling over with *yao* shoppers looking for a way to cool themselves. Stores lined both sides of the narrow street, and music blared in Mandarin, Taiwanese and English. The road was closed to traffic, overtaken by vendors with carts selling noodles and oyster omelets, cold juices and shakes. Others spread their merchandise on the ground over a blanket, hawking cheap toys and knick-knacks.

I slouched lower on the plastic table, faded black boots planted on a stool beneath, taking in the stench of cigarette smoke, stale beer, and sweat. I flipped my silver butterfly knife rhythmically between my fingers without thought, enjoying the feel of cold steel and the sound of blade and handles snapping in my hand.

Men glanced at me warily, touching the places where they hid their own weapons. Girls clustered closer as they edged past, chattering. One *yao* girl, barely fifteen, raised her kohl-smudged eyes from her heap of *chua bing* smothered in red beans and smiled at me, neon-purple bangs brushing against her lashes. Her friend elbowed her and loudly uttered something about delinquent *yao* boys, casting a pointed glare in my direction. They sashayed past, legs bare beneath short, ruffled skirts, the friend with her nose in the air. Smiling girl's pink mouth was now pursed in a pout.

"Hey," I called.

She half turned, careful not to spill her iced dessert. Her black brows were raised, widening her dark eyes. I winked at her, spinning my knife, then tossed it up in the air before catching it in one swift motion. She blushed, and her giggle carried to me even as her friend tugged her away, disappearing into the throngs.

Despite the distraction, I never lost sight of the two *you* girls bent over a round tub, trying to toss plastic balls into floating dishes. The prize was a koi—genetically engineered never to grow beyond two inches—in iridescent oranges, reds, and greens. Hell, they probably glowed in the dark. The girls were flanked by three bodyguards, beefy *yao* boys with muscular arms crossed against their bulging chests.

A *you* boy strutted toward the girls, his features obscured by his glass helmet from this distance. We called them Bowl Heads in derision, as their helmets looked like fishbowls. His sleek suit was black, with an indigo dragon breathing orange flames woven down one long sleeve. The suit ensured that he got the best oxygen available, that his temperature was regulated, that he was always plugged into the *you* communication system. The taller girl in the white and silver suit ignored him, intent on winning a koi in a jar, but her petite friend nodded to the bodyguards, and the *you* boy swaggered through.

I snorted under my breath.

They chatted, probably pulling up info on their com sys, assessing weight, height, and genetic makeup even as they exchanged first names. This was what it meant to be *you*, to *have*. To be genetically cultivated as a perfect human specimen before birth—vaccinated and fortified, calibrated and optimized. To have an endless database of information instantly retrievable within a second of thinking the query and displayed in helmet. To have the best air, food, and water, ensuring the longest possible life spans as the world went to rot around them.

Me, I'm like the other ninety percent of the *yaos* in this world. We *want* and are left wanting. I'd be lucky if I lived to thirty. I'm more than halfway there.

The *you* boy fiddled with his collar, then lifted off his helmet, handing it to one of the bodyguards with studied nonchalance. He coughed for a long time into his sleeve, attempting to adjust to the filth we breathed every day. What a rebel. He was really trying to impress. Without his helmet, I got a better look at him. His blond hair was chin length, streaked in red, his features Afro Asian. He looked about seventeen.

He pulled a cigarette from a sleeve pocket and lit it, inhaling deeply, tilting his head to blow out the smoke. He leaned toward the petite *you* girl, his expression flirtatious. I watched as the taller girl threw them a glance, then turned back toward the tub.

She was broad shouldered yet slender, her suit decorated in pink neon lines with a jeweled Hello Kitty stitched above her heart. Real gem stones, no doubt. The way she tensed her shoulders told me she wasn't pleased by the *you* boy's intrusion.

I tucked the knife away and retrieved two small items from a leather pouch strapped to my side. I wore a sleeveless black tee and black jeans to match. Not only did I blend in, but it allowed me to move with ease. I jumped off the table and stretched my arms overhead, flexing my shoulders.

Now or never.

I cut a quick path through the crowds, moving diagonally, thumping into others as they scurried out of my way. Steam rose from the *chou dofu* vendor stirring her spicy broth, and my eyes watered from the scent. I was behind the bodyguards within a minute. Their massive backs blocked me from my target. I tapped the middle one on his shoulder. He twisted, fists clenched.

"Move," I said.

"What?"

I cocked my elbow and punched him hard in the nose, breaking it. The oaf roared, covering his face as blood spurted. I barreled past him and slammed into the *you* boy, who was gaping, bug-eyed. The other two bodyguards swiped at me with clumsy hands, but I leaped out of the way, smashing the vial I held to the ground. Noxious smoke billowed around us. The bodyguards and the boy dropped to the ground like sacks of rice within ten seconds. Bet that *you* boy would regret taking off his helmet tomorrow morning. The petite girl screamed shrilly beside me as passersby shouted in alarm, but no help came as everyone steered clear of the fumes.

I lunged for the tall girl, pulling her tightly to my chest, and plunged the sleep spell into her hand, the only exposed part of her body. The needle hissed as it dispensed the drug. She sank against me and I hefted her into my arms, dashing into the dark alley behind us, finally allowing myself to take a breath when I cleared the smoke. She wasn't heavy, but all cumbersome limbs.

"Hey, you!" A man shouted, his running footsteps echoing behind me.

I cursed and spun around the corner into a black alley, pressing against the wall. My pursuer followed immediately. I stuck out my foot, and he tripped over it, thumping hard onto the uneven pavement.

I ran without looking back, weaving between the streets, the layout etched in my mind. The distant din of the night market reached me, accompanied by the shriek of police sirens as they inched their way through the crowds. No one followed. I burst onto the main street, at the far end of the market hailing a taxi. It screeched to a stop, spewing foul exhaust. I yanked open the door. "Take me to the end of the bus line," I said.

The driver nodded, raising an eyebrow as I gently laid my hostage on the backseat. "She drank too much," I muttered. "I tried to warn her."

He flicked a cigarette butt out the window before merging back into traffic. "Those *you* girls have everything, but they always want more."

I stared out the open window as the driver zipped through the streets with expertise, honking at pedestrians, hoverpeds, and motorcycles alike. "You her bodyguard?" he asked, catching my eye in the rearview mirror.

I shook my head.

"Ah, her boy toy then." He grinned. "Whatever pays the bills, right?"

Right. But I wanted more than just to pay the bills, to survive. I wanted to change the world.

Neon signs flickered in a kaleidoscope of colors, washing my vision in reds and blues, oranges and greens. I kept a hand on the *you* girl's arm so she wouldn't tumble over with the taxi driver's sudden braking. Her glass helmet reflected the lights around us, and I couldn't make out her features. I swallowed, suddenly afraid. There's no going back now. I jerked my face from her, loosening my grip when I realized I was squeezing her arm.

She was unresponsive, her chest barely rising with each breath. She'd be out until tomorrow morning at least.

The taxi slammed to a stop, and I threw my arms around the girl to keep her from falling onto the floor. "Here we are, end of the line," the driver said.

I handed him my cashcard, tied to a fake identity and bank account. "Thanks," I said. "Add ten for tip."

He smiled, the corners of his eyes creasing with deep lines, and saluted me. He couldn't have been more than twenty-five.

I got out and lifted the girl from the seat, kicking the door shut with my foot. The driver blared his horn twice before tearing off. It was almost midnight, and I needed to be within Yang Ming Shan as soon as possible. The end of the bus line was near the mountain's base. I shifted the girl so her head rested against

my shoulder, her helmet smooth and cold against my cheek, and
started my long climb home.

The half-moon was wane, obscured by clouds and pollution.
My watch face provided scant light, but I navigated the muddied
roads without trouble, stopping twice to catch my breath. Each
time I laid down my captive, setting her head on my thigh, not
knowing how else to place her. She seemed inhuman encased in
her glass helmet. Alien. The pink neon lines of her suit glowed in
the dark, and her exposed, soft hands lay limp at her sides. How
had we drifted so far from what it meant to be human? I could
remove her helmet, but it seemed too much of a violation. I had
to smile at the irony.

I rose once more, throwing the girl over my shoulder. She no
longer felt light—it was like hauling an elephant, and my arms
were dead weights. Finally, I spotted the outcropping of jagged
stones marking where I should turn off the path. Darkness enveloped me as I picked my way between thick brush and massive
trees. Twelve years ago, mud slides after a bad typhoon season
were followed immediately by a massive earthquake that swallowed teahouses, roads, and homes alike. Half of Yang Ming
Shan went up in flames. Survivors fled, and due to the economic
depression and rumors of the mountain being cursed, no investors ever bothered to rebuild.

Now the once-scenic getaway was deserted, lush and wild, its
only occupants the dead in overturned graves. And me. If anyone else lived on Yang Ming Shan, our paths never crossed.

I counted my steps, legs trembling with the effort. Near my

four hundredth, I spotted the first garden light glowing like a flower spirit. I had planted them for the last fifty steps leading home. Each light was solar powered. Sweat stung my eyes, but I was too close to stop. The heavy wooden door to the laboratory clicked open by my voice command, and I stumbled inside, laying the girl on the cot in the small office that served as my bedroom.

I slumped to the floor, arms draped over raised knees, and sat there until I caught my breath.

Leaving her, I stripped and washed myself in the makeshift shower, wishing I had cold water instead of the lukewarm spray that pattered over me. Every muscle shook as I soaped myself before drying off and pulling on some shorts. The front door could be activated by my voice alone, but I took no chances and rummaged through a metal desk, finding the key that I needed. I locked us in, then slipped the key on a string and tied it around my neck.

I didn't even look in on the *you* girl again before crashing onto the worn sofa in the main room, falling immediately into an exhausted sleep.

Something prickled my consciousness awake; it wasn't the brightness of day. My eyes snapped open to find the *you* girl peering at me, her bowl head not an inch away from my nose. I glimpsed her face for the first time. She'd had little work done that I could see: eyes halfway between almond shaped and slender, a rounded nose and rosebud mouth. Her eyes were a light brown, like the watered-down coffee I'd buy with fake cream. Her fingers were extended tentatively above my throat. The back of her hand was bruised where I had jabbed her with the needle. She jumped back when she saw that I had woken. I looked down and remembered the key, then cursed for not putting on any clothes the previous night.

"It was only a precaution," I said, my voice cracking. I cleared my throat and sat up. "You wouldn't have been able to get out even if you got it."

She stood over me, appearing even leaner in the daylight, all long lines and sharp angles.

"The back door's blocked," she said in perfect, educated Mandarin.

Her voice surprised me. Rich, like dark chocolate—more womanly than she looked.

"Mud slide," I said.

She nodded and drew her other hand from behind her back, revealing a pair of dull scissors I kept in the desk. "I could have killed you in your sleep."

"You would have had to try hard." I rose, reaching for a clean shirt draped over the back of a wooden chair. It was black, like most of my clothes. "Those scissors are from another century." I pulled on the shirt, then some blue jeans, and scrubbed a hand through my short hair, suddenly self-conscious.

Now what?

We stared at each other for a long moment. If she were a feline, her tail would be thrashing.

"How much do you want?" she asked.

I reached for the scissors, and she relinquished them without protest. "Are you hungry?" I asked.

Her eyes narrowed, and she shook her head.

"I know you must be thirsty. The sleep spell will do that to you." I crossed the spare chamber to the corner kitchen and pulled the refrigerator door open, grabbing a bottle of fancy *you* water, purified and enriched with gods knew what. A case of it cost more than most *yao* folks' weekly salary. "Here." I offered it to her.

She sat down in the wooden chair, turning the bottle in her hand, examining it.

"It's not tainted," I said. "The seal's unbroken."

She lifted her eyes. "How do I drink it?"

Ah.

"Haven't you ever taken—"

"No. Never in unregulated space."

"The air isn't as polluted up here," I lied.

"I can't call anyone in helmet."

"No." I knew the first thing she'd try upon waking was to call for help. "I've jammed the signals."

She blinked several times, and her nostrils flared.

I glanced away, tamping down my sympathy.

The girl fidgeted with her suit collar, finally lifting her helmet. It came off with a low hiss. Her ponytail sprang free, black and uncolored. The scent of strawberries filled the air, and I took a step back, caught off guard. I had expected *you* girls to be scentless at best or to smell clinical at worst, like some specimen kept too long in a jar.

Not like fresh, sweet strawberries.

Her eyes truly watered now as she breathed our polluted air for the first time in her life. She doubled over, coughing spastically. I grabbed the bottle from her hand and twisted it open.

"Drink."

She did so, sucking down the water as if it would save her life. Finally, she wiped her mouth with a handkerchief that had been tucked in her sleeve, then pressed it against her eyes. "How do you live breathing this every day?" she asked in a weak voice.

"We don't have to live for very long," I replied.

She dropped her handkerchief and stared at me with red-rimmed eyes. "That's not funny," she said.

I smiled. "I wasn't trying to be." I sat back down on the old sofa, so there was some distance between us.

She was pretty in a way I wasn't used to. Not engineered like most *you* girls bowing to the latest ethnic trends, narrowing their noses and rounding their eyes to look more European, then reshaping their lips fuller and plumping their breasts, hips, and rear when the exotic South American fad was in. The *yao* girls, lacking the funds for such drastic changes, resorted to painting their young faces in bright colors, using semipermanent tattoos, dying their hair or wearing wigs.

It was almost impossible to tell what a girl really looked like anymore.

She finished her water and cast a wary glance my way. "What's your name?"

"Seriously?" I laughed.

She lifted her shoulders. "I'd guess you're one year older than I am. Eighteen. Born in the Year of the Horse." She nodded at the black clothes strewn on the few pieces of furniture in the room. "Dark Horse, I'll call you."

I almost smiled, but instead pulled out my butterfly knife and began the familiar pattern of flipping it between my fingers and spinning it in my hand. It helped me to think. She tensed, clutching her thighs. She was afraid I might take advantage of her. I wouldn't, of course. Besides, doing it with a *you* girl was about as appealing as having sex with a giant clam. I imagined peeling the suit off of her body, revealing pale skin never touched by natural sunlight, and was disgusted by the thought.

"Why so Romeo?" Her throaty voice broke my reverie. She didn't mean Romeo as in romantic; she meant Romeo as tragic.

Why so Ro?

I took in my surroundings through her eyes. I lived in an abandoned laboratory that used to belong to Yang Ming Shan University, an experimental "home" run on sustainable energy. Back when some thought we could still salvage our planet by "going green." We might have, if enough people had cared. But they hadn't. The rich were too rich, the poor were too poor, and the middle class—let's be honest—were only poor people with bigger houses, driving better cars. Now that the majority of us didn't live past forty, we cared even less. I'd been on my own since thirteen, when my mom died. I'd lost my father when I was three. He had been killed in a construction accident.

My current home consisted of just three rooms: the office, a bathroom, and this main chamber, which included the small kitchen. It held a large, round dining table with a couple of mismatched stools, the ragged turquoise and yellow sofa that was at least four decades old, a metal desk, and the wooden chair she sat in. Large windows flanked the southern wall, revealing a thicket of jungle beyond.

I tossed my knife three times, savoring the snick and snap of the blade and handles, before shrugging. "It's easier to kidnap in black."

Bad joke. I think her eyes actually smoldered.

I jumped up and grabbed my ancient MacBook Plus from the desk, opening it. "Put your helmet back on," I said.

"Why?"

"You're calling your family."

She did as I asked, securing her helmet, then took such a deep, full breath that her breasts swelled against her suit. I pretended not to notice.

"You have one minute." I tapped the necessary commands into my laptop and nodded to her.

Her brown eyes widened, then focused. I could follow the entire conversation from her one-sided replies.

"*Ma!*" Her voice changed, sounding younger, helpless.

Although her helmet had darkened slightly, I still glimpsed the tears brightening her eyes, seeing her mother's face in the glass.

"*Mei you, mei you. Wo hao.*" No, he hasn't tortured or raped me.

She clasped her hands in front of her face, fingers trembling as if she could keep her mother's image there.

"Tell her I want three hundred million," I said.

Her pupils dilated, then shrank, and she saw me again.

"Now!"

"*Ta yao san yi,*" she whispered.

"Put it in this account." I gave her the cashcard number for the ghost account I had set up, and she recited it. "You have two hours."

"You liang ge xiao shi," she repeated.

Her mom began asking frantic questions.

Who is he? *"Wo bu zhi dao."*

Where are you? *"Bu zhi dao!"*

I typed a command and severed her connection.

She leaned forward, almost falling off of the chair, disoriented. Then tugged off her helmet, throwing it to the ground. It bounced on the bamboo rug and spun twice before I snatched it up.

"Shit! Are you crazy?"

She had pulled her legs into her chest on the chair, burying her face between her knees. Her shoulders heaved. When she lifted her head, her pale face was mottled.

"What if you had broken it?" I carefully placed her helmet on the dining table.

"Are *you* crazy? Three hundred million?"

"What? You probably have twice that waiting for you in your trust fund." The *you*s didn't lead the lives that they did without having a few billion to spare.

"What do you want with it?" she asked, crossing her arms, assessing me.

"What do *you* want with it?" I countered.

We stared at each other, both our breaths coming too quickly. Hers because she was unused to our foul air. Mine because I was rattled. *Damn* this *you* girl.

"How does my family know to trust you?" she demanded. "That you won't kill me anyway?"

"You know how it works." There was an unspoken rule between kidnappers and their targets. The victims always paid in full, and the criminals never killed anyone. Not yet anyway. But then, no one had ever asked for three hundred million before. That wasn't my problem. And if I were a betting man, the ransom would be in the ghost account within the hour.

"Can I use your bathroom?" she asked.

I nodded toward the door, and she disappeared within, shutting it behind her. I took the moment of privacy to pace the room and analyze my situation. I'd give her family two hours to hustle up the funds. Once cleared, I could deliver the girl back to the night market.

The shower had been running for some time, and I went to the bathroom door, which didn't lock. "The window's too small to crawl through, and the drop to the other side will break your legs, if not your neck," I shouted.

The water turned off after another minute. She came out, looking exactly the same and still smelling of strawberries.

"Do you need a towel?" I asked, hiding a smirk behind the last apple I had found in the refrigerator drawer.

"No, thank you," she said coolly, then proceeded to drink the vitapak I handed her with dainty sips. "Don't you have any solid foods to eat?"

"Does this look like a five-star *you* establishment to you?" I asked. "I've only got liquids." Because I couldn't afford anything more. "Although..." Suddenly remembering, I opened a kitchen cabinet. "I do have two *rou song bao* from the bakery."

I gave her one. "Don't blame me if you get a stomachache," I said, taking a big bite out of mine.

She stared at it for a long time, finally trying a nibble and chewing slowly before swallowing. Then she sat very still, as if waiting to die. I finished mine and brushed off my hands. "Well?" I was still hungry.

She took a full bite the next time, challenging me with a slant of her head. "It's good," she said. She glanced out the expansive windows. "Are we on Yang Ming Shan?" she asked.

"No," I lied. "Is that the only mountain you know in Taiwan?"

"I haven't traveled much out of Taipei." Her face took on an expression that looked like yearning as she gazed into the trees. "Can we go outside?"

I couldn't hide my surprise. "No."

"I've never been in the mountains before. I won't run away."

"You'd get lost. And die."

She walked to the giant window and pressed herself against it. I wondered what it was like, never having been in the mountains or seen the jungle so close—never to have gone outdoors without a glass bowl over my head.

"All right. Your helmet stays inside. If you're willing to breathe the air, we can step out for a while." It was a risk, but so was my entire plan. I was no kidnapper or thief—even if kidnapping and stealing were exactly what I was doing. I hadn't gotten this far worrying over risks.

She turned, silhouetted by the afternoon light, and actually smiled. I was beginning to like her despite myself.

"Come on. Stay close." I unlocked the heavy door, and it clicked open with my voice command. "I've got cucumbers and tomatoes to harvest anyway."

"What?"

I grabbed her hand, feeling the softness of her skin in my own rough palm. She jerked back her arm, startled, but my grip didn't

230

loosen. "Do you want to see or not?" I asked.

She nodded, jaw tense, two bright spots on her cheekbones.

I led her along the edge of the house, sweeping aside giant fronds and leaves, past a dozen massive cisterns that collected rainwater. The smell of wet earth filled my senses. We picked our way through the shaded dirt path and veered into a small clearing, where the view of the sky was unobstructed. The sun burned above us, a blistering orb tinged in orange.

The sky used to be blue. This was what my research on the undernet told me. Some even displayed actual photographs from another time—a pale blue skyline punctuated by skyscrapers or in a deeper hue over a calm sea, so two shades of blue melded like some old painting by a landscape artist. My mind kept returning to this image, the crisp purity of it. Unapologetic and true.

But what could you believe from reading the undernet? Images were more easily manipulated than a *you* girl's face. I didn't know anyone who had ever seen a blue sky. It wasn't until I had read a novel—published more than a century ago—where the author described something in *sky blue* that I let myself believe it, feeling wonder and joy and grief all at once.

I never did finish that book.

I suddenly felt the pressure of the *you* girl's hand clutching mine. Her flushed face was tilted up, eyes squinted against the dull sunlight. She coughed into her sleeve, and when she finally stopped, her breaths came quick and shallow. It was late afternoon, the summer day's humid heat oppressive.

"Are you all right?" I asked.

She turned to me, eyes gleaming, and said, "I've never seen the sky like this before."

"You mean without your helmet?"

"And so wide. It's always a dirty brown over Taipei," she said.

I led her into my small garden. Cucumbers dangled from a bamboo trellis I had made, nestled within their giant dark-green leaves. We stepped between the tomato plants, their fruits small and marred. I stooped down, and she crouched with me as I selected a tomato, dusting it off then taking a bite. More tangy than sweet. She stared as if I had plucked a rat off the ground and eaten that instead.

"The sky used to be blue," I said after I finished the tomato.

"That's what my grandfather says."

Grandfather. I'd never met my grandparents, didn't even know their names. They were long dead before I was born.

"He's seen it, then?" I tried to keep my voice from rising. "With his own eyes?"

"He thinks so. But he was very young." She ran her fingertips over the ridges and bumps of an orange tomato. "He says it feels like a dream when he remembers it."

Sweat beaded at her temples, and there was a sheen of perspiration above her upper lip. I swiped my arm across my forehead. "I can't believe how hot it gets," she said, licking her mouth.

I mirrored her without thinking, tasting the salt on my tongue. "This is what summers are like in Taiwan when you're not wearing an air-conditioned suit," I replied, and grabbed the woven basket near my feet.

"I'll help you," she said.

We spent the next twenty minutes in silence, filling the basket with imperfect tomatoes and cucumbers. The mountain breeze rustled the leaves around us, and the birds sang deep within the jungle's thicket. When we were done, the *you* girl's lips were leeched of color, and wisps of black hair that had escaped from her ponytail clung to her damp neck.

Her breaths still came too fast, like a frightened hare's. "I think we should go back inside," I said, lifting the basket.

She rose with me. "I want to try one."

I tilted the basket, and her hand grazed over the tomatoes and cucumbers, touching them as if they were gems instead of meager crops. She finally selected an oblong tomato, redder than the others, and brushed a thumb over its skin before taking a bite. She immediately made a face and shuddered.

I laughed. "No good?"

"It's more sour than I've ever tasted."

No doubt she'd only ever had perfectly grown specimens. We walked back toward the house, and she appeared thoughtful as she finished the fruit. "I like that it tastes...earthy," she finally said. I saw her eyes sweep our surroundings as we approached the front of the lab.

The door unlocked with my voice, and we stepped back inside the relative coolness of the building. I set the basket on the dining table and nodded at her helmet beside it. "You should put it back on."

"Later," she murmured, and walked back toward the windows, gazing outward.

I sat on a stool and tapped a few quick commands into my laptop. The funds had transferred in full. I let out a breath, releasing the tension I had held ever since stealing this *you* girl. Three hundred million had been a gamble, but a gamble worth taking. It was enough for me to suit up as a *you* boy and pretend to be one of them, to infiltrate their closed and elite society. It would be a start.

I wanted blue skies again.

"What are you going to do with the money?" She turned, her hands clasped in front of her.

I jumped at the sound of her voice and shut the MacBook. "I don't know. Redecorate." She gave me a leveled look, and I broke away first, taking in the chamber I had called home for the past year. I'd have to leave immediately. I would miss this place.

"I'd suggest a new wardrobe first, Dark Horse."

I laughed despite myself. "What's your name then?"

"Seriously?" She raised her eyebrows and smiled.

I shrugged. "What does it matter now?" I did like her. I wanted to know.

"Dai Yu," she replied.

"From the novel?"

Her smile widened in surprise, and it made her truly beautiful. "You've read it?"

I read voraciously, most often from the undernet, but had found an actual copy of *Dream of the Red Chamber* stuffed and forgotten in the desk drawer of a junk shop. The owner had given it to me for free, waving me off without a glance. Books weren't worth the paper they were printed on.

"You don't look the tragic heroine to me," I replied.

"Don't I?" She had been leaning against the glass and straightened now, squaring her shoulders. But not before I caught a glimpse of wistfulness in her eyes. Of longing. What more could a *you* girl possibly want when she already had everything?

"We better go," I said. "I need to return you to your family, and it'll be dark soon."

Dai Yu lifted her helmet and adjusted her collar before fitting it over her head. And in an instant she was something *other* to me, something less human. It was hard to believe there was an almost-normal girl beneath the glass. A smart one with a sense of humor.

"I'll have to give you the sleep spell again," I said apologetically.

"No. Blindfold me if you have to."

"I can't risk it. I've added something so you'll forget." I could see her eyes widen in panic, even with her helmet on. "Not everything. Just this...these past few days."

She shook her head. "Please don't."

But I took her hand, was already pulling her to the door. "It's safer for us both if you didn't remember anything. Trust me." I felt stupid the moment I uttered the last words.

We were out in the muggy humidity of the late afternoon again. It would take a few hours at least to walk to the mountain's base, and by then night would have fallen. Even if I was abandoning the lab, I still couldn't risk her remembering this place, remembering me.

The sunlight glinted off her helmet, and I was glad I couldn't see her features clearly as I tugged her to me. She resisted, but I was stronger. So she stepped forward instead, bunching the fabric of my shirt in one hand.

"But I *want* to remember," she said.

I grabbed her wrist, stuck the syringe into her open palm. Its hiss seemed too loud to my ears. "We all do," I whispered and caught her as she fell.

We all do.

What Arms to Hold Us

by Rajan Khanna

If gollies had ears, Ravi might have heard the other driver coming straight at him. Instead, the other golly's metal claw slammed into his golly's body, the impact registering through his mental link. In panic, he lashed out with his own golly's arm, throwing the other machine clear and deeper into the mine.

His mind raced. He'd heard of other drivers going on rampages. It was some kind of problem with the link, or with the drivers perhaps. But it always meant damage to the gollies, and possibly to the mine as well.

He'd expected the other driver to back off, go inactive as his minder severed the mental link, but instead, the other golly moved forward, swinging its arms in a frenzy. Through the goggle eyes, the rampaging golly resembled a large, squat metal man, all brass carapace and long, ape-like arms.

Ravi knew he needed to protect his golly. He raised its gripping hand and grabbed the other golly's cutting arm with the claw-like appendage. Then he raised his own cutting arm. For a moment he considered cutting the other golly, but he knew how valuable gollies were, and he feared what would happen if he damaged one. Instead, he swept his arm overhead, cutting into an overhang of rock with the moving blade. Then Ravi released the golly's grip and moved backward.

Rock fell down onto the golly's legs, fixing them in place. Ravi watched through the golly's eyes as it tried to pull them free. But they wouldn't move.

As his panic subsided, he spoke, through his own mouth, to his minder back in the pen. "Another golly attacked me. But he's contained now," he said.

"We should pull you out," Minder Charles said into his ear.

"No, wait," Ravi said. Now that the dust raised by the rampaging golly had cleared, he saw what lay revealed behind the rock he had cut.

In the shine of his wytchfire, rich primosite reflected back the bilious light. Golden-white primosite. The treasure of their modern age. The power source for all of the Imperium's wondrous creations. Even through the golly's eyes it seemed to have hidden depths.

Had he been able to, Ravi would have smiled. But golly faces couldn't smile. Instead, he spoke from his own mouth, telling the Minder back in the pen that he had found primosite to be collected, then he began the process of cutting into the vein, collecting the rich mineral. The other golly remained still, the link probably severed back in the pen.

When Ravi was pulled out, the other driver, a boy named Suresh, had already been removed. "What happened?" Ravi asked Minder Charles.

"Just a little problem with the link," Minder Charles said. "Nothing to worry about. You did a great job in stopping the golly, though."

That night as the others filed into the feeding station for the nightly rations, Ravi was allowed a special meal, a kind of soupy curry with gristly pieces of indeterminate origin lurking inside. It wasn't anything he'd ever had before—the approximation of things he had eaten in his childhood rather than a true Drinan dish—but there was the barest hint of home in its aroma and taste.

The Overseer had come to see him after the meal. "Good work today," he said. "Keep doing well and you might move up. Did you enjoy the meal?"

"Yes, sir," Ravi said. "If I may?" He knew he was being bold, but after stopping the rampaging golly and finding a vein of primosite, he felt it justified.

"Go on," the Overseer said, raising one gray eyebrow.

"May I write a letter back home?"

"You can write?" the Overseer asked.

Ravi nodded. "My sister, Astha, taught me."

The Overseer shrugged. "Then you can write a letter. I'll have someone bring you some paper. Deliver it to me in the morning."

"Yes, sir," Ravi said, and ran back off to his room.

Back at the flop, laid out like brown teeth next to the other boys, he composed his letter, trying to fit as much as possible into the space allotted. The tele-gollies could only handle a limited amount, or at least whatever was rationed per person.

Like everything, they ran on primosite, and it was costly.

"Dear Mami and Papu," he began. "I hope that you're doing well. I hope that the stipend you're receiving for my work has been helpful to you." He went on to tell them a little about his work and his living situation, embellishing a bit so they wouldn't worry. But he ended by talking of his recent success and how he hoped it would lead to something better for him. He even mentioned the gossip he'd overheard: that the Archmagus himself might be visiting them soon as part of his tour of the Imperium. He hoped his parents would be proud of him. He hoped they already were.

Afterward, the letter carefully secreted beneath his sleeping mat, he crawled over to Noosa's mat. "It's time for another lesson," he said.

Noosa shook his head and tried to roll over. "I *thought* you were busy with your letter."

"I was and now I'm not."

Noosa raised himself on his elbows. "If you can read and write, why do I have to?"

"Because I won't always be here," Ravi said. "I intend to move out of this stink hole soon enough. Maybe onto the railroad like Atul."

"You don't need to read or write to work the railroad."

"No, but one day I intend to have a nice job in an office. You should, too."

Noosa grumbled, but crawled with Ravi over to the window, where they went over letters by moonlight. After an hour or so of this, Ravi let Noosa return to sleep, and he crawled atop his mat, thinking for the first time in months that his exit was at least close at hand.

In the morning, Ravi handed the letter to Overseer Drudge, who folded it and stuffed it into his pocket. "It's good news for you, my lad," he said.

"Yes, sir?"

"We've decided to move you forward. You'll be at the front of the golly waves. The diggers have moved into new territory. You'll be one of the first to see it."

Ravi couldn't stop a smile from spreading across his face. "Thank you, sir," he said.

"Just keep up the good work," Drudge said. "There'll be more letters in the future for you if you do. And maybe a special meal or two."

"Yes, sir," Ravi said.

Magus Sharpe was in the Driving Room when Ravi arrived. Sharpe often stopped by to supervise the transfers and check on the links, but today his scowl seemed deeper than usual. He glared at Ravi as he entered the room. "You're late," he said, and cuffed Ravi on the back of the head.

Ravi didn't let it bother him. Minder Charles looked surprised as Ravi hopped into the transfer chair. "You're full of pep this morning," he said.

"Yes, sir," Ravi said, smiling, and closed his eyes as Charles slid the thin metal crown over his head. He felt the familiar charge and tingle as the primosite energy flowed through the machine. The hairs on his arms stood up.

Then he was seeing through the golly's eyes. They weren't as sharp as human eyes, but they picked up contrast better. He took a moment to check the golly's movements, make sure that the link was correct. He'd never had a problem before, but the rampaging golly was still fresh in his mind. He didn't want to jeopardize his new status at the front of the lines.

"Proceed to the foremost tunnel," the minder's voice said in his ear.

Ravi moved the golly forward.

Brassy heads swiveled as he passed them, and he knew the other boys were wondering where he was going. Why he was moving forward. Most of them probably didn't even know who he was, but he could feel their envy as if it were primosite energy radiating out into the close air of the mine.

He'd never been this far before, had never seen the front of the mining efforts. The tunnel's end was blocked by the bulk of the diggers just ahead—the large, powerful machines that bored through the rock powered, of course, by primosite. It was kind of funny when he thought about it. They used primosite power to mine more primosite to power more things.

But then of course there was much more than mining equipment to run. The railroads, where Atul was working, were one of the most recent destinations for the valuable ore. Then there were other machines, ones that the elite of the city used to do, well, almost everything if the other boys were to be believed. Primosite power was even said to cook their food, though such a thing seemed far too fantastic for him to believe.

He began his work, pushing the wytchfire lamp to full power, sweeping his gaze over the rock in front of him, readying the cutting arm.

The first few hours yielded very little. He'd thought that maybe the newly cut rock would be gleaming with primosite veins; instead, he found only a few small deposits. Barely enough to line the bottom of his bin. But he worked steadily, still hoping.

His windfall was not to be. By the time Minder Charles told him to withdraw, he had barely doubled his take from the beginning of the day. It was slim pickings, and as Charles pulled the cap from his head, he clenched his hands, his human hands, into fists.

As he exited the room, head low, he noticed that Suresh wasn't in his usual chair. A new boy was there. Maybe he was still in the Infirmary, Ravi thought. He forgot to ask, though, worried as he was. He anticipated the call into the Overseer's office and the removal of his newfound status at the front.

"It's your first day," Noosa said at the evening meal, his mouth full of lentils. "Maybe they're letting you warm up."

"Do you think that's likely?" Ravi said. "You've been here longer than I have. You know how things work."

Noosa shrugged. "Then they're waiting for you to screw up even more first." He wiped at his nose, and Ravi saw a trickle of blood across his hand. Atul had had nosebleeds as well, before he moved on to the railroads. The Minders said it was a result of the dry air. Ravi was lucky he had avoided them.

The next day Ravi was still unable to find any significant primosite deposits. As the other boys gathered for the evening meal, he was summoned to the Overseer's office. Ravi stood before the man's desk, his brown hands clenched together in front of him. Drudge read over some papers on his desk before finally looking up at Ravi. His skin was like pale stone, but his eyes were a piercing blue. He shook his head ever so slightly. "I have to say I am disappointed in you."

Ravi felt the blood rush to his face, and he lowered his eyes.

"We moved you to the Front because we thought, because *I thought*, that you could bring us more primosite. But based on the latest figures"—he picked up a sheet of paper and ran a finger over it—"hardly up to snuff."

"I—I'm sorry," Ravi began. "I've been trying."

Drudge stood up and came around his desk, looking down at Ravi. The great, pale roll of his neck ballooned over his tight collar like the belly of a frog. "I suggest you try harder," he said, quietly but firmly. "I thought that maybe you would be able to follow in the footsteps of your brother. Prove yourself a boon to us. But now…"

Ravi felt as if he had eels wriggling in his belly. Dark, shameful eels that bit at him from the inside. "I can do it," he insisted.

"See that you do," the Overseer said. "You may have heard that the Archmagus may visit us soon. If he does, he will be taking an interest in our people and our figures. If you don't make the grade, you'll be sent to the back of the mines, and there will be no special meals and no letters home. Understood?"

Ravi nodded. The Overseer dismissed him, and he walked back to the mess like a dead thing, the eels now turned to cold, heavy bricks inside of him. Worse still, the meal had finished being served, and all that was left were scraps. He spooned the tasteless food into his mouth and chewed mechanically.

That night he dreamed of Atul and his work on the railroad. He imagined his brother riding atop a great silvery snake of chrome and brass, primosite energy crackling off it as it slid against the rails. "Come aboard," Atul said. He leaned off the side of the engine and held out a thin, brown arm to Ravi. "Come on."

Ravi reached for his hand, but the engine was moving so fast and Atul's hand seemed so thin, so small. He reached for it, but it slipped right through his grasp, soft, dry fingers slipping away like silk. Ravi's fingers closed on empty air.

He turned to watch Atul go, tears forming in his eyes, but to his shock and horror, his brother fell from the top of the engine, falling away below into a great, black chasm that had appeared below it.

He woke in a clinging sweat. As he was wiping it from his stubbly head, he felt the scar at the back of his skull, rubbed it. It was a reminder, a mark of who he was. He was a driver. He moved gollies. Would he be stuck doing that forever?

He rolled over and tried to go back to sleep.

Magus Sharpe was once again in the Driving Room when Ravi and the others arrived. They were lined up in the front of the room and the Magus stood before them, his red-robed arms crossed over his chest, his face stern and scowling. "Listen up, you wogs," he said. "This hostel is about to come under a great deal of scrutiny. The Archmagus will be arriving here within the next two weeks. We don't know when he will arrive, but when he does, he will be inspecting the whole facility. He will be reviewing primosite loads, golly damage reports; he will be inspecting all of you, your crowns and your chairs. He might even ask you to operate your gollies for him. If so, you will do anything he says.

"He will be attended by his retinue, which means that things will be more crowded when they arrive. All non-working time will be restricted to your flop, and rations will be cut to help support our larger numbers.

"You will act at all times with respect and dignity. I know it is not natural to you, but do your best to imitate your betters. If you do not, if you embarrass this facility and the fine people who run it, you will face me." This last he said with a grim smile. Then he waved a hand, indicating that they should continue.

Minder Charles would not meet his eyes when Ravi slid into the driving chair. Ravi inhaled as the crown was lowered onto his head, and he took control of the golly with a sense of determination churning inside of him.

Still, a primosite vein eluded him for most of the morning, and he was starting to feel his head ache from the strain of searching. It had been three days now since he'd been positioned at the Front, and he had so far turned up nothing significant. If he failed here, they would send him to the back, where the pickings were even slimmer and where he'd have no chance of finding anything worth presenting. He would remain in the mines, and he wouldn't see Atul for a long time. If ever. Condemned to remain in this hell.

The pain and the frustration hammered away at him until, for the first time, he lost control and lashed out with the golly's arm. Rock sparked and flew away, and because it fulfilled some kind of primal urge, he did it again. Then again.

By the time he had controlled himself—that kind of behavior was punished because it could damage the gollies—a large chunk of rock had been gouged from the cavern wall.

Inside, Ravi saw primosite gleaming.

He turned up his light, and yes, there it was. A primosite vein. A juicy primosite vein. Almost as big as the one that had earned him the Front.

He thought he might be able to make the golly smile this time. He started delicately cutting at the vein when the ground around him started to shake.

His delight twisted into fear as he realized what was happening.

A cave-in.

He turned, looking for the others around him, but he was alone. He started moving back, making his way to where it was safe.

But the vein... if he left it now, there was no telling if he could return. Even if the Front were still clear, he might not find it. Or maybe someone else would before he could claim it.

His indecision cost him. Chunks of rock fell from the cavern ceiling, some bouncing against the brass of the golly, and Ravi felt the impacts through the link they shared.

He began to move back to the rear of the mining group, but vision was hard with all the dust kicked up from the collapse.

He stomped blindly, not knowing in which direction he needed to go, trying in vain to wave the dust away but hoping that he would make it to safety.

Then the golly pitched over, and his vision went dark. Stones rattled across the golly's back. With a shudder that he felt all over, more rock fell, heavier and harder, until he couldn't move any part of the golly.

"Help," he said, back in the pen. "A cave-in. I'm... I'm trapped." In a moment the crown was removed from his head, and he was back in the pen, the minder's pale face in front of his own.

"There was no moving the golly?" Charles said.

Ravi shook his head. His hands curled into fists. He had seen primosite. He had been so close. Now it was lost. And if they found out he was responsible for the cave-in, and the loss of the golly, he would be punished.

"You'd better return to the flop," Charles said. "You won't be able to do anything until they can free your golly."

Ravi fled, head down, past the beds full of boys, their eyes staring vacantly. As he climbed the stairs to where all the boys slept, he wiped a trickle of blood from his nose.

At the evening meal, Ravi sat next to Noosa, as usual, darkness shadowing his thoughts. He wondered if they would be able to discover that the cave-in was his fault. He wondered if his golly was damaged. He wondered if the loss in productivity would be attributed to him. Despite the blandness of the stewed beans, his mouth tasted bitter.

"Did you hear what Itchy said?" Noosa asked. He was all smiles. He'd received a letter from home, and his minder had read it to him before the evening meal.

Ravi shook his head, happy to focus on something else.

"He said that Little Osef moved on to the girl's pen."

"That's ridiculous," Ravi said.

"He said that he's teaching the girls how to operate gollies."

"Itchy likes to tell tales." It wasn't even a good one. Everyone knew that girls weren't allowed to drive gollies. He'd heard that some learned to operate tele-gollies, but he'd never heard of a girl in the mines.

"Well, I wouldn't mind a job like that," Noosa said. "Can you imagine? One of him, all those girls…" He pulled a piece of paper from his pocket and mimed fanning himself.

Ravi frowned. "What's that?"

Noosa flashed a sly smile. He leaned forward. "It's my letter from home."

"They gave it to you?"

Noosa's smile widened. "Nah. But someone stopped by to see Minder Frederick before I left, and I swiped it. I thought you could help me read it. Something real."

"Okay," Ravi said. He was hoping that it would distract him from thoughts of the mine. At the very least it was a window into a world that he didn't normally see.

When they were back at the flop, Noosa brought out the letter, and together they went through it, word by word. Noosa had heard it already from his minder, but he was happy to read it again. Ravi understood. He wished he had copies of the letters from home.

As they went through it, Ravi realized that it was similar to his own letters—inquiries about how Noosa was, talk of the family, weather, village life—but as Ravi read on, he realized it sounded too typical. Lines from the letter sounded so familiar, as if they could have come from one of his letters. As Noosa tussled with the last few sentences, Ravi read through it a second time, noticing the lack of specific details. Activities, events, even people were mentioned generally. The family was doing well, not individuals. When talking about the village, there were again no mentions of specific people and no references to local holidays. With a start, Ravi realized that there was nothing to indicate that it really was from Noosa's family. It could have been handed to any of the boys there, and they would believe it was for them.

"What's wrong?" Noosa said, looking at him.

"Nothing," Ravi said. "I just...have a headache."

"Me, too," Noosa said. "They've been getting worse lately. Do you think it's from all the reading?"

"No," Ravi said. "Not at all. It must be something else."

Noosa shrugged and carefully placed the letter underneath his sleeping mat. "Thanks," he said, then rolled over to go to sleep.

Ravi did the same, but his sleep was troubled.

He talked to some of the other boys at the morning meal the next day. Asked them about their letters. Discretely, he hoped. All indicated similar topics. One or two claimed that specific family members had been named, but on further questioning, Ravi thought they might just be remembering wrong, as the content seemed largely the same from letter to letter.

He remembered asking Minder Charles once if he had ever been to Drina.

"Me?" Charles said, surprised. "No. I can't say that I have. Though I have spent a lot of time here with you lot. Drinans and Arvins and Chand alike. Why?"

"Just wondering," Ravi had said.

Then the transfer crown had come down, and Ravi's world became the golly.

Minder Charles looked worried as Ravi reported to him the next morning. "Is everything all right?" Ravi asked.

"No," Charles said. "Your golly still hasn't been recovered. And we fear that it might be damaged. The Overseer approved you to be linked to a new golly."

"A new one?"

Charles smiled. "The Overseer tells me it's newly constructed. But you'll need to be linked to it."

"What do I have to do?" Ravi said.

"It will take most of day," Charles said. "You'll need to visit the doctor, and he'll need to do an examination of you. Then the Magus will create the link."

"Then I can get back into the mines?"

Charles frowned. "The examination... it will take a lot out of you. You'll need some time to recover. And the link will take some time to set up. If everything goes well, we'll get you in as soon as possible."

Ravi nodded, but inside, his thoughts swirled darkly. The Archmagus was coming to visit soon. What if Ravi's numbers were far below the other boys'? He wouldn't stay in the mines forever. He couldn't.

He reported to the doctor as told. Dr. Umber was a tall, thin man, with pale skin and paler hair that came down into a sharp point over his forehead. "Lie down on the table," he instructed. Ravi did so.

"Now, we'll need to take some time with you to get you ready for the new golly," Umber said. "To make it easier on you, I'll be putting you to sleep. Just relax. You'll be done in no time." Umber's smile revealed yellow teeth. As Ravi was staring at them, the man slid a needle into his arm. He felt the cold metal slide underneath his skin. Then as the pain built, he felt a cold flush in the limb and then nothing.

When he woke, his head ached and his limbs felt like sodden logs. Moving golly limbs seemed easier than moving his own. As he rubbed his head, he felt a fresh bandage on the back of his head, near where his original scar was. He winced at the fresh pain as his fingers caressed the new wound. Something to do with the link, no doubt.

"You back with us?" Dr. Umber said, leaning over him. "Good. We're all done here. You can return to the common room now. Your head may be a little sore, but that will pass. If you feel anything more than what you're feeling now, let one of the Minders know. Okay?"

Ravi nodded.

He passed Magus Sharpe on the way out. The Magus scowled at him. Probably for the extra work that Ravi was causing. Ravi ignored him and went straight to his flop.

It was still a few hours until the evening meal, so he lay down on his mat. He realized that this had been the most time he'd spent not driving a golly since he had arrived at the pen. His thoughts swarmed like dark flies. He thought of the letters. Were they all shams? The letters kept the boys working hard. With the idea that money was being sent back to their families. Did that mean the money wasn't reaching them? Was it deliberate or just laziness?

He chewed on this until it was time for the evening meal, and then he rejoined the other boys at the long wooden tables. "Where you been?" Noosa asked.

"They're giving me a new golly," Ravi said.

"Really?" Noosa said, and Ravi heard the envy in his voice. He was disturbed by a coughing fit. "What's the matter? You wreck the last one?"

"It got stuck in a cave-in," Ravi insisted.

Noosa shrugged. "You'll need it to catch up," he said, his mouth full of beans. "You must be dropping behind."

When they returned to the flop and Ravi curled up on his mat, he couldn't stop thinking about the letters. If they were lying about them, what else were they lying about?

It became too much for him to bear, there on his mat. He carefully rose to his feet and padded over to the flop's door. Drivers weren't allowed out of the flop at night, but some of the boys were able to sneak out from time to time, mostly to scavenge for food scraps or whatever else they could find. Itchy had even found a mouse (some said a rat) once that they'd tried to train before it had run off.

Carefully, Ravi slipped through the doorway and down the stairs. He crept along the hallways, stopping whenever he heard footsteps. The boots that the minders and the other staff wore heralded their appearance. Meanwhile, his bare feet made almost no noise.

He headed for where he had once been told the tele-golly was. There, maybe he would find answers. He slipped through hallway after hallway, often ducking into doorways or around corners to avoid detection.

At last he came to the door that was supposed to lead out of their part of the facility. Beyond lay the girls' quarters as well as the tele-golly. None of the drivers had ever seen beyond this door.

He reached a trembling, thin hand out to the handle.

Then fingers gripped his shoulder and he jumped, his heart beating impossibly fast. He shook so much he thought he would explode.

He looked back into the face of Magus Sharpe.

Sharpe grabbed him firmly by the hand and dragged him down the hallway. Ravi could barely hear, could barely think over the sound of his heart pounding, the beats reverberating through his body. His skin flushed with blood and heat, and he followed without a struggle.

He was caught.

Magus Sharpe opened a door and pushed him inside. Then closed it behind him. Ravi huddled on the ground, his arms up, waiting for the blows to fall.

"What were you doing?" the magus demanded.

"I was... I was looking for the tele-golly."

"Why?"

Ravi could not meet the magus's eyes. "I just—"

Sharpe bent down until he was level with Ravi and gripped him by the shoulders. "Why?"

Ravi squeezed his eyes shut. Some of the boys said the magus had powers other than those that joined boys to gollies.

"Ravi," Sharpe said.

"I was looking for a letter," Ravi blurted.

Sharpe frowned, then let Ravi go. "One of yours?"

"Anyone's," Ravi said. "I wanted to see what it said."

Sharpe narrowed his eyes. "You know, don't you? About the letters."

Ravi remained silent. He had said too much.

Magus Sharpe seemed lost in other thoughts. Then his eyes snapped back to Ravi. "You're right," he said. "The letters aren't real. They're written here. They're not from your families."

"What?" Ravi said. He couldn't believe the magus was telling him this.

"You're a clever one, Ravi," the magus said. He nodded. "You can help me."

"Help you how?"

"You are in a unique position right now, Ravi. Today you were linked to a new golly. One that's still here."

"Tomorrow they'll send it to the mines."

"I think not."

"Why?"

"Tomorrow the Archmagus visits."

"I don't understand," Ravi said.

"You know that something is wrong here," Sharpe said. "You know about the letters. Doesn't it make you want to stop all of this? I've been working, with others, to stop it."

"The mining?"

"The whole system. The primosite. The Imperium. Every day boys and girls like you are being stolen from their families. No stipends are being sent to them. They bring you to places like this where they work you—on the gollies or on other machines. But it wears you down. Most golly drivers don't live to manhood. Eventually it will drain you enough that it will kill you. And then another boy will take your place."

"I don't believe you," Ravi said.

"It's true," the man said. "I could show you a room where they bring those boys too worn down by this. The younger you are, the easier it is, but as you age, it takes more and more out of you. Which is why they need an endless supply of children."

Ravi shook his head. They were supposed to be freed if they worked hard enough. Given pensions. Freedom to return to their families. Or else respected jobs in the Imperium. But he thought about all of the faces of the minders and the overseers. They were pale faces. The only brown he saw was the skin of the other boys.

Cold settled into the pit of Ravi's stomach. This secret was big. Too big. He was in danger. "Please," he said. "Let me go back. I won't say anything to anyone."

Sharpe shook his head. "Don't you see, Ravi? This needs to be stopped. And I can only do so much from the inside. I need your help. Your help to make things change. To make them better for boys like you."

Ravi thought of Noosa, thought of his younger cousins back home. "What can I do?" Ravi asked. "I'm just a driver."

"Exactly," Sharpe said.

Sharpe took Ravi to another room. This one was large and painted all over—floors, ceiling, and walls—with symbols much like those on the transfer crowns. Standing in a large circle was a golly. Ravi couldn't help staring at it. It looked different through his own eyes. Its brassy body was massive. Two thick legs held it up and the two powerful arms sprang from the torso like tree branches. The goggle-like eyes lent it a serious look.

"This is where I form the links," Magus Sharpe said. "Earlier today, I linked you to your new golly."

"How?" Ravi asked.

"The particulars would take too long to explain, but there's a ritual. And…it requires your brain tissue."

"What?" Ravi said.

Sharpe looked at him, then away. "That's how the link is created. We take a piece of your brain, and they put it in the golly. It's how control is established."

Ravi rubbed at the new bandage on the back of his head. "They took part of my brain?"

"They do it to all of you," Sharpe said. "Every one."

And they did it to me twice, Ravi thought. Sharpe held out the crown. "We can see if you can make the transfer."

"What about the chair? And the machines?"

Sharpe shook his head. "The chair just facilitates the transfer. The only necessary element is the crown. It is made with a primosite alloy."

Ravi let Sharpe place the crown on his head. A moment later he was seeing through the eyes of the golly. He moved the head down, looking at the top of Magus Sharpe's head. Then he saw himself lying on the floor. Was he really that thin? His long, brown limbs crossed over his bony chest. His mop of black hair fell in a messy heap around his head. The magus's words from earlier came back to him—about the boys dying. All of them.

He spoke and saw his mouth move. "I want to see what happened to Atul," he said.

The magus shook his head and moved to the crown, ready to remove it.

Ravi moved the golly toward Sharpe, blocking his body. "Show me."

Sharpe gritted his teeth. Then nodded. "But first you have to come back."

Ravi pulled the golly away, and a moment later he was back in his body, the magus holding the crown. "Follow me," he said.

Magus Sharpe led him through corridors and rooms unfamiliar to him. The boys were not allowed in these. Sharpe wheeled out a long cart with a blanket on it. "Get on," he said. "And be quiet."

Ravi did so, and the magus wheeled him farther into the corridors. They turned once, then again, and he heard a door opening. Then they stopped, and Sharpe pulled the blanket down from his face. Ravi sat up to see rows and rows of long metal tables. The room was cold, too. He could see his breath puff out in front of him, and his skin bubbled with gooseflesh.

Sharpe pushed Ravi to a wall of small, square metal doors. The magus looked at him with his piercing eyes, then opened one of the doors. He pulled out a long tray upon which was a boy—all brown skin and gangly limbs. He was dead. It was Suresh, the driver who had had the fit. Ravi walked to the next door and opened it, pulled out the tray. Another boy who had supposedly moved on.

"They are brought here when they start to fail," the magus said. "The minders make up some story about them moving on, but the truth is that your bodies just can't handle it. All that primosite energy. They use boys like you because you work best with the transfers, but it also burns you down like a candle."

Ravi thought of all the boys in his village who had been sent to places like this. All the other villages in Drina, in Arvind, in Chand. And maybe other places, too, where the Imperium had spread. So many children. They could always bring in more.

"It's an evil system," Magus Sharpe said. "And the Archmagus is one of the men behind it. He helped develop the binding, using the brain tissue to link you to the gollies. He's the one who produced the crowns. He is one of the men who must be stopped."

"What do you want me to do?" Ravi said. Tears had begun to well in his eyes. He clenched his fists at his side, thinking of all the boys who had been brought to the room, thinking of Atul, of his mother and father and the dreams that they had for their children.

"I want you to kill the Archmagus," Sharpe said.

The morning of the Archmagus's visit, Ravi came down with a sudden illness. Sharpe had coached him what to say, what symptoms to give to Minder Charles. He moaned and twisted in the driving chair. Magus Sharpe, at the back of the room, quickly came over. "We can't have him like this, not with the visit today," Sharpe said. "I want him kept away from the Driving Room and from the Greeting Ceremony."

Minder Charles had acquiesced to the magus's wishes. Like everyone else in the whole facility, he seemed on edge and anxious for the Archmagus's arrival.

They sent Ravi to the infirmary, but not before Sharpe slipped him a primosite crown. Ravi hid it down his loose pants, then beneath the table when he arrived. To Ravi's surprise, Noosa was already there. "What's wrong?" he asked, wondering if Noosa was also in on the plan.

"I feel weak," Noosa said. His brown face was ashen, and dark circles ringed his eyes.

"Me, too," Ravi lied. So it was happening to Noosa, too. Ravi remembered the nosebleeds, the coughs, the headaches.

"Looks like I'm going to fall behind, too," Noosa said. He frowned. "One of us needs to get out of here. If I don't make it, you have to. This place is shit. It sucks the life from you."

"Noosa…," Ravi said. "Hold on." He went to check to make sure that no one was around, then told his friend everything. About the letters and what he'd been told by Magus Sharpe.

Noosa began by shaking his head, but then his face fell. "If you had told me this a week ago, I wouldn't have believed you. But now…" He slammed his fist against the cot. "Damn it! It's not fair."

"But if I can help to stop it…"

"Do you really think it will work? Can you trust him?"

"I don't know," Ravi said. "What other choice do I have?"

An attendant soon came in to give them a draught of medicine, then returned to other duties. Noosa was about to take his when Ravi snatched it from his hand and shook his head. He poured both draughts down the privy. "You need to stay awake," he said. Whatever happened, he knew that he had to get Noosa out with him before he died. "Just rest," Ravi said. "I need to go do something, but I'll come back."

For the first time since he had been taken from his home, for the first time since becoming a golly driver, things were utterly quiet. It was almost peaceful. But the thought of what he must do roiled within him.

Magus Sharpe had drilled the map of the facility into him. "You must get to the Hall where the ceremony is taking place. It will be guarded, but they won't be able to stop you in your golly. You must dispatch the guards quickly and make your way into the Hall. They will try to stop you. And they will have weapons. But remember: You won't be there; your golly will. It's strong and it's tough, and you should be able to make it to the Archmagus. Remember, this is the man behind much of what happens here. He is responsible for your brother's death and all the others. He deserves this."

Ravi had nodded, but the thought of it had kept him up for most of the night. Could he really kill a man? Even a man who had been partially responsible for Atul's death? Thinking of Atul made the tears come, and his fists would clench and he would tell himself that yes, the man should die. But then, after some time, doubt would creep in again.

He wondered what would happen afterward. After he killed the Archmagus, they would surely know that it was his golly. They would search for him. Magus Sharpe had assured him that he would help Ravi escape, but would he be able to? And where would he go? What would become of Magus Sharpe? And what of the other drivers? Would they be sent back into their gollies as if nothing had happened?

He realized with a chill that he still didn't know much about Magus Sharpe or his friends. He'd said they aimed to bring down the system, but what did that mean for the drivers? Would they matter? Would they be sacrificed? Would he? He didn't have any answers.

He ran the map through his head again. His golly had been

positioned to make it easier for him to reach the Hall. Assuming everyone was in the Hall as they were expected to be, no one would notice him until he was upon them.

He rose from his cot and checked to make sure that he was alone. The place was deadly still.

He took out the crown that Sharpe had slipped him. It was a simple metal band sized to fit his head, engraved with symbols that enabled the transfer to happen. The only problem was that he wouldn't be able to remove the crown once it was on. He would stay in the golly until someone took it off. Hopefully, Sharpe would find him first. If not…

He thought about where he should be when he made the transfer. In his cot? Or somewhere else? If somewhere else, how would Sharpe find him? They hadn't discussed it. Ravi felt a tightening in his throat.

With the crown in one sweaty hand, Ravi crept out of the infirmary and up the hallway. He listened as hard as he could for any sound, but all was silence. The map of the facility was still fresh in his head. He made his way to the room that Sharpe had taken him to, where his golly was. There, at its feet, he lay down and placed the crown on his head. Before his hands had even fallen, he was in the golly. Once more he looked down at himself, at the collection of brown sticks that was his body. Such a fragile thing. He could imagine using the golly's powerful arms to crush the life from the Archmagus. To tear him apart. He could crush rock—flesh and bone would be nothing to him.

It would certainly get people's attention. The Archmagus's death would even be heard of in Drina, if the Imperium let the word get out. And Sharpe's Resistance would make themselves known. But Ravi could only think of the other drivers. Poor Noosa and the others. Did Sharpe really care for them? The Imperium's path was wrong—he knew that now—but did that make Sharpe's path better?

Ravi bent the golly down and, carefully using its arms, lifted his body. It was remarkably light. Lighter than he would have imagined.

Then he moved the golly out of the room. To his right was the corridor leading to the Hall and the Archmagus. Ravi turned left, driving the golly down the corridor, back to the infirmary. But the golly wouldn't fit through the door, and the powerful arms of the construct weren't delicate enough to remove the crown from his body without crushing his head. Ravi realized the vulnerability of his situation. He tapped at the door to the infirmary, but there was no answer.

"What are you doing?" Ravi heard, the noise registering in his human ears. He turned the golly to see Magus Sharpe, his familiar scowl now returned.

"I want to save Noosa as well," Ravi said.

"We don't have time for this. We're too close. Put your body down and get ready to do what we agreed."

"What happens to Noosa?" Ravi said. "What happens to the others?"

"Don't you want to stop the system?" Sharpe said.

"But will it? Won't they just appoint another Archmagus? And what if they choose to punish everyone here?"

"You just have to have faith and trust me," Sharpe said, his face softening.

Something clicked into place inside of Ravi. "That's just it. I don't."

Sharpe's face turned hard. "If you don't cooperate, I'll send the Archmagus's guards after you. Noosa, too. I don't want to, but this is too important. This is bigger than you and your friends."

A brown streak moved across the golly's field of vision. Noosa. He held a metal instrument in his hand, and he swung at Magus Sharpe's head. Only, weak as he was, it fell short and instead glanced off the man's shoulder.

Sharpe turned and smacked Noosa hard, sending him careening into the wall. Noosa hit with a cracking sound, then crumpled to the ground like a bag of twigs.

Ravi moved the golly forward.

"Wait!" Sharpe held up his hands. "Let me check on him." He moved over to Noosa's still form, bending over him. He stood up and faced the golly. "I'm sorry," he said. "I never wanted this to happen."

Even through the golly's eyes Ravi could read the expression on Magus Sharpe's face. Noosa was dead.

Horror, sadness, and most of all rage flooded into him and through the link, as if the golly was filled with nothing but a chaotic flux of emotions.

Ravi moved the golly forward, his anger directed at Magus Sharpe, raising the cutting arm. Sharpe turned to move, but the golly's arms were long, and Ravi had already set them in motion.

The arm moved through the air, straight for Sharpe's head, and Ravi could imagine it cutting into it like a ripe melon. He wanted Sharpe to pay. Wanted to kill him the way he had killed Noosa.

At the last minute, though, he diverted the arm, sending it into the wall instead, tearing a huge chunk out in a shower of dust. He wanted Sharpe to pay, wanted the Archmagus to pay, but he couldn't bring himself to kill them. Who knew what that would set in motion?

He saw movement at the end of the hallway: guards reacting to the sound of the broken wall. Sharpe was already moving toward them. Running to safety with other white faces.

Still burning with fury, Ravi turned the golly and pushed it as fast as he could down the hallway to where the map had indicated an exit.

The door was closed, locked, but carefully holding his body in one golly arm, he pushed at the door with the other, and with a screech of metal, it tore outward. The guards stationed outside went scurrying for safety. They were equipped to fight off people, not gollies. Still, he held one arm protectively over his body.

More guards came forward, taking up positions near the perimeter fence. They raised weapons and fired at him. Cracks filled the air, then pings as the bullets bounced off the golly's skin. Being careful to protect his body, he walked right through the gunfire, cutting through the stone perimeter fence as easily as he cut rock. Then he collapsed the fence behind him to discourage pursuit.

The sun was bright outside the facility. Through the golly's eyes, Ravi could see grassy fields and hills in the distance. He didn't know where he was—somewhere in the countryside—but out there was freedom. But not just for him. Somehow there had to be freedom for them all.

Together, Ravi and the golly moved off into the daylight to find it.

Solitude

by Ursula K. Le Guin

My mother, a field ethnologist, took the difficulty of learning anything about the people of Eleven-Soro as a personal challenge. The fact that she used her children to meet that challenge might be seen as selfishness of selflessness. Now that I have read her report I know that she finally thought she had done wrong. Knowing what it cost her, I wish she knew my gratitude of her for allowing me to grow up as a person.

Shortly after a robot probe reported people of the Hainish Descent on the eleventh planet of the Soro system, she joined the orbital crew as back-up for the three First Observers down on-planet. She had spent four years in the tree-cities nearby Huthu. My brother In Joy Born was eight years old and I was five; she wanted a year or two of ship duty so we could spend some time in a Hainish-style school. My brother had enjoyed the rainforests of Huthu very much, but though he could brachiate he could barely read, and we were all bright blue with skin-fungus. While Borny learned to read and I learned to wear clothes and we all had antifungus treatments, my mother became as intrigued by Eleven-Soro as the Observers were frustrated by it.

All this is in her report, but I will say it as I learned it from her, which helps me remember and understand. The language had been recorded by the probe and the Observers had spent a year learning it. The many dialectical variations excused their accents and errors, and they reported that language was not a problem. Yet there was a communication problem. The two men found themselves isolated, faced with suspicion or hostility, unable to form any connection with the native men, all of whom lived in solitary houses as hermits or in pairs. Finding communities of adolescent males, they tried to make contact with them, but when they entered the territory of such a group the boys either fled or rushed desperately at them trying to kill them. The women, who lived in what they called "dispersed villages," drove them away with volleys of stones as soon as they came anywhere near the houses. "I believe," one of them reported, "that the only community activity of the Sorovians is throwing rocks at men."

Neither of them succeeded in having a conversation of more than three exchanges with a man. One of them mated with a woman who came by his camp; he reported that though she made unmistakable and insistent advances, she seemed disturbed by his attempts to converse, refused to answer his questions, and left him, he said, "as soon as she got what she came for."

The woman Observer was allowed to settle in an unused

268

house in a "village" (auntring) of seven houses. She made excellent observations of daily life, insofar as she could see any of it, and had several conversations with adult women and many with children; but she found that she was never asked into another woman's house, nor expected to help or ask for help in any work. Conversation concerning normal activities was unwelcome to the other women; the children, her only informants, called her Aunt Crazy-Jabber. Her aberrant behavior caused increasing distrust and dislike among the women, and they began to keep their children away from her. She left. "There's no way," she told my mother, "for an adult to learn anything. They don't ask questions, they don't answer questions. Whatever they learn, they learn when they're children."

Aha! said my mother to herself, looking at Borny and me. And she requested a family transfer to Eleven-Soro with Observer status. The Stabiles interviewed her extensively by ansible, and talked with Borny and even with me—I don't remember it, but she told me I told the Stabiles all about my new stockings—and agreed to her request. The ship was to stay in close orbit, with the previous Observers in the crew, and she was to keep radio contact with it, daily if possible.

I have a dim memory of the tree-city, and of playing with what must have been a kitten or a ghole-kit on the ship; but my first clear memories are of our house in auntring. It is half underground, half aboveground, with wattle-and-daub walls. Mother and I are standing outside it in the warm sunshine. Between us is a big mud puddle, into which Borny pours water from a basket; then he runs off to the creek to get more water. I muddle the mud with my hands, deliciously, till it is thick and smooth. I pick up a big double handful and slap it onto the walls where the sticks show through. Mother says, "That's good! That's right!" in our new language, and I realize that this is work, and I am doing it. I am repairing the house. I am making it right, doing it right. I am a competent person.

I have never doubted that, so long as I lived there.

We are inside the house at night, and Borny is talking to the ship on the radio, because he misses talking the old language, and anyway he is supposed to tell them stuff. Mother is making a basket and swearing at split reeds. I am singing a song to drown out Borny so nobody in the auntring hears him talking funny, and anyway I like singing. I learned this song this afternoon in Hyuru's house. I play every day with Hyuru. "Be aware, listen, listen, be aware," I sing. When Mother stops swearing she listens, and then she turns on the recorder. There is a little fire still left from cooking dinner, which was lovly pigi root, I never get tired of pigi. It is dark and warm and smells of pigi and of burning duhur, which is a strong, sacred smell to drive out magic and bad feelings, and as I sing "Listen, be aware," I get sleepier and sleepier and lean against Mother, who is dark and warm and smells like Mother, strong and sacred, full of good feelings.

Our daily life in the auntring was repetitive. On the ship, later, I learned that people who live in artificially complicated situations call such a life "simple." I never knew anybody, anywhere I have been who found life simple. I think a life or a time looks simple when you leave out the details, the way a planet looks smooth, from orbit.

Certainly our life in the auntring was easy, in the sense that our needs came easily to hand. There was plenty of food to be gathered or grown and prepared and cooked, plenty of temas to pick and rett and spin and weave for clothes and bedding, plenty of reeds to make baskets and thatch with; we children and other children to play with, mothers to look after us, and a great deal to learn. None of this is simple, though it's all easy enough, when you are aware of the details.

It was not easy for my mother. It was hard for her, and complicated. She had to pretend she knew the details while she was learning them, and had to think how to report and explain this way of living to people in another place who didn't understand it. For Borny it was easy until it got hard because he was a boy. For me it was all easy. I learned the work and played with the children and listened to the mothers sing.

The First Observer had been quite right: there was no way for a grown woman to learn how to make her soul. Mother couldn't go listen to another mother sing, it would have been too strange. The aunts all knew she hadn't been brought up well, and some of them taught her a good deal without her realizing it. They had decided her mother must have been irresponsible and had gone on scouting instead of settling in an auntring, so that her daughter didn't get educated properly. That's why even the most aloof of the aunts always let me listen with their children, so that I could become an educated person. But of course they couldn't ask another adult into their houses. Borny and I had to tell her all the songs and stories we learned, and then she would tell them to the radio, or we told them to the radio while she listened to us. But she never got it right, not really. How could she, trying to learn it after she'd grown up, and after she'd always lived with magicians?

"Be aware!" She would imitate my solemn and probably irritating imitation of the aunts and the big girls. "Be aware! How many times a day do they say that? Be aware of what? They aren't aware of *what* the ruins are, their own history—they aren't aware of each other! They don't even talk to each other! Be aware, indeed!"

When I told her the stories of the Before Time that Aunt Sadne and Aunt Noyit told their daughters and me, she often heard the wrong things in them. I told her about the people, and she said, "Those are the ancestors of the people here now." When I said, "There aren't any people here now," she didn't understand. "There are persons here now," I said, but she still didn't understand.

Borny liked the story about the Man Who Lived with Women, how he kept some women in a pen, the way some persons keep rats in a pen for eating, and all of them got pregnant, and they each had a hundred little babies, and the babies grew up as horrible monsters and ate the man and the mothers and each other. Mother explained to us that that was a parable of the human overpopulation of this planet thousands of years ago. "No, it's not," I said, "it's a moral story."—"Well, yes," Mother said. "The moral is, don't have too many babies."—"No, it's not," I said. "Who could have a hundred babies even if they wanted to? The man was a sorcerer. He did magic. The woman did it with him. So of course their children were monsters."

The key, of course, is the word *tekell*, which translates so nicely into the Hainish word *magic*, an art or power that violates natural law. It was hard for Mother to understand that some persons truly consider most human relationships unnatural; that marriage, for instance, or government, can be seen as an evil spell woven by sorcerers. It is hard for her people to believe in magic.

The ship kept asking if we were all right, and every now and then a Stabile would hook up the ansible to our radio and grill Mother and us. She always convinced them that she wanted to stay, for despite her frustrations, she was doing the work the First Observers had not been able to do, and Borny and I were happy as mudfish, all those first years. I think Mother was happy too, once she got used to the slow pace and indirect way she had to learn things. She was lonely, missing other grown-ups to talk to, and told us that she would have gone crazy without us. If she missed sex she never showed it. I think, though, that her report is not very complete about sexual matters, perhaps because she was troubled by them. I know that when we first lived in the auntring, two of the aunts, Hedimi and Behyu, used to meet to make love, and Behyu courted my mother; but Mother didn't understand, because Behyu wouldn't talk the way Mother wanted to talk. She couldn't understand having sex with a person whose house you wouldn't enter.

Once when I was nine or so, and had been listening to some of the older girls, I asked her why didn't she go out scouting. "Aunt Sadne would look after us," I said, hopefully. I was tired of being the uneducated woman's daughter. I wanted to live in Aunt Sadne's house and be just like the other children.

"Mothers don't scout," she said, scornfully, like an aunt.

"Yes, they do, sometimes," I insisted. "They have to, or how could they have more than one baby?"

"They go to settled men near the auntring. Behyu went back to the Red Knob Hill Man when she wanted a second child. Sadne goes and sees Downriver Lame Man when she wants to have sex. They know the men around here. None of the mothers scout."

I realized that in this case she was right and I was wrong, but I stuck to my point. "Well, why don't you go see Downriver Lame Man? Don't you ever want sex? Migi says she wants it all the time."

"Migi is seventeen," Mother said dryly. "Mind your own nose." She sounded exactly like all the other mothers.

Men, during my childhood, were a kind of uninteresting mystery to me. They turned up a lot in the Before Time stories, and the singing-circle girls talked about them; but I seldom saw any of them. Sometimes I'd glimpse one when I was foraging, but they never came near the auntring. In summer the Downriver Lame Man would get lonesome waiting for Aunt Sadne and would come lurking around, not very far from the auntring— not in the bush or down by the river, of course, where he might be mistaken for a rogue or stoned—but out in the open, on the hillsides, where we could all see who he was. Hyuru and Didsu, Aunt Sadne's daughters, said she had had sex with him when she went out scouting the first time, and always had sex with him and never tried any of the other men of the settlement.

She had told them, too, that the first child she bore was a boy, and she drowned it, because she didn't want to bring up a boy and send him away. They felt queer about that and so did I, but it wasn't an uncommon thing. One of the stories we learned was about a drowned boy who grew up underwater, and seized his mother when she came to bathe, and tried to hold her under till she too drowned; but she escaped.

At any rate, after the Downriver Lame man had sat around

for several days on the hillsides, singing long songs and braiding and unbraiding his hair, which was long too, and shone black in the sun, Aunt Sadne always went off for a night or two with him, and came back looking cross and self-conscious.

Aunt Noyit explained to me that Downriver Lame Man's songs were magic; not the usual bad magic, but what she called the great good spells. Aunt Sadne never could resist his spells. "But he hasn't half the charm of some men I've known," said Aunt Noyit, smiling reminiscently.

Our diet, though excellent, was very low in fat, which Mother thought might explain the rather late onset of puberty; girls seldom menstruated before they were fifteen, and boys often weren't mature till they were considerably older than that. But the women began looking askance at boys as soon as they showed any signs at all of adolescence. First Aunt Hedimi, who was always grim, then Aunt Noyit, then even Aunt Sadne began to turn away from Borny, to leave him out, not answering when he spoke. "What are you doing playing with the children?" old Aunt Dnemi asked him so fiercely that he came home in tears. He was not quite fourteen.

Sadne's younger daughter Hyuru was my soulmate, my best friend, you would say. Her elder sister Didsu, who was in the singing circle now, came and talked to me one day, looking serious. "Borny is very handsome," she said. I agreed proudly.

"Very big, very strong," she said, "stronger than I am."

I agreed proudly again, and then I began to back away from her.

"Yes you are," I said, "I'll tell your mother!"

Didsu shook her head. "I'm trying to speak truly. If my fear causes your fear, I can't help it. It has to be so. We talked about it in the singing circle. I don't like it," she said, and I knew she meant it; she had a soft face, soft eyes, she had always been the gentlest of us children. "I wish he could be a child," she said. "I wish I could. But we can't."

"Go be a stupid old woman, then," I said, and ran away from her. I went to my secret place down by the river and cried. I took the holies out of my soulbag and arranged them. One holy—it doesn't matter if I tell you—was a crystal that Borny had given me, clear at the top, cloudy purple at the base. I held it a long time and then I gave it back. I dug a hole under a boulder, and wrapped the holy in duhur leaves inside a square of cloth I tore out of my kilt, beautiful, fine cloth Hyuru had woven and sewn for me. I tore the square right from the front, where it would show. I gave the crystal back, and then sat a long time there near it. When I went home I said nothing of what Didsu had said. But Borny was very silent, and my mother had a worried look. "What have you done to your kilt, Ren?" she asked. I raised my head a little and did not answer; she started to speak again, and then did not. She had finally learned not to talk to a person who chose to be silent.

Borny didn't have a soulmate, but he had been playing more and more often with the two boys nearest his age, Ednede who was a year or two older, a slight, quiet boy, and Bit who was only eleven, but boisterous and reckless. The three of them went off somewhere all the time. I hadn't paid much attention, partly because I was glad to be rid of Bit. Hyuru and I had been practicing being aware, and it was tiresome to always have to be aware of Bit yelling and jumping around. He never could leave anyone quiet, as if their quietness took something from him. His mother, Hedimi, had educated him, but she wasn't a good singer or storyteller like Sadne and Noyit, and Bit was too restless to listen even to them. Whenever he saw me and Hyuru trying to slow-walk or sitting being aware, he hung around making noise till we got mad and told him to go, and then he jeered, "Dumb girls!"

I asked Borny what he and Bit and Ednede did, and he said, "Boy stuff."

"Like what?"

"Practicing."

"Being aware?"

After a while he said, "No."

"Practicing what, then?"

"Wrestling. Getting strong. For the boygroup." He looked gloomy, but after a while he said, "Look," and showed me a knife he had hidden under his mattress. "Ednede says you have to have a knife, then nobody will challenge you. Isn't it a beauty?" It was metal, old metal from the People, shaped like a reed, pounded out and sharpened down both edges, with a sharp point. A piece of polished flint-shrub wood had been bored and fitted on the handle to protect the hand. "I found it in an empty man's-house," he said. "I made the wooden part." He brooded over it lovingly. Yet he did not keep it in his soulbag.

"What do you *do* with it?" I asked, wondering why both edges were sharp, so you'd cut your hand if you used it.

"Keep off attackers," he said.

"Where was the empty man's-house?'"

"Way over across Rocky Top."

"Can I go with you if you go back?"

"No," he said, not unkindly, but absolutely.

"What happened to the man? Did he die?"

"There was a skull in the creek. We think he slipped and drowned."

He didn't sound quite like Borny. There was something in his voice like a grown-up; melancholy; reserved. I had gone to him for reassurance, but came away more deeply anxious. I went to Mother and asked her, "What do they do in the boygroups?"

"Perform natural selection," she said, not in my language but in hers, in a strained tone. I didn't always understand Hainish anymore and had no idea what she meant, but the tone of her voice upset me; and to my horror I saw she had begun to cry silently. "We have to move, Serenity," she said—she was still talking Hainish without realizing it. "There isn't any reason why a family can't move, is there? Women just move in and move out as they please. Nobody cares what anybody does. Nothing is anybody's business. Except hounding the boys out of town!"

I understood most of what she said, but got her to say it in my language; and then I said, "But anywhere we went, Borny would be the same age, and size and everything."

"Then we'll leave," she said fiercely. "Go back to the ship."

I drew away from her. I had never been afraid of her before: she had never used magic on me. A mother has great power, but there is nothing unnatural in it, unless it is used against the child's soul.

Borny had no fear of her. He had his own magic. When she told him she intended leaving, he persuaded her out of it. He wanted to go join the boygroup, he said; he'd been wanting to for a year now. He didn't belong in the auntring any more, all women and girls and little kids. He wanted to go live with other boys. Bit's older brother Yit was a member of the boygroup in the Four Rivers Territory, and would look after a boy from his auntring. And Ednede was getting ready to go. And Borny and Ednede and Bit had been talking to some men, recently. Men weren't all ignorant and crazy, the way Mother thought. They didn't talk much, but they knew a lot.

"What do they know?" Mother asked grimly.

"They know how to be men," Borny said. "It's what I'm going to be."

"Not that kind of man—not if I can help it! In Joy Born, you must remember the men on the ship, real men—nothing like these poor, filthy hermits. I can't let you grow up thinking that that's what you have to be!"

"They're not like that," Borny said. "You ought to go talk to some of them, Mother."

"Don't be naïve," she said with an edgy laugh. "You know perfectly well that women don't go to men and *talk*."

I knew she was wrong; all the women in the auntring knew all the settled men for three days' walk around. They did talk with them when they were out foraging. They only kept away from the ones they didn't trust; and usually those men disappeared before long. Noyit had told me, "Their magic turns on them." She meant the other men drove them away or killed them. But I didn't say any of this, and Borny said only, "Well, Cave Cliff Man is really nice. And he took us to the place where I found those People things"—some ancient artifacts that Mother had been excited about. "The men know things the women don't," Borny went on. "At least I could go to the boygroup for a while, maybe.

I ought to. I could learn a lot! We don't have any solid information on them at all. All we know anything about is this auntring. I'll go and stay long enough to get material for our report. I can't ever come back to either the auntring or the boygroup once I leave them. I'll have to go to the ship, or else try to be a man. So let me have a real go at it, please, Mother?"

"I don't know why you think you have to learn how to be a man," she said after a while. "You know how already."

He really smiled then, and she put her arm around him.

What about me? I thought. I don't even know what the ship is. I want to be here, where my soul is. I want to go on learning to be in the world.

But I was afraid of Mother and Borny, who were both working magic, and so I said nothing and was still, as I had been taught.

Ednede and Borny went off together. Noyit, Ednede's mother, was as glad as Mother was about their keeping company, though she had said nothing. The evening before they left, the two boys went to every house in the auntring. It took a long time. The houses were each just within sight or hearing of one or two of the others, with bush and gardens and irrigation ditches and paths in between. In each house the mother and the children were waiting to say good-bye, only they didn't say it; my language has no word for *hello* or *good-bye*. They asked the boys in and gave them something to eat, something they could take with them on the way to the Territory. When the boys went to the door everybody in the household came and touched their hand or cheek. I remembered when Yit had gone around the auntring that way. I had cried then, because even though I didn't much like Yit, it seemed so strange for somebody to leave forever, like they were dying. This time I didn't cry; but I kept waking and waking again, until I heard Borny get up before the first light and pick up his things and leave quietly. I know Mother was awake, too, but we did as we should do, and lay still while he left, and for a long time after.

I have read her description of what she calls "An adolescent male leaves the Auntring: a vestigial survival of ceremony."

She had wanted him to put a radio in his soulbag and get in touch with her at least occasionally. He had been unwilling. "I want to do it right, Mother. There's no use doing it if I don't do it right."

"I simply can't handle not hearing from you at all, Borny," she had said in Hainish.

"But if the radio got broken or taken or something, you'd worry a lot more, maybe with no reason at all."

She finally agreed to wait half a year, till the first rain; then she would go to a landmark, a huge ruin near the river that marked the southern end of the Territory, and he would try and come to her there. "But only wait ten days," he said. "If I can't come, I can't." She agreed. She was like a mother with a little baby, I thought, saying yes to everything. That seemed wrong to me; but I thought Borny was right. Nobody ever came back to their mother from boygroup.

But Borny did.

Summer was long, clear, and beautiful. I was learning to star-watch; that is when you lie down outside on the open hills in the dry season at night, and find a certain star in the eastern sky, and watch it cross the sky till it sets. You can look away, of course, to rest your eyes, and doze, but you try to keep looking back at the star and the stars around it, until you feel the earth turning, until you become aware of how the stars and the world and the soul move together. After the certain star sets you sleep until dawn wakes you. Then as always you greet the sunrise with aware silence. I was very happy on the hills those warm great nights, those clear dawns. The first time or two Hyuru and I starwatched together, but after that we went alone, and it was better alone.

I was coming back from such a night, along the narrow valley between Rocky Top and Over Home Hill in the first sunlight, when a man came crashing through the bush down onto the path and stood in front of me. "Don't be afraid," he said. "Listen!" He was heavyset, half naked; he stank. I stood still as a stick. He had said "Listen!" just as the aunts did, and I listened. "Your brother and his friend are all right. Your mother shouldn't go there. Some of the boys are in a gang. They'd rape her. I and some others are killing the leaders. It takes a while. Your brother is with the other gang. He's all right. Tell her. Tell me what I said."

I repeated it word for word, as I had learned to do when I listened.

"Right. Good," he said, and took off up the steep slope on his short, powerful legs, and was gone.

Mother would have gone to the Territory right then, but I told the man's message to Noyit, too, and she came to the porch of our house to speak to Mother. I listened to her, because she was telling things I didn't know well and Mother didn't know at all. Noyit was a small, mild woman, very like her son Ednede; she liked teaching and singing, so the children were always around her place. She saw Mother was getting ready for a journey. She said, "House on the Skyline Man says the boys are all right."

When she saw Mother wasn't listening, she went on; she pretended to be talking to me, because women don't teach women: "He says some of the men are breaking up the gang. They do that, when the boygroups get wicked. Sometimes there are magicians among them, leaders, older boys, even men who want to make a gang. The settled men will kill the magicians and make sure none of the boys gets hurt. When gangs come out of the Territories, nobody is safe. The settled men don't like that. They see to it that the auntring is safe. So your brother will be all right."

My mother went on packing pigi-roots into her net.

"A rape is a very, very bad thing for the settled men," said Noyit to me. "It means the women won't come to them. If the boys raped some women, probably the men would kill *all* the boys."

My mother was finally listening.

She did not go to the rendezvous with Borny, but all through the rainy season she was utterly miserable. She got sick, and old Dnemi sent Didsu over to dose her with gagberry syrup. She made notes while she was sick, lying on her mattress, about illnesses and medicines and how the older girls had to look after sick women, since grown women did not enter one another's houses. She never stopped working and never stopped worrying about Borny.

Late in the rainy season, when the warm wind had come and the yellow honey-flowers were in bloom on all the hills, the Golden World time, Noyit came by while Mother was working in the garden. "House on the Skyline Man says things are all right in the boygroup," she said, and went on.

Mother began to realize then that although no adult ever

entered another's house, and adults seldom spoke to one another, and men and women had only brief, often casual relationships, and men lived all their lives in real solitude, still there was a kind of community, a wide, thin, fine network of delicate and certain intention and restraint: a social order. Her reports to the ship were filled with this new understanding. But she still found Sorovian life impoverished, seeing these persons as mere survivors, poor fragments of the wreck of something great.

"My dear," she said—in Hainish; there is no way to say "my dear" in my language. She was speaking Hainish with me in the house so that I wouldn't forget it entirely.—"My dear, the explanation of an uncomprehended technology as magic *is* primitivism. It's not a criticism, merely a description."

"But technology isn't magic," I said.

"Yes, it is, in their minds; look at the story you just recorded. Before-Time sorcerers who could fly in the air and undersea and underground in magic boxes!"

"In *metal* boxes," I corrected.

"In other words, airplanes, tunnels, submarines; a lost technology explained as supernatural."

"These *boxes* weren't magic," I said. "The *people* were. They were sorcerers. They used their power to get power over other persons. To live rightly a person has to keep away from magic."

"That's a cultural imperative, because a few thousand years ago uncontrolled technological expansion led to disaster. Exactly. There's a perfectly rational reason for the irrational taboo."

I did not know what *rational* and *irrational* meant in my language; I could not find words for them. *Taboo* was the same as *poisonous*. I listened to my mother because a daughter must learn

284

from her mother, and my mother knew many, many things no other person knew; but my education was very difficult, sometimes. If only there were more stories and songs in her teaching, and not so many words, words that slipped away from me like water through a net!

The Golden Time passed, and the beautiful summer; the Silver Time returned, when the mists lie in the valleys between the hills, before the rains begin; and the rains began, and fell long and slow and warm, day after day after day. We had heard nothing of Borny and Ednede for over a year. Then in the night the soft thrum of rain on the reed roof turned into a scratching at the door and a whisper, "Shh—it's all right—it's all right."

We wakened the fire and crouched at it in the dark to talk. Borny had got tall and very thin, like a skeleton with the skin dried on it. A cut across his upper lip had drawn it up into a kind of snarl that bared his teeth, and he could not say *p*, *b*, or *m*. His voice was a man's voice. He huddled at the fire trying to get warmth into his bones. His clothes were wet rags. The knife hung on a cord around his neck. "It was all right," he kept saying. "I don't want to go on there, though."

He would not tell us much about the year and a half in the boygroup, insisting that he would record a full description when he got to the ship. He did tell us what he would have to do if he stayed on Soro. He would have to go back to the Territory and hold his own among the older boys, by fear and sorcery, always proving his strength, until he was old enough to walk away— that is, to leave the Territory and wander alone till he found a place where the men would let him settle. Ednede and another boy had paired, and were going to walk away together when the rains stopped. It was easier for a pair, he said, if their bond was sexual; so long as they offered no competition for women, settled men wouldn't challenge them. But a new man in the region anywhere within three days' walk of an auntring had to prove himself against the settled men there. "It would 'e three or four years of the sa'e thing," he said, "challenging, fighting, always watching the others, on guard, showing how strong you are, staying alert all night, all day. To end up living alone your whole life. I can't do it." He looked at me. "I'ne not a 'erson," he said. "I want to go ho'e."

"I'll radio the ship now," Mother said quietly, with infinite relief.

"No," I said.

Borny was watching Mother, and raised his hand when she turned to speak to me.

"I'll go," he said. "She doesn't have to. Why should she?" Like me, he had learned not to use names without some reason to.

Mother looked from him to me and finally gave a kind of laugh. "I can't leave her here, Borny!"

"Why should you go?"

"Because I want to," she said. "I've had enough. More than enough. We've got a tremendous amount of material on the women, over seven years of it, and now you can fill the information gaps on the men's side. That's enough. It's time, past time, that we all got back to our own people. All of us."

"I have no people," I said. "I don't belong to people. I am trying to be a person. Why do you want to take me away from my soul? You want me to do magic! I won't. I won't do magic. I won't speak your language. I won't go with you!"

My mother was still not listening; she started to answer angrily. Borny put up his hand again, the way a woman does when she is going to sing, and she looked at him.

"We can talk later," he said. "We can decide. I need to slee."

He hid in our house for two days while we decided what to do and how to do it. That was a miserable time. I stayed home as if I were sick so that I would not lie to the other persons, and Borny and Mother and I talked and talked. Borny asked Mother to stay with me; I asked her to leave me with Sadne or Noyit, either of whom would certainly take me into their household. She refused. She was the mother and I the child and her power was sacred. She radioed the ship and arranged for a lander to pick us up in a barren area two days' walk from the auntring. We left at night, sneaking away. I carried nothing but my soulbag. We walked all next day, slept a little when it stopped raining, walked on and came to the desert. The ground was all lumps and hollows and caves, Before-Time ruins; the soil was tiny bits of glass and hard grains and fragments, the way it is in the deserts. Nothing grew there. We waited there.

The sky broke open and a shining thing fell down and stood before us on the rocks, bigger than any house, though not as big as the runs of the Before Time. My mother looked at me with a queer, vengeful smile. "Is it magic?" she said. And it was very hard for me not to think that it was. Yet I knew it was only a thing, and there is no magic in things, only in minds. I said nothing. I had not spoken since we left my home.

I had resolved never to speak to anybody until I got home again; but I was still a child, used to listen and obey. In the ship, that utterly strange new world, I held out only for a few hours, and then began to cry and ask to go home. Please, please, can I go home now.

Everyone on the ship was very kind to me.

Even though I thought about what Borny had been through and what I was going through, comparing our ordeals. The difference seemed total. He had been alone, without food, without shelter, a frightened boy trying to survive among equally frightened rivals against the brutality of older youths intent on having and keeping power, which they saw as manhood. I was cared for, clothed, fed, so richly I got sick, kept so warm I felt feverish, guided, reasoned with, praised, befriended by citizens of a very great city, offered a share in their power, which they saw as humanity. He and I had both fallen among sorcerers. Both he and I could see the good in the people we were among, but neither he nor I could live with them.

Borny told me he had spent many desolate nights in the Territory crouched in a fireless shelter, telling over the stories he had learned from the aunts, singing the songs in his head. I did the same thing every night on the ship. But I refused to tell the stories or sing to the people there. I would not speak my language, there. It was the only way I had to be silent.

My mother was enraged, and for a long time unforgiving. "You owe knowledge to our people," she said. I did not answer, because all I had to say was that they were not my people, that I had no people. I was a person. I had a language that I did not speak. I had my silence. I had nothing else.

I went to school; there were children of different ages on the ship, like an auntring, and many of the adults taught us. I learned

Ekumenical history and geography, mostly, and Mother gave me a report to learn about the history of Eleven-Soro, what my language calls the Before Time. I read that the cities of my world had been the greatest cities ever built on any world, covering two of the continents entirely, with small areas set aside for farming; there had been 120 billion people living in cities, while the animals and the sea and the air and the dirt died, until the people began dying too. It was a hideous story. I was ashamed of it and wished nobody else on the ship or in the Ekumen knew about it. And yet, I thought, if they knew the stories I know about the Before Time, they would understand how magic turns on itself, and that it must be so.

After less than a year, Mother told us we were going to Hain. The ship's doctor and his clever machines had repaired Borny's lip; he and Mother had put all the information they had into the records; he was old enough to begin training for the Ekumenical Schools, as he wanted to do. I was not flourishing, and the doctor's machines were not able to repair me. I kept losing weight, I slept badly, I had terrible headaches. Almost as soon as we came aboard the ship, I had begun to menstruate; each time the cramps were agonizing. "This is no good, this ship life," she said. "You need to be outdoors. On a planet. On a civilized planet."

"If I went to Hain, "I said, "when I came back, the persons I know would all be dead hundreds of years ago."

"Serenity," she said, "you must stop thinking in terms of Soro. We have left Soro. You must stop deluding and tormenting yourself, and look forward, not back. Your whole life is ahead of you. Hain is where you will learn to live it."

I summoned up my courage and spoke in my own language:

"I am not a child now. You have no power over me. I will not go. Go without me. You have no power over me!"

Those are the words I had been taught to say to a magician, a sorcerer. I don't know if my mother fully understood them, but she did understand that I was deathly afraid of her, and it struck her into silence.

After a long time she said in Hainish, "I agree. I have no power over you. But I have certain rights; the right of loyalty; of love."

"Nothing is right that puts me in your power," I said, still in my language.

She stared at me. "You are like one of them," she said. "You are one of them. You don't know what love is. You're closed into yourself like a rock. I should never have taken you there. People crouching in the ruins of a society—brutal, rigid, ignorant, superstitious—each one in a terrible solitude—and I let them make you into one of them!"

"You educated me," I said, and my voice began to tremble and my mouth to shake around the words, "and so does the school here, but my aunts educated me, and I want to finish my education." I was weeping, but I kept standing with my hands clenched. "I'm not a woman yet. I want to be a woman."

"But Ren, you will be!—ten times the woman you could ever be on Soro—you must try to understand, to believe me—"

"You have no power over me," I said, shutting my eyes and putting my hands over my ears. She came to me then and held me, but I stood stiff, enduring her touch, until she let me go.

The ship's crew had changed entirely while we were onplanet. The First Observers had gone on to other worlds; our backup was now a Gethenian archeologist named Arrem, a mild,

290

watchful person, not young. Arrem had gone down onplanet only on the two desert continents, and welcomed the chance to talk with us, who had "lived with the living," as heshe said. I felt easy when I was with Arrem, who was so unlike anybody else. Arrem was not a man—I could not get used to having men around all the time—yet not a woman; and so not exactly an adult, yet not a child: a person, alone, like me. When this crisis came, Arrem came to my mother and took counsel with her, suggesting that she let me go back down onplanet. Borny was in on some of these talks, and told me about them.

"Arrem says if you go to Hain you'll probably die," he said. "Your soul will. Heshe says some of what we learned is like what they learn on Gethen, in their religion. That kind of stopped Mother from ranting about primitive superstition.... And Arrem says you could be useful to Ekumen, if you stay and finish your education on Soro. You'll be an invaluable resource." Borny sniggered, and after a minute I did too. "They'll mine you like an asteroid," he said. Then he said, "You know, if you stay and I go, we'll be dead."

That was how the young people of the ships said it, when one was going to cross the light-years and the other was going to stay. Good-bye, we're dead. It was the truth.

"I know," I said. I felt my throat get tight, and was afraid. I had never seen an adult at home cry, except when Sut's baby died. Sut howled all night. Howled like a dog, Mother said, but I had never seen or heard a dog; I heard a woman terrible crying. I was afraid of sounding like that. "If I can go home, when I finish making my soul, who knows, I might come to Hain for a while," I said, in Hainish.

"Scouting?" Borny said in my language, and laughed, and made me laugh again.

Nobody gets to keep a brother. I knew that. But Borny had come back from being dead to me so I might come back from being dead to him; at least I could pretend I might.

My mother came to a decision. She and I would stay on the ship for another year while Borny went to Hain. I would keep going to school; if at the end of the year I was still determined to go back onplanet, I could do so. With me or without me, she would go on to Hain then and join Borny. If I ever wanted to see them again, I could follow them. It was a compromise that satisfied no one, but it was the best we could do, and we all consented.

When he left, Borny gave me his knife.

After he left, I tried not to be sick. I worked hard at learning everything they taught me in the ship school, and I tried to teach Arrem how to be aware and how to avoid witchcraft. We did slow-walking together in the ship's garden, and the first hour of the untrance movements from the Handdara of Karhide on Gethen. We agreed that they were alike.

The ship was staying in the Soro system not only because of my family, but because the crew was now mostly zoologists who had come to study a sea animal on Eleven-Soro, a kind of cephalopod that had mutated toward high intelligence, or maybe it already was highly intelligent; but there was a communication problem. "Almost as bad as with the local humans," said Steadiness, the zoologist who taught and teased us mercilessly. She took us down twice by lander to the uninhabited islands in the Northern Hemisphere where her station was. It was very strange to go down to my world and yet be a world away from my aunts and sisters and my soulmate; but I said nothing.

I saw the great, pale, shy creature come slowly up out of the deep waters with a running ripple of colors along its long coiling tentacles and ringing shimmer of sound, all so quick it was over before you could follow the colors or hear the tune. The zoologist's machine produced a pink glow and a mechanically speeded-up twitter, tinny and feeble in the immensity of the sea. The cephalopod patiently responded in its beautiful silvery shadowy language. "CP," Steadiness said to us, ironic—Communication Problem. "We don't know what we're talking about."

I said, "I learned something in my education here. In one of the songs, it says," and I hesitated, trying to translate it into Hainish, "it says, thinking is one way of doing, and words are one way of thinking."

Steadiness stared at me, in disapproval I thought, but probably only because I had never said anything to her before except "Yes." Finally she said, "Are you suggesting that it doesn't speak in words?"

"Maybe it's not speaking at all. Maybe it's thinking."

Steadiness stared at me some more and then said, "Thank you." She looked as if she too might be thinking. I wished I could sink into the water, the way the cephalopod was doing.

The other young people on the ship were friendly and mannerly. Those are words that have no translation in my language. I was unfriendly and unmannerly, and they let me be. I was grateful. But there was no place to be alone on the ship. Of course we each had a room; though small, the *Heyo* was a Hainish-built explorer, designed to give its people room and privacy and comfort and variety and beauty while they hung around in a solar system for years on end. But it was designed. It was all human-made—everything was human. I had much more privacy than I had ever had at home in our one-room house; yet there I had been free and here I was in a trap. I felt the pressure of people all around me, all the time. People around me, people with me, people pressing on me, pressing me to be one of them, to be one of them, one of the people. How could I make my soul? I could barely cling to it. I was in terror that I would lose it altogether.

One of the rocks in my soulbag, a little ugly gray rock that I had picked up on a certain day in a certain place in the hills above the river in the Silver Time, a little piece of my world, that became my world. Every night I took it out and held it in my hand while I lay in the bed waiting to sleep, thinking of the sunlight on the hills above the river, listening to the soft hushing of the ship's systems, like a mechanical sea.

The doctor hopefully fed me various tonics. Mother and I ate breakfast together every morning. She kept at work, making our notes from all the years on Eleven-Soro into her report to the Ekumen, but I knew the work did not go well. Her soul was in as much danger as mine was.

"You will never give in, will you, Ren?" she said to me one morning out of the silence of our breakfast. I had not intended the silence as a message. I had only rested in it.

"Mother, I want to go home and you want to go home," I said. "Can't we?"

Her expression was strange for a moment, while she misunderstood me; then it cleared to grief, defeat, relief.

"Will we be dead?" she asked me, her mouth twisting.

"I don't know. I have to make my soul. Then I can know if I can come."

"You know I can't come back. It's up to you."

"I know. Go see Borny," I said. "Go home. Here we're both dying." Then noises began to come out of me, sobbing, howling. Mother was crying. She came to me and held me, and I could hold my mother, cling to her and cry with her, because her spell was broken.

From the lander approaching I saw the oceans of Eleven-Soro and in the greatness of my joy I thought that when I was grown and went out alone I would go to the seashore and watch the sea-beasts shimmering in their colors and tunes till I knew what they were thinking. I would listen, I would learn, till my soul was as large as the shining world. The scarred barrens whirled beneath us, ruins as wide as the continent, endless desolations. We touched down. I had my soulbag, and Borny's knife around my neck on its string, a communication implant behind my right earlobe, and a medicine kit Mother had made for me, "No use dying of an infected finger, after all," she had said. The people on the lander said goodbye, but I forgot to. I set off out of the desert, home.

It was summer; the night was short and warm; I walked most of it. I got to the auntring about the middle of the second day. I went to my home cautiously, in case somebody had moved in while I was gone; but it was just as we had left it. The mattresses were moldy, and I put them and the bedding out in the sun, and started going over the garden to see what had kept growing by it-self. The pigi had got small and seedy, but there were some good roots. A little boy came by and stared; he had to be Migi's baby. After a while Hyuru came by. She squatted down near me in the garden in the sunshine. I smiled when I saw her, and she smiled, but it took us a while to find something to say.

"Your mother didn't come back," she said.

"She's dead," I said.

"I'm sorry," Hyuru said.

She watched me dig up another root.

"Will you come to the singing circle?" she asked.

I nodded.

She smiled again. With her rose brown skin and wide-set eyes, Hyuru had become very beautiful, but her smile was exactly the same as when we were little girls. "Hi, ya!" she sighed in deep contentment, lying down on the dirt with her chin on her arms. "This is good!"

I went on blissfully digging.

That year and the next two, I was in the singing circle with Hyuru and two other girls. Didsu still came to it often, and Han, a woman who settled in our auntring to have her first baby, joined it too. In the singing circle the older girls pass around the sto-ries, songs, knowledge they learned from their own mother, and young women who have lived in other auntrings teach what they learned there; so women make each other's souls, learning how to make their children's souls.

Han lived in the house where old Dnemi had died. Nobody in the auntring except Sut's baby had died while my family lived there. My mother had complained that she didn't have any data on death and burial. Sut had gone away with her dead baby and never came back, and nobody talked about it. I think that turned my mother against the others more than anything else. She was angry and ashamed that she could not go and try to comfort Sut and that nobody else did. "It is not human," she said. "It is pure animal behavior. Nothing could be clearer evidence that this is a broken culture—not a society, but the remains of one. A terrible, an appalling poverty."

I don't know if Dnemi's death would have changed her mind. Dnemi was dying for a long time, of kidney failure I think; she turned a kind of dark orange color, jaundice. While she could get around, nobody helped her. When she didn't come out of her house for a day or two, the women would send their children in with water and a little food and firewood. It went on so through the winter; then one morning little Rashi told his mother Aunt Dnemi was "staring." Several of the women went to Dnemi's house, and entered it for the first and last time. They sent for all the girls in the singing circle, so that we could learn what to do. We took turns sitting by the body or in the porch of the house, singing soft songs, child-songs, giving the soul a day and a night to leave the body and the house; then the older women wrapped the body in bedding, strapped it on a kind of litter, and set off with it toward the barren lands. There it would be given back, under a rock cairn or inside one of the ruins of the ancient city. "Those are the lands of the dead," Sadne said. "What dies stays there."

Han settled down in that house a year later. When her baby began to be born she asked Didsu to help her, and Hyuru and I stayed in the porch and watched, so that we could learn. It was a wonderful thing to see, and quite altered the course of my thinking, and Hyuru's too. Hyuru said, "I'd like to do that!" I said nothing, but thought, so do I, but not for a long time, because once you have a child you're never alone. And though it is of the others, of relationships, that I write, the heart of my life has been my being alone.

I think there is no way to write about being alone. To write is to tell something to somebody, to communicate to others. CP, as Steadiness would say. Solitude is non-communication, the absence of others, the presence of a self sufficient to itself.

A woman's solitude in the auntring is, of course, based firmly on the presence of others at a little distance. It is a contingent, and therefore human, solitude. The settled men are connected as stringently to the women, though not to one another; the settlement is an integral though distant element of the auntring. Even a scouting woman is part of the society—a moving part, connecting the settled parts. Only the isolation of a woman or man who chooses to live outside the settlements is absolute. They are outside the network altogether. There are worlds where such persons are called saints, holy people. Since isolation is a sure way to prevent magic, on my world the assumption is that they are sorcerers, outcast by others or by their own will, their conscience.

I knew I was strong with magic, how could I help it? and I began to long to get away. It would be so much easier and safer to be alone. But at the same time, and increasingly, I wanted to know something about the great harmless magic, the spells cast between men and women.

I preferred foraging to gardening, and was out on the hills

a good deal; and these days, instead of keeping away from the men's-houses, I wandered by them, and looked at them, and looked at the men if they were outside. The men looked back. Downriver Lame Man's long, shining hair was getting a little white in it now, but when he sat singing his long, long songs I found myself sitting down and listening, as if my legs had lost their bones. He was very handsome. So was the man I remembered as a boy named Tret in the auntring, when I was little, Behyu's son. He had come back from the boygroup and from wandering, and had built a house and made a fine garden in the valley of Red Stone Creek. He had a big nose and big eyes, long arms and legs, long hands; he moved very quietly, almost like Arrem doing the untrance. I went often to pick lowberries in Red Stone Creek Valley.

He came along the path and spoke. "You were Borny's sister," he said. He had a low voice, quiet.

"He's dead," I said.

Red Stone Man nodded. "That's his knife."

In my world, I had never talked with a man. I felt extremely strange. I kept picking berries.

"You're picking green ones," Red Stone Man said.

His soft, smiling voice made my legs lose their bones again.

"I think nobody's touched you," he said. "I'd touch you gently. I think about it, about you, ever since you came by here early in the summer. Look, here's a bush full of ripe ones. Those are green. Come over here."

I came closer to him, to the bush of ripe berries.

When I was on the ship, Arrem told me that many languages have a single word for sexual desire and the bond between mother and child and the bond between soulmates and the feeling for one's home and worship of the sacred; they are all called love. There is no word that great in my language. Maybe my mother is right, and human greatness perished in my world with the people of the Before Time, leaving only small, poor, broken things and thoughts. In my language, love is many different words. I learned one of them with Red Stone Man. We sang it together to each other.

We made a brush house on a little cove of the creek, and neglected our gardens, but gathered many, many sweet berries.

Mother had put a lifetime's worth of nonconceptives in the little medicine kit. She had no faith in Sorovian herbals. I did, and they worked.

But when a year or so later, in the Golden Time, I decided to go out scouting, I thought I might go places where the right herbs were scarce; and so I stuck the little noncon jewel on the back of my left earlobe. Then I wished I hadn't, because it seemed like witchcraft. Then I told myself I was being superstitious; the noncon wasn't any more witchcraft than the herbs were, it just worked longer. I had promised my mother in my soul that I would never be superstitious. The skin grew over the noncom, and I took off my soulbag and Borny's knife and the medicine kit, and set off across the world.

I had told Hyuru and Red Stone Man I would be leaving. Hyuru and I sang and talked together all one night down by the river. Red Stone Man said in his soft voice, "Why do you want to go?" and I said, "To get away from your magic, sorcerer," which was true in part. If I kept going to him I might always go to him. I wanted to give my soul a body of larger world to be in.

Now to tell of my scouting years is more difficult than ever. CP! A woman scouting is entirely alone, unless she chooses to ask a settled man for sex, or camps in an auntring for a while to sing and listen with the singing circle. If she goes anywhere near the territory of a boygroup, she is in danger; and if she comes on a rogue she is in danger; and if she hurts herself or gets into polluted country, she is in danger. She has no responsibility except to herself, and so much freedom is very dangerous.

In my right earlobe was the tiny communicator; every forty days, as I had promised, I sent a signal to the ship that meant "all well." If I had wanted to leave, I would send another signal. I could have called for the lander to rescue me from a bad situation, but though I was in bad situations a couple of times I never thought of using it. My signal was the mere fulfillment of a promise to my mother and her people, the network I was no longer part of, a meaningless communication.

Life in the auntring, or for a settled man, is repetitive, as I said; and so it can be dull. Nothing new happens. The mind always wants new happenings. So for the young soul there is wandering and scouting, travel, danger, change. But of course travel and danger and change have their own dullness. It is finally always the same otherness over again; another hill, another river, another man, another day. The feet begin to turn in a long, long circle. The body begins to think of what it learned back home, when it learned to be still. To be aware. To be aware of the grain of dust beneath the sole of the foot, and the skin of the sole of the foot, and the skin of the sole of the foot, and the touch and scent of the air on the cheek, and the fall and motion of the light across the air, and the color of the grass on the high hill across the river, and the thoughts of the body, of the soul, the shimmer and ripple of colors and sounds in the clear darkness of the depths, endlessly moving, endlessly changing, endlessly new.

So at last I came back home. I had been gone about four years.

Hyuru had moved into my old house when she left her mother's house. She had not gone scouting, but had taken to going to Red Stone Creek Valley; and she was pregnant. I was glad to see her living there. The only house empty was an old half-ruined one too close to Hedimi's. I decided to make a new house. I dug out the circle as deep as my chest; the digging took most of the summer. I cut the sticks, braced and wove them, and then daubed the framework solidly with mud inside and out. I remembered when I had done that with my mother long, long ago, and how she had said, "That's right. That's good." I left the roof open, and the hot sun of late summer baked the mud into clay. Before the rains came out, I thatched the house with reeds, a triple thatching, for I'd had enough of being wet all winter.

My auntring was more a string than a ring, stretching along the north bank of the river for about three kilos; my house lengthened the string a good bit, upstream from all the others. I could just see the smoke from Hyuru's fireplace. I dug it into a sunny slope with good drainage. It is still a good house.

I settled down. Some of my time went to gathering and gardening and mending and all the dull, repetitive actions of primitive life, and some went to singing and thinking the songs and stories I had learned here at home and while scouting, and the things I had learned on the ship, also. Soon enough I found why women are glad to have children come to listen to them, for songs and stories are meant to be heard, listened to. "Listen!" I would say to the children. The children of the auntring came and went, like the little fish in the river, one or two or five of them, little ones, big ones. When they came, I sang or told stories to them. When they left, I went on in silence. Sometimes I joined the singing circle to give what I had learned traveling to the older girls. And that was all I did; except that I worked, always, to be aware of all I did.

By solitude the soul escapes from doing or suffering magic; it escapes from dullness, from boredom, by being aware. Nothing is boring if you are aware of it. It may be irritating, but it is not boring. If it is pleasant the pleasure will not fail so long as you are aware of it. Being aware is the hardest work the soul can do, I think.

I helped Hyuru have her baby, a girl, and played with the baby. Then after a couple of years I took the noncom out of my left earlobe. Since it left a little hole, I made the hole go all the way through with a burnt needle, and when it healed I hung in it a tiny jewel I had found in a ruin when I was scouting. I had seen a man on the ship with a jewel hung in his ear that way. I wore it when I went out foraging. I kept clear of Red Stone Creek Valley. The man there behaved as if he had a claim on me, a right to me. I liked him still, but I did not like that smell of magic about him, his imagination of power over me. I went up into the hills, northward.

A pair of young men had settled in old North House about the time I came home. Often boys got through boygroup by pairing, and often they stayed paired when they left the Territory. It helped their chances of survival. Some of them were sexually paired, others weren't; some stayed paired, others didn't. One of

303

this pair had gone off with another man last summer. The one that stayed wasn't a handsome man, but I had noticed him. He had a kind of solidness I liked. His body and hands were short and strong. I had courted him a little, but he was very shy. This day, a day in the Silver Time when the mist lay on the river, he saw the jewel swinging in my ear, and his eyes widened.

"It's pretty, isn't it?" I said.

He nodded.

"I wore it to make you look at me," I said.

He was so shy that I finally said, "If you only like sex with men, you know, just tell me." I really was not sure.

"Oh, no," he said, "no. No." He stammered and then bolted back down the path. But he looked back; and I followed him slowly, still not certain whether he wanted me or wanted to be rid of me.

He waited for me in front of a little house in a grove of redroot, a lovely little bower, all leaves outside, so that you would walk within arm's length of it and not see it. Inside he had laid sweet grass, deep and dry and soft, smelling of summer. I went in, crawling because the door was very low, and sat in the summer-smelling grass. He stood outside. "Come in," I said, and he came in very slowly.

"I made it for you," he said.

"Now make a child for me," I said.

And we did that; maybe that day, maybe another.

Now I will tell you why after all these years I called the ship, not even knowing if it was still there in the space between the planets, asking for the lander to meet me in the barren land.

When my daughter was born, that was my heart's desire and

the fulfillment of my soul. When my son was born, last year, I knew there is no fulfillment. He will grow toward manhood, and go, and fight and endure, and live or die as a man must. My daughter, whose name is Yedneke, Leaf, like my mother, will grow to womanhood and go or stay as she chooses. I will live alone. This is as it should be, and my desire. But I am of two worlds; I am a person of this world, and a woman of my mother's people. I owe my knowledge to the children of her people. So I asked the lander to come, and spoke to the people on it. They gave me my mother's report to read, and I have written my story in their machine, making a record for those who want to learn one of the ways to make a soul. To them, to the children I say: Listen! Avoid magic! Be aware!

AFTERWORD

by Joe Monti

Mi abuelita, Lucia, passed away when she was ninety-six. She was Quichua—she grew up in the Chaco Mountains in Argentina. She moved to Buenos Aires, where she was brought to a wealthy Jewish immigrant family to be a handmaiden to their young daughter, who was about nine, like she was. Two of her seven older brothers also accompanied her to be groundsmen. They were sixteen and eighteen. This was the 1920s. Lucia knew three languages: Quichua, Spanish, and Yiddish. Lucia married *mi abuelito*, Francisco, whose family had immigrated to Argentina from Italy when he was ten.

My parents met at a dance. They had both emigrated to the United States months earlier, my father from a small town in Italy that was bombed accidentally by Americans during World War II and still retains echoes of Aeneas and the war he left behind. My mother knew some Italian, and my parents were able to find common ground at a church hall in the Bronx.

I look a lot like my mother, and as I'm pale with an Italian last name, no one looks further or expects to find anything more varied. I felt that way until I was in my teens. Yet the food and culture were always there from her side.

Now I'm married. My wife is Chinese American. Her parents emigrated to Queens. My wife and I met in high school in racially segregated Yonkers, New York. So my son can fill in a few boxes on forms.

While the specifics may be unique, this wonderful, blended, messed-up world is the one I know best and is very much what I see around me here on the East Coast. In 2009 a heated discussion on race in fantasy and science fiction was boiling up. This became known as RaceFail 09. A few months later, the discussion of whitewashing covers in young adult literature arose, initially from Justine Larbalestier's *Liar* but continued on in other examples and dovetailed with RaceFail. It was a reminder that even an industry as progressive and genial as publishing needed to get schooled. There was a lot more heated discussion, largely on the blogosphere, about the portrayal of race in teen literature and its effects on the fantasy and science fiction community.

Conflicts online tend to gravitate toward flame wars, and even though there were some very measured and smart responses being written, it was largely reactive. But the butterfly effect was happening. Whitewashed covers were changed, editors in publishing started looking for more books by people of color, and review attention increased. These are good foundations.

Yet when another incident arose from an ignorant essay by

a prominent writer, I was about to get online and rant, and instead called Toby Buckell and suggested we do something constructive and gather some of the writers we know and get them each to contribute a story to an anthology about a wonderful, blended, messed-up future not as a role model, but a touchstone. Having people of color/Caucasian/LGBT protagonists in stories by these writers is not a brick thrown at a window; it is the continued paving of a path.

We're contributing a portion of the money we're making here to the Carl Brandon Society's Octavia E. Butler Memorial Scholarship Fund to encourage new writers of color into the field by attending one of the Clarion writing workshops. It's like this: You may think that a grilled banana, peanut butter, bacon, and honey sandwich is not for you until you eat one. Then it's essential. Likewise a Chinese pork bun or a creamy Indian korma, a Ukranian borscht (I prefer it hot), a Moroccan tagine, and on and on. You don't know what you're missing until you've had it.

The children of the revolution are always ungrateful, and the revolution must be grateful that it is so. —Ursula K. Le Guin

ABOUT THE
CONTRIBUTORS

EDITORS

TOBIAS S. BUCKELL is a Caribbean-born professional blogger and SF/F author who grew up in Grenada, the British Virgin Islands, and the US Virgin Islands. He is a Clarion graduate, Writers of the Future winner, and John W. Campbell Best New Writer Award Finalist for science fiction, and he has been nominated for a Nebula Award. His work on *Halo* books has been selected as a YALSA Best Book for Young Adults (BBYA). Buckell lives in Ohio with his wife and two children.

JOE MONTI is a literary agent. Before becoming an agent he was the children's fiction buyer at Barnes & Noble Inc., held an executive sales position at Houghton Mifflin, and was an editorial director at Little, Brown Books for Young Readers. There, several of the books he acquired have become *New York Times* bestsellers, and one was nominated for the National Book Award and was awarded the Michael L. Printz Award. Monti lives in New Jersey with his wife and son.

STORY CONTRIBUTORS

PAOLO BACIGALUPI is a Michael L. Printz Award winner and a National Book Award Finalist for his young adult novel *Shipbreaker*. He has been awarded the Hugo and Nebula Awards for his debut novel, *The Windup Girl*. He is also a winner of the Theodore Sturgeon Memorial Award, the John W. Campbell Award, and a three-time winner of the Locus Award. His next novel is a follow-up to *Shipbreaker* titled *The Drowned Cities*. He lives in western Colorado with his wife and son.

K. TEMPEST BRADFORD's science fiction and fantasy stories have been published in *Strange Horizons*, *Electric Velocipede*, the Federations anthology, and several other publications. She also writes plays, poetry, and nonfiction, and has been an editor for Peridot Books, *The Fortean Bureau*, *Sybil's Garage*, and *Fantasy Magazine*.

RAHUL KANAKIA is a science fiction writer whose stories have appeared in *Clarkesworld*, *Daily Science Fiction*, *Redstone*, *Nature*, and *Lady Churchill's Rosebud Wristlet*. He lives in Oakland, California, where he works as an international development consultant.

RAJAN KHANNA is a graduate of the 2008 Clarion West Writers Workshop and is a member of the New York City–based writing group Altered Fluid. His fiction has appeared or is forthcoming in *Shimmer Magazine*, *GUD*, and *The Way of the Wizard*, among others. He has also received Honorable Mention in the *Year's Best Fantasy & Horror* and the *Year's Best Science Fiction*. He lives in Harlem, New York.

URSULA K. LE GUIN is the author of several dozen books for adults, teens, and children. Her fiction publications include eleven volumes of short stories, twelve children's books, and nineteen novels, including the six books that comprise the Earthsea cycle. Among the honors her writing for young readers has received are: a National Book Award, a Newbery Honor, and the Margaret A. Edwards Award for her lifetime contribution to young adult readers. Le Guin's story "Solitude" was bestowed the Nebula Award. She lives in Portland, Oregon.

KEN LIU's fiction has appeared in *F&SF*, *Asimov's*, *Strange Horizons*, *Lightspeed*, and *Clarkesworld*, among other publications. His work has been nominated twice for the Nebula and the Hugo Awards, and several of his stories have been selected for inclusion in various *Year's Best* anthologies. He lives near Boston with his wife and daughter.

MALINDA LO's first novel, *Ash*, a retelling of Cinderella with a lesbian twist, was a finalist for the William C. Morris YA Debut Award, the Andre Norton Award for YA fantasy and science fiction, and the Lambda Literary Award. Her second novel, *Huntress*, a companion novel to *Ash*, is an ALA Best Book for Young Adults. Her next work is a young adult science fiction duology, beginning with *Adaptation* (Fall 2012). She lives in Northern California with her partner and their dog.

ELLEN OH's first book, *Prophecy: The Dragon King Chronicles*,

313

will be published in the winter of 2013. Transplanted from Brooklyn, New York, she is a lawyer, a writer, and a college instructor now living near Washington, D.C., with her husband and three daughters.

CINDY PON's debut, *Silver Phoenix: Beyond the Kingdom of Xia*, is a young adult fantasy inspired by ancient China. The novel has received starred reviews from *Booklist* and *VOYA* and was named one of the top SF/fantasy reads for youth in 2009 by *Booklist*. She is also a student of Chinese brush painting.

GREG VAN EEKHOUT was born and raised in Los Angeles, California, in neighborhoods with hippies, criminals, working people, and movie studios. His parents are Dutch Indonesian. His novel *The Boy at the End of the World* has been nominated for the Nebula Award.

DANIEL H. WILSON was born in Tulsa, Oklahoma, and earned a BS in computer science from the University of Tulsa. After earning a PhD in robotics from Carnegie Mellon University in Pittsburgh, he moved to Portland, Oregon, where he has authored several books. His novel *Robopocalypse*, which is excerpted in this anthology, was a national bestseller and a YALSA Alex Award recipient. The novel will be adapted for the screen by Stephen Spielberg in 2014. His next novel, *Amped*, has been optioned for film.